## Leo Tolstoy

COUNT LEO TOLSTOY was born on September 9, 1828, in Yasnaya Polyana, Russia. Orphaned at nine, he was brought up by an elderly aunt and educated by French tutors until he matriculated at Kazan University in 1844. In 1847, he gave up his studies and, after several aimless years, volunteered for military duty in the Army, serving as a junior officer in the Crimean War before retiring in 1857. In 1862, Tolstoy married Sophie Behrs, a marriage that was to become, for him, bitterly unhappy. His diary, started in 1847, was used for self-study and self-criticism, and it served as the source from which he drew much of the material that appeared not only in his great novels *War and Peace* (1869) and *Anna Karenina* (1877), but also in his shorter works. Seeking religious justification for his life, Tolstoy evolved a new Christianity based upon his own interpretation of the Gospels. Yasnaya Polyana became a Mecca for his many converts. At the age of eighty-two, while away from home, the writer's health broke down in Astapovo, Riazan, and he died there on November 20, 1910.

# THE COSSACKS

A NEW TRANSLATION BY
ANDREW R. MacANDREW

WITH AN AFTERWORD BY
F. D. REEVE

# and THE RAID
## LEO TOLSTOY

A SIGNET CLASSIC
Published by THE NEW AMERICAN LIBRARY

SIGNET CLASSICS *are published by*
*The New American Library of World Literature, Inc.*
*501 Madison Avenue, New York 22, New York*

PRINTED IN THE UNITED STATES OF AMERICA

# CONTENTS

# THE COSSACKS
## and THE RAID

"Sure," Dake said. "You stay here and I'll be back right away. I just want to show Uncle Eroshka the spot."

"The best place," Ergushev said. "We can see everything, and it's impossible to see us. It's the most convenient spot."

# THE COSSACKS

1 Moscow has grown quiet. The squeak of wheels is heard only occasionally in the wintry streets. The windows are no longer lighted. The streetlamps have been extinguished. Peals of church bells floating over the slumbering city mark the approaching morning. The streets are empty. Now and then a night cabman's sleigh cuts into the sand-covered snow with narrow runners, and then, stopping at the next corner, the driver dozes off while waiting for a fare. A little old woman passes by on her way to church where unevenlyplaced candles are burning, the red reflections of their lights playing on the gilt mountings of the icons. Laborers are getting up to go to work after the long winter's night.

But to the elegant set, it's still evening.

Through a chink in the shutter a light oozes from a window of Chevalier's Restaurant. By the entrance, parked along the curb, there stand a carriage and several sleighs, private and for hire. A three-horse post coach waits there too. The porter, wrapped in his coat, his head tucked between his shoulders, huddles behind the corner of the house.

"Haven't they had enough of their stupid chatter yet?" wonders a footman, with drawn face, as he sits waiting in the hall. "This always happens when I'm on duty."

The voices of three young diners come from the adjoining, brightly lit room. They are seated at a table that holds opened bottles of wine and the remains of supper. One of them, small, neat and ugly, sits looking out of his tired, kindly eyes at the one about to leave. Another, a tall man, is stretched out on a sofa by the table, fiddling with the winder of his watch. The third man has left the table. He is pacing the room, his short, fur-lined coat already on. He stops from time to time, takes an almond and cracks the shell. His fingers are strong, rather large, with well-tended nails. He keeps smiling at something. His cheeks and his eyes are aglow. He speaks heatedly, gesticulates, but obviously has difficulty finding the right words: they seem inadequate to express his feelings. He keeps smiling.

"Now I can tell all," said the one leaving. "I'm not try-ing to justify myself but I do wish you would understand me the way I understand myself instead of applying clichés. You say I've treated her badly?" he said, ad-dressing the man with the kindly eyes.

"Yes, you have," the small, ugly man replied, and his face looked even more kindly and more tired as he said it.

"I wonder why you say that," said the man departing. "You mean that being loved is as great a happiness as to love, and that once it happens to a man, it should suffice for the rest of his life?"

"Yes, it should indeed. It's more than enough to satis-fy a man," the small man said, opening and closing his eyes.

"But why shouldn't a man be in love too?" The one leaving plunged into thought and glanced at his friend as though he was in some way sorry for him. "Why not? Because love doesn't automatically arrive, that's why. No, no, to be loved is a misfortune; it makes for feelings of guilt if one can't repay it in kind, if one's incapable of loving in return."

"Oh. . . ." He made a helpless gesture with his hand. "If only it all would happen reasonably, the way we wish it to . . . but things are so incongruous, so mixed up. I feel as if I'd stolen affection. And you think so, too. Yes, you do—don't deny it. But would you believe, of all the many stupid, wicked things I've managed to do in my life, this is one I do not and cannot repent. I never lied to her or to myself, before or after. I thought I'd finally fallen in love with her, but then I realized that it was self-deception, that it wasn't love, that I couldn't continue. But she did continue. Do you really think I'm to blame because I could not? What was I supposed to do?"

"Well, it's over with," the friend said, lighting a cigar to combat his fatigue. "All I can say is that you've yet to love and know nothing of the meaning of love."

The man in the fur-lined coat wanted to say something. He seized his head between his hands, but failed to find the proper words.

"It's true, I've never been in love. But why? I have a need to love in me, and there's nothing stronger than that. But then, does that kind of love exist? I always sense something incomplete. . . . Well, what's the use of denying it? I've made a mess of my life and, as you say, it's finished now. I must start a new life. . . ."

"Which you'll mess up, too," said the third man, playing with the winder of his watch.

But the man departing didn't hear him. "I'm both sorry and glad to leave," he said, "but I don't know why it should make me sad."

And the man about to set out on a journey started to talk about himself without noticing that the topic failed to interest the other two. A man reaches the height of egotism during moments of spiritual ecstasy. He feels then that there is nothing in the world more important and more fascinating than himself.

A young servant wearing a sheepskin, with a scarf tied around his head, appeared in the door.

"The coachman says he can't wait any longer, sir," he said. "The horses have been ready since before midnight and it's four now."

Dmitri Andreyevich Olenin looked toward his serf Vania and saw in the scarf tied around his head, his felt boots and his sleepy face, another side of life—the side that was summoning him now toward work, hardship, accomplishment.

"You're right," Olenin said, fingering his coat to see if it were properly buttoned. "Good-by then!"

And despite his friends' suggestion that he mollify the coachman with a tip, he put on his fur cap and stood in the middle of the room. The friends embraced and Olenin took a glass of champagne from the table and emptied it. Then he took the small, ugly man's hand, blushing.

"Never mind, I'll say it . . . I must be frank with you

because I like you. . . . You do love her, don't you? I've always thought so."

"Yes," the small man said, and his smile became even meeker.

"I'm sorry, gentlemen, I've been ordered to turn off the lights," said the sleepy waiter who'd been sitting in the hall. He couldn't understand why these gentlemen kept repeating the same things over and over again. "On whose account shall I enter the bill? On yours, sir?" he said addressing the tall one and knowing the reply in advance.

"Yes," the tall man said. "How much?"

"Twenty-six rubles, sir."

The tall man pondered something for a moment, then slipped the bill into his pocket without saying a word.

In the meantime, the two others went on talking as before.

"Good-by—you're a good fellow," the meek-eyed man said.

They were both on the verge of tears as they made their way out.

"Oh, yes," Olenin said, blushing, to the tall one, as though he'd suddenly remembered, "would you mind settling my account with Chevalier and then write me. . . ."

"Certainly, certainly," the man said putting on his gloves. "How I envy you!" he added unexpectedly when they were outside.

Olenin got into the sleigh, wrapped himself in his coat and said; "All right, let's go!" And he moved aside, as though to make room for the one who had said he envied him. Olenin's voice was uncertain.

The tall man said, "Good-by, Dmitri, I wish you . . ."

He wished only one thing—that Dmitri Olenin would drive off as rapidly as possible, and he did not finish his sentence.

They were silent for a moment. Then one of the three said "good-by" once more, one of them gave the order for the coachman to start, and Olenin's sleigh moved off.

"Elizar! The sleigh," one of the remaining men called. The coachmen stirred, clicked their tongues, and pulled at the reins. A half-frozen carriage squeaked on the snow.

"Nice fellow, Olenin," one of the two staying behind said. "But why did he decide to go to the Caucasus, and with the army? I wouldn't do it for anything. By the way, you dining at the club tomorrow?"

"I am."

And each went his way.

Olenin felt too hot in his fur coat. He slipped down into the bottom of the sleigh and unfastened it. The shaggy horses dragged themselves from street to street, past houses Olenin had never seen before, and he felt that only those leaving on long journeys passed through them. Around him, everything was dark, soundless, and bleak. His head buzzed with memories, fondness, regret, and tears pressed pleasantly against his eyelids.

2  "I LIKE them, I like them very much, they're nice fellows! I feel fine!" he kept repeating, still feeling like crying. But why did he want to cry? Who was nice? Whom did he like? He wasn't at all sure. Now and then he would scrutinize some house, surprised at the curious way it was built; then he would wonder why Vania and the coachman, with whom he had nothing in common, were sitting so close to him and being swayed and jerked by the tugs of the side-horses stretching the frozen traces, just as he was. And then he repeated again: "They're nice people. I like them." Once he even said aloud: "Good going! Wonderful!" and was himself surprised that he'd said it. He wondered, "Could I be drunk?" And, indeed, he'd downed a couple of bottles himself—but it wasn't the wine alone. He recalled all the protestations of friendship which, bashfully, as though by chance, had slipped out before his departure. He recalled the pressure of a hand holding his, meaningful looks, silences and the sound of a voice saying, "Good-by, Dmitri." He remembered his own determined frankness. And it all had a signifi-

cance for him that moved him deeply. Before his departure, not only his friends, but even those who were indifferent or even hostile to him, all, as though by agreement, seemed to have decided to think better of him, to like him more, to forgive him everything, as one forgives a repentant, dying man. "Perhaps he won't ever return from the Caucasus," Olenin thought of himself, and it seemed to him that he loved his friends and also that he loved someone else. And he grew very sorry for himself. But it was not love for his friends that softened his heart, nor was it love for a woman—he'd never loved yet. It was love for himself, a warm, hopeful feeling, a love for everything that was good in him—and for the moment he felt everything in him to be good—and it was this love that made him cry and mutter disconnected words.

Olenin was a young man who had never managed to complete a university course, who did not work (he held a merely nominal post in some government department), who had squandered half his inheritance, a man who, at the age of twenty-four, had yet to decide on a career. He was known to Moscow society as nothing more than a young-man-about-town.

At eighteen, Olenin had found himself free as only a young Russian of the 1840's, left early without parents, could be. He was without physical or moral fetters: he could do as he pleased, had no obligations, was bound by nothing. He had no family, no country, no religion, no wants. He believed in nothing, respected nothing. But, although he believed in nothing, he was not in the least gloomy, bored, opinionated. On the contrary, he was constantly being carried away by something. Although he'd decided that there was no such thing as love, each time he was in the presence of a pretty young woman, he felt overwhelmed. He'd known for a long time that honors and position were nonsense, yet, despite himself, he was delighted when at a ball Prince Sergei came up to him and said a few nice things. However, he gave himself to his enthusiasms only so long as they didn't obligate him. As soon as he felt that one of his impulses would require labor and effort, he instinctively disengaged himself from the feeling or the pursuit and regained his freedom. This is how he approached society, work, the management of his estate, music, which he had considered studying at one time, and also women, whose love he didn't believe in. He was trying to decide where to invest all the youthful energy that is given to a man only once in a lifetime —in learning, in art, in love of a woman, or in some practical activity. It was not a question of the strength of his brain, of his heart, or of the qualities acquired by education, but the unique enthusiasm, the ineffable power conferred upon a man that enables him to mold himself— and, he may feel, the whole world—into whatever he decides. True, there are people devoid of this *élan,* people who, as soon as they enter life, get into harness and pull conscientiously until the end of their lives. But Olenin felt too strongly the presence of this all-powerful god of youth within himself—the ability to transform himself into one single desire, one single thought, the ability to want and to accomplish, the ability to dive into the bottomless abyss without knowing why. He was aware of this feeling, proud of it, and although he did not know it, it made him happy. Thus far he had loved only himself, and he could not help loving himself because he expected only good things of himself and had not had time to become disappointed. Leaving Moscow, he was possessed of that happy mood wherein a young man suddenly tells himself that everything that has happened to him so far is unreal, accidental, unimportant, that until that moment he has not tried to live. Now that he was leaving Moscow, he was making a new start, and from then on there would be no mistakes, no regrets, nothing but certain happiness.

It always happens on long journeys that during the first two or three stops the imagination remains in the place left behind until suddenly, with the first morning met on the road, it leaps ahead to the place of destination and proceeds to build the palaces of the future there. So it happened with Olenin.

Once the city had been left behind, he looked around at the snow-covered fields, feeling happy to be there all by himself, pulled his fur coat tighter about him, and dozed off. The leave-taking had touched him, and memories of the past winter season in Moscow with the people he had come across flashed through his mind. Now and then, however, unpleasant thoughts and regrets butted unbidden into his imaginings.

He thought of the friends who had seen him off and of his relations with the girl they had talked about. She was rich. "How could he possibly love her knowing that she was in love with me?" Olenin mused, and unpleasant suspicions crossed his mind. "When one comes to think of it, there's a lot of dishonesty in men. But why couldn't I fall in love with her?" he wondered. "They all tell me I haven't loved. Am I a cripple emotionally?" And he started to recall all his enthusiasms.

He recalled that during the early days of his Moscow life he had spent many an evening with the sister of a friend. They would sit at a table, under a lamp that shed its light on her slender fingers engaged in some needlework, and on the lower part of her delicate face. Then he remembered their conversations, dragged-out and conventional like some fashionable game, and his own feeling of revolt against the artificiality of it all. A voice inside him had kept repeating, "No, this isn't it," and sure enough, it wasn't.

Then he remembered dancing a mazurka at a ball with the beautiful D——. "Yes, that night I was in love, all right. And I was so happy! And I remember how miserable I was when, waking up the next day, I realized that I was free. So it seems that love won't come and tie me hand and foot. . . . No, no, there's no such thing as love. The girl from the estate next to ours who used to tell Dubrovin, the Count, and me how much she loved the stars was not *it* either."

Then he thought of the way he had run his estate and again could find nothing on which he could dwell with pleasure. "How long will they talk about my departure?" he wondered suddenly, although he couldn't have explained whom he meant by "they." Then came a thought that made him wince and let out an incoherent sound: he remembered the six hundred and seventy-eight rubles he owed his tailor, the words he had used to persuade Monsieur Capelle to wait another year and the expression of bewilderment and resignation on the tailor's face. "My God, my God," Olenin repeated, screwing up his face and trying to chase away the unpalatable thought. "And still, despite all that, she loved me. . . . And had I married her I would have no debts, whereas now I owe Vasiliev." And he relived the last night's gambling with Vasiliev at the club, to which he had gone straight from her; he relived his humiliating requests for a continuation of the game and Vasiliev's icy refusals. "One year of austerity and all those debts'll be paid, damn 'em . . .!" But this reassurance notwithstanding, he immediately started again to add up all his outstanding debts, to recall when they were due, and to wonder whether he could pay them on time. "Why, besides Chevalier, I owe money to Morel." And he recalled the night he'd contracted a rather large debt. It was a night-long party with drinking and gypsies, with some visitors from Petersburg: Sashka B——(an aide-de-camp to the Tsar), Prince D——and that self-important old man. . . .

"And why are those gentlemen so pleased with themselves? What qualifies them to feel they are an elite to whose company others should feel so flattered to be admitted? Can such a thing as being an aide-de-camp to the Tsar give one such ideas? And they look down on the rest of mankind and consider other people stupid and vulgar. But I made it clear to them that I had no desire whatsoever to be admitted to their circle. Still, I guess the head waiter was very impressed by my familiar tone, by my being on first-name terms with an Imperial aide-de-camp like that Sashka. . . . Yes, and none of them managed to outdrink me on that occasion . . . I even taught the gypsies a new song and everyone listened to me. Yes, though I've committed my share of stupidities, I'm not really all that bad. . . ."

By morning Olenin had reached the third station. He had his tea, helped Vania to move his luggage, and sat down, neat, erect and practical, knowing where each item of luggage could be found, where his money was, how much of it he had at his disposal, where he'd put his passport and his post coach ticket—and he was so much impressed by his own efficiency that it made him feel fine and he looked forward to the long journey ahead as if it were an extended pleasure trip.

Throughout the morning and into the afternoon he became immersed in all sorts of computations: how many miles he'd covered; the distance to the next station; how long to the first town, to dinner, to tea, to Stavropol; and what fraction of the trip had been covered at that particular moment. At the same time, he also calculated how much money he had, how much there would be left, how much was required to settle all his debts, and what proportion of his income he could spend per month. After his evening tea, he reckoned that there remained seven-elevenths of the total distance to Stavropol, that he could settle his debts within seven months of austerity, and that their total sum amounted to one-eighth of his total assets. This calmed him and he settled down in the sleigh and dozed off again. His imagination was now in the future, in the Caucasus. And his visions of the future were combined with the shadows of characters from novels set in the Caucasus, with pictures of Circassian women, mountains, awesome precipices, and waterfalls in that land of dangerous living. It all appeared to him vaguely, unclearly; but beckoning glory and the danger of death were the main ingredients of this future. At one moment he, Olenin, displaying incredible daring and a strength that left everyone stunned, kills and subdues fantastic numbers of mountain tribesmen; the next moment he becomes a mountaineer himself and fights with his fellow tribesmen for independence from the Russians. Investigating one of these scenes more closely, he finds some of his old Moscow acquaintances. Sashka is there fighting and, whether he's on the Russian side or on that of the mountain tribesmen, he's always against Olenin. And even the tailor, Monsieur Capelle, managed somehow to take part in his triumphal march. Now, if old errors and humiliations happened to crop up against this background, the thought seemed rather pleasant since obviously they could not recur over there, among the mountains and streams, the perils and the Circassian girls. He had already atoned for them by making a full self-confession. One vision, the dearest of all to the young man, was mingled with the other pictures of the future: the vision of a woman. And the woman now appeared to him as a shapely Circassian slave girl with a long plait of hair and eyes filled with infinite submission. He imagined a lonely hut in the mountains with *her* before the door. She is waiting for him and he is riding back to her covered with blood, dust, and glory, thinking of her kisses, of her shoulders, of her sweet voice, and her submissiveness. She is enchanting in her wild, primitive ignorance. And he begins educating her during the long winter evenings. She is intelligent, gifted and quick, and rapidly assimilates all the indispensable subjects. She masters foreign languages with surprising ease and soon can read books in French. *Notre Dame de Paris,* for instance, pleases her very much. She also learns to speak French, and in a drawing room she displays more natural poise than a lady of highest society. She can sing with simplicity, strength, and passion. . . .

"Good God, what nonsense!" he mutters under his breath as the post coach reaches a way-station and he is forced to change sleighs and distribute tips. But soon, once more, his imagination seeks out the interrupted nonsense, and he sees again Circassian girls, glory, his triumphal return to Russia, his appointment as aide-de-camp, his beautiful wife. "But there's no such thing as love," he reminds himself, "and honors are sheer nonsense. . . . But what about the six hundred and seventy-eight rubles? What about the conquest of territory that would give me more wealth than I'll need for the rest of my life? Of course, it wouldn't be right to keep all that wealth for myself, I'll have to share it. With whom, though? Well, I'll give the six hundred and seventy-eight rubles to Capelle and then I'll see. . . ." And now, shadowy visions begin to veil his thoughts until Vania's voice and the cessation of the motion of the sleigh interrupt his healthy, youthful sleep and, without awareness, he climbs into another sleigh at yet another station and continues on his way.

The next day, the same thing: the same stations, the same morning teas, the same moving hindquarters of the horses, the same brief exchanges with Vania, the same undefined daydreaming and dozing, and at night the same tired, healthy, youthful sleep.

**3** THE farther from Central Russia Olenin traveled, the more remote seemed his memories of the past; and the closer he came to the Caucasus, the more cheerful he felt. "Why not stay away for good and never show myself in society again," the thought flashed through his head at times. "These people I see here aren't people of consequence—none of them knows me and none of them will ever go to Moscow and meet those who do know me and find out about my past. And no one of our circle will ever find out how I've lived among these people." A completely new sensation of freedom overwhelmed him among the primitive creatures he was meeting in the course of his trip, creatures he didn't consider quite *people,* as his Moscow acquaintances were. The more primitive they were, the fewer the trappings of civilization surrounding them, the freer he felt. Stavropol, which he had to go through, depressed him. Advertising signs, some of them even in French, ladies out driving in carriages, cabbies waiting in the market place, a gentleman in an elegant coat and hat walking along an avenue and looking over the passers-by—all made a painful impression upon him. "Perhaps he knows someone I know. . . ." And again he visualized the club, the tailor, the cards, his Moscow acquaintances. . . .

After Stavropol, however, things brightened considerably: the country was wild enough, beautiful and warlike, and Olenin felt more and more cheerful. Everyone he met, Cossacks, coachmen, station masters, appeared to be simple creatures with whom he could joke and talk effortlessly and unaffectedly without having to consider what class they might belong to. They were all members of the human race toward which, *in toto,* Olenin unconsciously extended his affection. And they, in turn, were very friendly toward him.

In the Don Cossack country, Olenin had already discarded sleighs and started to travel on wheels, and beyond Stavropol it became so warm that he discarded his overcoat. It was spring here, and this unexpected spring filled Olenin with joy. At night he was no longer allowed to leave the Cossack villages because it was said to be unsafe. A loaded gun was carried in the post coaches, and Vania began to feel distinctly uneasy. Olenin, on the contrary, felt more and more sprightly. At one stopover the station master told them of a horrible murder that had recently occurred on the road. Then they began to come across armed men. "This is where it starts!" Olenin told himself, expecting at any time now to see the snow-capped mountains about which he'd heard so much. Then, one evening, the Nogay driver pointed his whip to where mountains could just be discerned among the clouds. Olenin looked intently, but the sky was overcast and the clouds concealed the mountains almost entirely. He made out something gray, white, fleecy and, try as he might, he couldn't discover anything attractive about the vista. And these were the mountains he'd read and heard so much about. He decided that they looked much like the clouds, and that all the talk about their peculiar beauty was just as false as admiration for Bach or as fictitious as the love of women. And he ceased looking forward to the mountains. Then early the next morning the cold woke him on the road, and he turned his head indifferently to the right. It was an absolutely clear morning, and he saw—seemingly sixty feet away—the immaculate, gigantic white bulk of the mountains, with their delicate contours and the neat, elaborate outline of their summits against the far-off sky. When he realized how far off they were and they, in turn, from the sky, how immense they were; and when he felt the impact of their infinite beauty—he grew frightened as if confronted by an apparition or something out of a dream. He shook himself, trying to awaken. The mountains remained, as before.

"What's that? What is it?" he asked the driver.

"Why, the mountains," the Nogay driver said indifferently.

"I've been looking at them too for quite a while," Vania

said. "Beautiful, aren't they? They wouldn't believe it back home."

As the three-horse carriage moved rapidly along a level road, the mountains seemed to race along the horizon, their rose-colored peaks gleaming in the rising sun. At first they simply amazed Olenin, then they gladdened him. But as he gazed more and more intently at the snowy chain rising not from among other black mountains, but straight out of the steppe, the beauty of it spoke directly to him, and then he really *felt* the mountains. From that moment on, whatever he saw or thought or felt bore their majestic imprint. All his Moscow recollections, his shame and repentance, all his stereotyped visions and expectations of the Caucasus vanished once and for all.

"Now it has begun," a solemn voice seemed to say, and the road along which they were driving, the remote line of the Terek River, the Cossack villages and the people around—all this now seemed to have become altogether real and was no longer a joke. He looked up at the sky and thought of the mountains. He looked at himself, at Vania and again at the mountains.

Here come two Cossacks on horseback. Their holstered rifles swing rhythmically across their backs. The bay and gray legs of the horses form a complicated pattern. And behind them the mountains. . . . The rising sun glittering on the Terek beyond the reeds, and behind it the looming mountains. . . . Hostile riders raiding the steppes on this side of the Terek, but here I am driving along, afraid of nothing. I am armed and young and strong and there, ahead, are the mountains. . . .

4 THE settlements of the Greben Cossacks extend for fifty miles along the Terek. The countryside is uniform. The Terek, which separates the Cossacks from the hill people, is still turbulent and fast flowing here, although it

begins to grow somewhat wider and smoother. It deposits grayish sand on its low, reedy right bank while it erodes its steep, although not very high, left bank with its roots of century-old oaks, rotting plane trees, and young brushwood. Along the right bank lie pacified but still restless Tartar villages. On the left bank, about half a mile from the river, each of them five or six miles from one another, are the Cossack advance posts. Formerly these Cossack settlements were situated on this left bank, but the Terek's course has deviated northward every year, away from the mountains, and has eaten away this bank, so that now there remain only abandoned sites, orchards and vineyards thickly overgrown with blackberry bushes and wild vines. No one lives there any longer, and the only tracks one finds in the sand are those of deer, wolves, hares, and pheasants who seem to have taken a fancy to these spots. The Cossack settlements are connected with one another by roads cut straight through this forest as if by cannon shells. Along these roads Cossack patrols and guarded watchtowers form a cordon. The Cossacks' domain consists of a narrow strip, about seven hundred yards wide, of fertile, wooded ground. To the north begin the sand drifts of the Nogay and Mozdok steppes, which fuse far northward into the Turmen, Astrakhan and Kirghiz steppes. Southward flows the Great Chechen, the Kochkalov range, the Black Mountains, another range and, beyond, one can see the snow-capped mountains no one's ever crossed. And it is within this fertile wooded strip of rich land that the warlike, handsome, prosperous tribe of Orthodox Old Believers—the Greben Cossacks—have lived since time immemorial.

A long time ago, ancestors of the Old Believers fled from Russia and settled among the Chechens beyond the Terek, on the Greben range, the first range of the wooded mountains of Great Chechenia. Living among the Chechens, the Cossacks intermarried and adopted many of their customs, though they retained their Russian language in all its purity and their religion. There is still a legend among the Cossacks that Tsar Ivan the Terrible came to the Terek, summoned the Cossack elders from the Greben range, and granted them land on the north bank of the Terek. He is supposed to have exhorted them to remain friendly toward Russia and promised them not to force them against their will to become his subjects or to abandon their faith. To this day the Cossack families feel a kinship with the Chechens and share their predilection for freedom, idleness, looting, and war. Russian influence shows itself largely in its unattractive aspects: interference in elections, requisitioning of church bells, and the passage of Russian troops through the territory. The Cossack feels less natural hatred for a hostile hillman who may have killed his brother than for the soldier who's been quartered with him to defend his village but who fills his house with tobacco smoke. For the enemy from the mountains he has respect, while he has nothing but scorn for the soldier he considers an oppressor. In a Cossack's eyes, a Russian muzhik is something alien, something wild and despicable, something of which he had a foretaste in the traders and settlers from the Ukraine, for whom he has scornful names. Standards of Cossack fashion in dress are set by Circassians. The best weapons are obtained from mountain tribesmen, and the fastest horses are bought or stolen from them. A young Cossack likes to show off his knowledge of the Tartar language and at times may even address another Cossack in Tartar. Nevertheless, this small Christian tribe, lost in one small corner of the world, surrounded by half-savage Mohammedans and by soldiers from the North, feels it's quite civilized, considers that only a Cossack is a human being, and professes deep contempt for all others. The Cossack spends most of his time patrolling roads, raiding enemy territory, hunting and fishing. He is almost never home. His presence in the settlement is an exception and then, usually, he's having himself quite a time. Every Cossack makes his own wine and drunkenness is not so much an inherent tendency as a sort of sacred obligation, nonconformity to which would be considered betrayal.

A woman for a Cossack is someone to be made use of for his comfort. Only unmarried girls are allowed to play and dance. Once married, a woman is expected to slave for her husband until extreme old age, and he sets Oriental standards of obedience and toil for her. As a result of this attitude toward the woman, she has developed impressively both physically and morally and, despite her apparent subjection, has—as in the Orient in general—an infinitely greater importance in the family than her Western counterpart. Her aloofness from social life and the habit of performing work which would seem more fitting for a man give her greater authority in the household. A Cossack who deems it indecent to speak affectionately to his wife, or even to simply chat with her, may be very much aware of her true superiority when left alone face to face with her. The house, all the belongings, everything, is maintained through her efforts. And although a Cossack firmly professes the belief that work is a disgrace, fit only for a woman or a Nogay hired hand, he feels vaguely that everything he has, everything he calls his own, is the product of this labor, and that it is within the power of a woman, his mother or his wife, whom he considers his servant, to deprive him of everything. Moreover, the constant physical work demanding a man's strength and the responsibilities they are left to face have given the Greben Cossack women an independent, masculine character and have strikingly devolped their physical vigor, common sense, determination, and strength of will. Greben Cossack women are for the most part stronger, cleverer, handsomer, and smarter than their men. The beauty of these women is especially remarkable because of the combination of dark Circassian features with the broad and powerful build of Northern women. They dress like Circassian women: a Tartar smock, an overgarment with wide sleeves, and soft slippers. But they tie kerchiefs around their heads in Russian fashion. Neatness, cleanliness, and good taste in dress and in the furnishings of their houses are of prime importance to them. In their relations with men, the women, especially unmarried women, enjoy complete freedom.

The heart of the Greben Cossack territory is Novomlinsk Village. In it, more than in any other village, the customs of the old Greben Cossacks have been preserved, and its women are famous for their beauty throughout the whole of the Caucasus. Its main means of livelihood are its orchards, vineyards and fields of watermelons and pumpkins, fishing, hunting and the growing of corn and millet, and war booty.

The Village is about two miles from the Terek and is separated from it by thick woodland. On one side of the road running through the Village is the river, on the other, the green masses of the vineyards and orchards and beyond them the sand dunes of the Nogay steppe. The Village is surrounded by an earth rampart covered with thorny brambles. One enters it through an arched gateway with a thatched roof. Near the gates stands a wooden gun carriage with an ugly cannon that was captured by the Cossacks somewhere once and hasn't been fired for a hundred years or more. Sometimes there's a uniformed Armed Cossack sentry by the gate and sometimes not; and if the sentinel is there, he may or may not present arms to a passing officer. Under the archway a white board bears the following inscription in black paint: NUMBER OF HOUSEHOLDS: 266; MALE POPULATION: 897; FEMALE POPULATION: 1012. All the Cossack houses are built on stilts, three feet or so above the ground. They have neat, thatched roofs and high, carved gables. And if not all are new, they are at least in good repair, clean, with tall porches, in all different shapes; they are not built in rows but are gracefully scattered along pretty, winding lanes. In front of the large windows of many of these houses, beyond the vegetable gardens, rise dark green poplars and acacias with tender light-green leaves and fragrant white flowers and, nearby, bold and gleaming yellow sunflowers and curly vines.

In the wide central square three stores sell lengths of bright material, sunflower and pumpkin seeds, green beans and gingerbread. Behind a tall fence, taller and wider than the other houses, is the commanding officer's house with its casement windows. The streets of the Village are generally rather empty, especially on weekdays in the summer. The young men are on patrol duty or taking part in a raid; the older ones are fishing, hunting, or helping their women in the orchards or vegetable gardens. Only the very old and the very young and those who are sick remain at home.

**5** IT was one of those evenings that can be experienced only in the Caucasus. The sun had moved behind the mountains, but it was still light. A third of the sky glowed red and the white mass of the mountains was sharply outlined against it. The air was rarefied, motionless, and full of sound. The miles-long shadow of the mountains lay on the steppe. The steppe, the land beyond the river, the roads—all were deserted. If by chance some riders appeared, the Cossack patrols and the Chechens in their villages would be sure to be watching them and wondering who these suspect characters might be.

At nightfall, the people, fearful of one another, flock to their dwellings, leaving the deserted country to beast and bird which have no fear of man. Cossack women who have been tying up vines chat briskly as they hurry to reach their homes before sunset. And, as with the rest of the countryside, the vineyards become deserted now while the village itself comes alive. People flock toward it from all directions, on foot, on horseback, and in screeching carts. Girls with twigs in their hands chat cheerily as they run to meet their cattle waiting by the gates in a cloud of dust and mosquitoes brought from the steppe. The well-fed cows and buffaloes scatter through the streets, led by women in bright-colored jackets whose sharp exchanges, giggles, and shouts are interspersed with the lowing of the beasts. An Armed Cossack has managed to obtain permission to leave the patrol. He rides toward his hut and, without dismounting, leans down and knocks on the window. Soon the pretty head of a young Cossack woman appears, and they exchange warm, smiling words. Further, a high-cheekboned, tattered Nogay laborer, just arrived from the steppe with a load of reeds, is turning his squeaking oxcart into the broad, well-swept yard of the Cossack captain. He lifts the yoke from the oxen who stand tossing their heads, while the captain shouts something to him in Tartar. A Cossack girl with a bundle of firewood tries to squeeze by close to a fence so as to avoid a huge puddle that extends almost the width of the street. She's barefoot and holds her skirt up, showing her white legs. A Cossack back from the hunt shouts to her teasingly, aiming his gun at her: "Lift it higher, don't be so bashful!" And the girl lets down her skirt and drops the load. An old fisherman, his trousers rolled up, his shirt unbuttoned on his gray chest, is on his way home. He carries his net over one shoulder, with silvery carp still jumping around in it. He takes a short cut by climbing over a neighbor's broken fence. His coat gets caught and he gives it a tug. A woman drags a dry branch along, and around a corner the blows of an ax resound. Wherever there's a smooth spot, Cossack children are spinning their tops and shrieking. Women climb over fences to save walking around. From every chimney rises pungent smoke from fuel made of straw and dung. Every house is alive with the increased activity that precedes the stillness of the night.

Like all the others, Grandma Ulitka, the wife of the captain's assistant who is also the schoolteacher, stands by her gate and waits for the cattle that her daughter Marianka has gone to get and is now driving down the street. Almost before she has time to open her gate, a huge buffalo cow surrounded by mosquitoes pushes mooing through it. She is followed by slowly moving, well-fed cows, which stare at their mistress out of their big eyes as they pass, rhythmically swishing their sides with their tails. Marianka, a tall and strikingly beautiful girl, goes through the gate, throws away her switch, latches the gate behind her, and runs nimbly to sort the animals out and drive them into the proper sheds.

"Take your sandals off, you creature from Hell," her mother shouts. "Look how you've worn them out. . . ."

Marianka does not seem at all offended at being called a creature from Hell. In fact, she seems to take it as a term of endearment and cheerfully goes on with her job. Her face is shaded by a kerchief tied round her head. She wears a pink smock and a green jacket. She disappears inside a shed, following the big buffalo cow, and her voice, gentle and persuasive, can be heard addressing the animal. "Come on, can't you stand still. . . . Come on, come on, you silly great lump. . . ."

Then the girl and the old woman emerge from the shed, each carrying a large jug of milk, the daily yield, to the dairy. Soon smoke is pouring out of the dairy's clay chimney: clotted cream is being made. The girl stays to keep the fire going while her mother comes out and walks toward the gate. Darkness is falling over the village now. The air is filled with the combined smell of vegetables, cattle, and smoke. By the gates, along the street, everywhere, Cossack girls are darting around, carrying rag torches. From the yards come the chewing and snorting sounds of the cows, who have been eased of their milk, and in the streets one hears the calling voices of women and children only. A drunken male voice is hardly ever heard on weekdays.

An old Cossack woman, tall and manly, came out of the yard across the street and asked Grandma Ulitka to light the rag in her hand.

"So, Grandma, all through for the day?" she asks Ulitka.

"The girl's stoking the fire. . . . You want a light?" Ulitka is very glad to oblige.

The two women enter the house. Their hands, rough and unaccustomed to handling small objects, shake as they open the precious matchbox, for matches are a luxury in the Caucasus. The mannish-looking woman installs herself on the doorstep with the obvious intention of having a little gossip.

"Is your man at the school?" the visitor inquires.

"He's still teaching all those kids. He says in his letter he'll be home for the holidays."

"He's a clever man. It comes in useful, y'know."

"Sure it comes in useful."

"And my Luke's on patrol and they won't let him come home." The visitor knows that Ulitka is well aware of this situation, but that doesn't bother her. She wants to talk of her son Luke. She's only recently fitted him out for armed service and wants to marry him off to the schoolteacher's daughter Marianka.

"He's on patrol?"

"He's on patrol, all right. Not been home since the last holidays. The other day I managed to send him some shirts with Fomushkin. Says he gets on fine with his superiors. Says they're after all those raiders again. Luke says he likes it over there."

"Good," Ulitka said, "you've got yourself a regular Ball-of-Fire there!"

Luke had been nicknamed Ball-of-Fire for his daring and courage, and he was popular in the village because he'd jumped into a stream and saved a drowning boy. Ulitka used his nickname to say something pleasant to his mother.

"Yes, thank God, I've a good son. Everybody likes him. Still, I'd like to marry him off. Then I can die in peace."

"Oh, there're plenty of girls in the village," Ulitka said slyly, having a difficult time slipping the lid over the matchbox with her calloused fingers.

"There're plenty of girls, sure," Luke's mother said, shaking her head, "but none like your Marianka. It'd be a waste of time to look for another like her."

Ulitka knows what the other's up to. True, Ulitka holds Luke in good esteem, but she avoids the subject because, in the first place, she's the wife of the second highest-ranking officer in the regiment and is rich, whereas Luke's late father was simply a rank-and-file Cossack. In the second place, she doesn't look forward to losing her daughter too soon. But the main reason for her reticence is that propriety demands it.

"Well, when my Marianka grows up, I hope she'll be sought after," she says modestly, with detachment.

"I'll send matchmakers as soon as she's ready," the mannish woman says. "As soon as I'm through with the vineyards, I'll send 'em along to make the bows to you and Ilya Vasilievich."

"What's Ilya to say in all this? I'm the one to approach," Ulitka says proudly, "but all in good time."

Luke's mother realizes from Ulitka's stern expression that all further talk on the subject is unwelcome. She lights her rag torch with a match.

"Don't turn me down, then—remember," she says. "But now I must go and light my fire."

As she crosses the street, carrying the burning rag in her hand, she meets Marianka, who greets her with a nod. "She's good enough for a king," the woman thinks, looking at the beautiful girl. "She's grown enough, she's ready to be married off into a good family. She's ready for Luke now."

In the meantime, Grandma Ulitka had her own worries and she remained sitting on her doorstep deep in thought until Marianka called to her.

6 THE Cossack males spend their time patrolling the countryside, manning the defense posts, raiding enemy territory. Luke stood on the watchtower of the Nizhne-prototsk post, on the very bank of the Terek. Leaning on the railing, he scrutinized the horizon beyond the river with squinted eyes. From time to time he looked down at his comrades below and occasionally exchanged a few words with them. The sun was nearing the snowy range that loomed white above the fleecy clouds. The lower parts of the clouds, near the foot of the mountains, were growing darker. The transparency of evening was spreading through the air. Cool currents came from the wild, wooded thickets, but around the watchtower it was still hot. The voices of the Cossacks resounded louder and hung in the air. The swift, brown waters of the Terek stood out more sharply against the stationary banks. The water was beginning to subside at this time of year, and here and there, wet, yellow-brown sand gleamed on the banks and in the shallows. The country directly across the river from the defense post was deserted; nothing but short reeds stretched far away to the very foot of the mountains. A little to the side, the clay huts of a Chechen village, with their flat roofs and funnel-shaped chimneys, could be seen on the low river bank. Luke's sharp eyes followed the remote red-and-blue-clad figures of the

Chechen women coming and going in their pacified village. He watched them moving through light that was smoky from the evening fires.

The Cossacks were expecting a raid at any moment by hostile hill people coming across the river from the Tartar side. May is especially propitious for these raids: the woods along the Terek are so thick then that a man on foot has difficulty working his way through them, while the river itself is shallow enough in places for a horseman to ford. Indeed, two days earlier, a Cossack had arrived with a circular from the regimental commander, warning the posts that scouts had come across a hostile raiding party of eight men about to attempt a crossing of the river. Special vigilance was ordered.

But it didn't look as though the guard post was on the alert. The Cossacks behaved as though at home: their horses were unsaddled, they walked around unarmed, some were fishing, others were getting drunk, others again were out hunting. The only saddled horse, that of the man on sentry duty, was ambling about among the brambles at the edge of the forest, and only the sentry was fully dressed and armed with gun and saber. The Cossack in charge of the post, a tall, spare man with a very long back and short arms and legs, was sitting on a small mound of earth by a hut. His shirt was open, and his features expressed the special boredom and laziness of a man in command: his eyes were closed, and his head kept falling from the outstretched palm of one hand onto the other. A middle-aged Cossack with a pepper-and-salt beard was lying in his undershirt by the river, staring blankly at the waters as they swirled and foamed monotonously. Others, also overcome by the heat, sprawled around in various stages of undress: some were rinsing their clothes in the Terek, others were splicing a line, others again were simply lying on the hot sand of the bank, humming a tune to themselves.

One Cossack with a gaunt, very sun-tanned face lay by the hut, apparently dead drunk. A couple of hours earlier this must have been a shady spot, but now the man was fully exposed to the fierce, slanting rays of the sun.

Luke, who stood on the watchtower, was a tall, handsome youth of twenty or so. He looked very much like his mother. His build, despite his youthful angularity, indicated physical strength and his still very boyish features revealed a strong will. Although he had been conscripted into the Armed Cossacks only recently, his expression and his composure showed that he had already managed to acquire the proud bearing that is characteristic of the Cossacks and in general of people who constantly bear arms, and that he was fully aware of his own worth. His Circassian coat was torn in some places, his cap was pushed back Chechen-fashion. His attire was not costly, but he wore it with that special Cossack smartness that they copy from the Chechen warriors. A real Chechen brave's clothes are always baggy, torn, careless—only his arms are costly. But the certain way these ragged clothes must be worn and belted is by no means within everyone's grasp, and a Cossack or a mountaineer can spot it immediately. Luke had this dashing air of a brave. His hands folded under his saber and his eyes half-closed, he kept scrutinizing the Chechen village. Although, taken separately, his features were not handsome, the over-all impression left by his proud carriage and his dark-browed, intelligent face was that of a handsome man.

"Look at all the women over there in that village," he announced in a clear voice, lazily baring his white teeth and not addressing anyone in particular.

Nazar, who was stretched out under the watchtower, hurriedly lifted his head.

"Must be going for water," he commented.

"Wouldn't it be fun to fire a round," Luke said, snorting. "See 'em start running. . . ."

"You couldn't reach that far."

"Oh yeah? Mine would reach well beyond 'em," Luke said. "Oh," he said, angrily swishing away the mosquitoes that pestered him, "I can't wait for my holiday—I'll go and visit Girey-Khan and get plastered on some of that Tartar wine. . . ."

A rustling in the thicket drew the attention of the Cossacks. A pied mongrel with some setter in him, violently wagging his mangy tail, came running toward the post. Luke recognized the dog of his neighbor, Uncle

Eroshka, and soon made out the figure of the hunter himself standing in the thicket.

Uncle Eroshka was a Cossack of gigantic proportions. His snow-white beard was strikingly broad, as were his shoulders and his chest. But his powerful limbs were so well-proportioned that, as he emerged out of the forest, there being no other man there to compare him to, he did not seem unusually large. He wore a tattered coat, home-made deerskin sandals, and a white cloth cap. Over one shoulder he carried a blind for hunting pheasants and a bag with a chicken in it for luring hawks. Over his other shoulder a wild cat he'd killed was slung on a strap. In his belt were stuck small pouches with ammunition and gunpowder, a bag with a loaf of bread, a horsetail to swish away the mosquitoes, a hunting knife in a torn sheath covered with bloodstains, and two dead pheasants. He looked at the post and halted.

"Hey, Lam!" he called the dog in such a carrying bass voice that the echo resounded far and wide over the forest. He threw a huge flint gun over his shoulder and pushed back his cap.

"Having a good time, lads?" he said, addressing the Cossacks in the same strong, cheerful voice. He formed the words quite effortlessly, but they were as loud as though he had been shouting at the top of his lungs to communicate with someone across the river.

"Hi, Uncle!" young Cossack voices replied from all sides.

"Seen anything? Tell me . . . ," Eroshka said wiping his red, sweaty brow with the sleeve of his coat.

"Say, Uncle, you should see the hawk that's living in that plane tree over there," Nazar said, winking and jerking his shoulder, as though nudging the others in complicity. "As soon as the sun goes down it starts circling all around."

"Come on now," the old man said skeptically.

"Really, Uncle, you have to wait and watch for him," Nazar said with a snort of laughter.

Everyone laughed.

No hawk had been spotted, but the young Cossacks at the post liked to tease Uncle Eroshka, and they did so every time he came to see them.

"Shut up, you fool. Always the same stories," Luke said, looking down at Nazar from his watchtower. Nazar gave it up immediately.

"If you want me to watch for it, I'll watch for it," the old man said, to the great joy of the Cossacks. "And what about boars, seen any?"

"That all you think we have to do—watch for boars?" the Cossack in charge of the post said. He welcomed a little distraction. He was scratching his long back with both hands. "We're after Chechen raiders, not boars, Uncle. What about you—heard anything of 'em?" he added, frowning without particular reason and showing his close-set white teeth.

"Raiders? Haven't heard a thing," the old man said. "And what about giving us a drink of wine, my lad. I'm quite done in, you know. I'll bring you some fresh meat . . . you'll see. Now, how's about a drink?"

"Well, you going to watch for hawks tonight?" the Cossack in charge asked, ignoring Eroshka's request.

"I plan to ambush some varmint tonight, and maybe, God willing, I'll kill something for the holiday. You can have some."

"Uncle, hey, Uncle!" Luke called out sharply from his tower, and all the Cossacks turned to look up. "Up the stream a ways there's a good herd of boar, and I'm not fooling either. The other day one of us shot one there. That's the truth," he said, hitching up his rifle on his back, and his tone indicated that he was serious.

"So there you are, Luke!" the old man said lifting his head. "Where did he shoot it?"

"Haven't you found the spot? Looks like you're too young and inexperienced, Uncle," Luke said lightly. But immediately he added seriously: "Just by the ditch. We were going along the ditch when I heard this crackling. My gun was in its holster, but Ilya banged away at it . . . I'll take you to the spot, Uncle, it's not far off.

"Time to relieve me, Uncle Mosev," Luke said determinedly, almost imperiously, to the man in charge, and without waiting for an order, he started climbing down from the watchtower.

"All right, come down," the chief said, looking around.

"Your turn, Gurka? Go on, then. You know," he said, addressing the old man, "this Luke's become pretty handy with a rifle. Won't stay home any more. Keeps roving around just like you. He killed one the other day."

**7** THE sun had already disappeared, and the night shadows were advancing from the forest side. The Cossacks were winding up their chores around the post before going into the hut for supper. Alone, the old man was waiting for the hawk under the plane tree. From time to time he gave a jerk at a string tied to the chicken he was using as a lure. But the hawk wouldn't swoop down. Luke, humming one song after another, was leisurely setting pheasant traps among the thickest brambles. Although he was a big man with big hands, it was obvious that he could do delicate chores as well as rough work.

"Hey, Luke!" he heard Nazar's piercing voice from afar. "It's suppertime, they've gone in for supper."

Carrying a live pheasant under his arm, Nazar made his way through the undergrowth and emerged on the footpath.

"Ah," Luke said, "where'd you get that cock? Bet it was in my trap."

Nazar was the same age as Luke, and like him had been serving with the Armed Cossacks since spring.

He was plain, smallish and thin. His voice was squeaky and piercing. He and Luke were neighbors back home.

Luke was sitting in the grass cross-legged, splicing a rope.

"No idea whose trap. Maybe yours."

"Was it behind the pit by the plane tree? It's mine all right. I set it yesterday." Luke looked at the captured pheasant and patted its dark, bluish head, which the bird kept stretching out in terror, rolling its eyes. Luke took it into his hands.

"We'll stew it with rice tonight," he said. "You go and pluck it."

"Shall we eat it by ourselves or give some to the chief?"

"He has plenty."

"Say," Nazar said, "I don't like killing 'em."

"Give it here."

Luke drew a small knife he carried under his dagger and made a quick short movement. The pheasant fluttered, but before it had time to open its wings wide, the bleeding head bent sideways and jerked spasmodically.

"That's all there is to it," Luke said, letting the bird drop. "It'll make a nice meaty stew."

Nazar glanced at the bird and shivered slightly.

"Say, Luke," he said, picking up the pheasant, "that devil'll send us out again tonight."

He was referring to the chief of the post.

"It was Fomushkin's turn," Nazar said again, "but he sent him for the wine, and we'll have to spend the night patrolling again. You'd think he had no one but us. . . ."

Luke got up and went toward the post, whistling something. "Take the rope with you," he shouted back.

Nazar picked up the cord.

"I'll tell 'im tonight," Nazar said. "What about telling him we won't go—we're exhausted and that's that. Perhaps you should tell 'im, he'll listen to you. It can't go on like this!"

"What're you fussing about?" Luke said, apparently thinking of something else. "If they were kicking us out of the Village every night that would be something to beef about—there you could be having a good time or something. But here? What's the difference where we are, inside the post or lying in ambush? You're funny."

"And when are you going home?"

"I'll go on the holiday."

"Gurka says that your Dunia is going around with Fomushkin," Nazar announced suddenly.

"So what? Let her go around with him," Luke said, uncovering his even white teeth although not really smiling. "I'll find myself another."

"Gurka says he comes to her place one day, and her husband's not around. Fomushkin's sitting there and eating pie. So Gurka sits and sits, and then he had to be on his way. As he passes under the window he hears her say: 'So the old fool's finally left. Say, sweetie, would you like another piece of pie? And,' she says to him, 'don't bother to go home tonight, sweetie-pie.' And Fomushkin says, 'All right.'"

"I don't believe it," Luke said.

"It's the truth, I swear to God."

"So she got herself another guy," Luke said after a silence. "Good for her. There's plenty of others around. I've had enough of her anyway."

"You son-of-a-gun!" Nazar said. "Why don't you try Marianka? Why isn't she going out with anyone?"

Luke frowned. "Why Marianka?" he said. "They're all the same."

"I'd like to see you try with her. . . ."

"Why her? There's plenty of them in the Village."

And Luke started whistling again as he walked toward the post, tearing leaves from the branches as he went. Passing through the bushes, he suddenly stopped by a smooth twig and cut it off with the knife he had used to kill the pheasant. "A nice ramrod," he said, making the sapling whistle in the air.

The Cossacks were having their supper in the clay-plastered hut. They were sitting cross-legged on the earth floor around a low Tartar table.

When it came time to assign the duties for the night, one of the men got up, walked to the half-open door, and shouted to the chief: "Whose turn is it to go out tonight?"

"Whose turn?" the chief of the post repeated. "Well, Burlak has been, Fomushkin has been," he said somewhat hesitantly. "Well, what about you, Nazar, and Luke? And Ergushev—I guess he's slept it off, his wine?"

"You've not slept it off, so why should he?" Nazar muttered in a low voice.

The men laughed.

Ergushev was the Cossack who'd been sprawled dead drunk by the hut. He had just staggered into the hut and stood there rubbing his eyes.

In the meantime, Luke got up and started to inspect his gun.

"And hurry up," the chief of the post said. "Eat your supper quickly and go."

Without waiting for an acknowledgment of his order and apparently placing little trust in the Cossacks' compliance with his demand for promptness, he added, shutting the door of the hut: "I wouldn't be sending you out like this without special orders, but an officer may turn up at any moment—and you know there's a party of eight raiders around."

"Well, I guess we'd better go," Ergushev said. "Nothing doing. Discipline . . . can't be helped in such times. I guess we'd better be on our way."

And Luke, holding a large piece of the pheasant in both hands in front of his mouth, kept looking in turns at the chief and at Nazar. He seemed quite uninterested in whether he went out on night duty or not, and to be laughing at both of them. Before they left for their ambush, Uncle Eroshka entered the hut. He had stayed under the plane tree until nightfall, waiting in vain for the hawk.

"Say, lads," he said, his bass resounding in the low-ceilinged room, "I'm going out with you. While you're ambushing your Chechens, I'll ambush my pigs."

8 IT was completely dark when Uncle Eroshka and the three men on duty, wearing leather capes, their rifles slung on their shoulders, went along the Terek toward the place of ambush. Nazar had almost refused to go but Luke had grown angry, and without further delay they were on their way. After a short while they turned and followed a faint path that took them to the edge of the river.

By the bank rested a big black log that must have been cast up by the current; the reeds around it were freshly flattened.

"What about here?" Nazar said. "Shall we lie in wait here?"

"Sure," Luke said. "You stay here and I'll be back right away. I just want to show Uncle Eroshka the spot."

"The best place," Ergushev said. "We can see everything, and it's impossible to see us. It's the most convenient spot."

Nazar and Ergushev spread out their leather capes and installed themselves behind the log. Luke and Uncle Eroshka walked on.

"It's around here, not far at all, Uncle," Luke said, walking noiselessly ahead of the old man. "I'll show you where the boars have passed through. I'm the only one who knows."

"Show me, show me, lad. You sure know your way about," the old man whispered back.

A few steps farther on, Luke stopped, bent over a little puddle, and let out a whistle. "Here's where they came to drink, see, Uncle?" he said, pointing at a fresh hoof mark.

"God bless you, good lad," the old man whispered. "Here's where the pigs rolled in the mud. I'll stay here and you can run along."

Luke flung his leather cape over his shoulder and walked back along the riverbank, throwing quick glances to his left at the wall of reeds and to his right at the waters of the Terek seething under the bank. "He too must be sitting in ambush or crawling around somewhere," he thought, visualizing an imaginary Chechen. A sudden crack of branches and a splash in the water made him stop and grab his rifle. A boar leaped out from under the bank. For one second his dark body was clearly outlined above the glossy surface of the water. Then it disappeared among the reeds. Luke had taken aim, but before he could fire, the boar had disappeared in the thicket. Luke spat in disgust and walked on. Approaching the ambush, he stopped and whistled softly. A similar soft whistle answered him, and he joined his comrades.

Nazar, all curled up, was already asleep. Ergushev was sitting up by him. He moved aside slightly to make room for Luke.

"This is a nice place to sit in ambush," he said. "You show him the spot?"

"I did," Luke said, spreading his leather cape out

under him. "You hear the boar crashing around? I roused him—a big one—over by the water. . . . Must be the same one."

"I heard it crashing around. I realized right away it was an animal, and I said to myself, Luke has roused one. Now," he said, wrapping himself up in his cape, "I'm going to have a snooze, and you give me a shake when the cocks crow. We've got to do it properly. Then you'll have your snooze and I'll sit up. That's the way. . . ."

"Thanks," Luke said, "but I'm not even sleepy."

The night was warm, dark, and windless. Stars were shining only from one side of the sky, of which the larger part was overcast by a single huge black cloud that started by the mountains and slowly spread farther and farther despite the absence of wind. Its edges were sharply outlined against the deep starry portion of the sky. In front of him, Luke could see only the river and the horizon beyond it. Behind and on either side he was surrounded by a wall of reeds. From time to time the reeds would rustle without any apparent cause. Seen from below, their swaying tufts looked like leafy branches against the clear sky. At his feet was the bank, beneath which torrential waters rushed by, while beyond them the glossy, brownish main current of the river flowed slowly, rippling monotonously over the shallows. And still farther, everything, the water, the bank and the remote mountains, fused into an impenetrable darkness. On the surface of the water shadowy shapes slipped past, which the Cossack's experienced eye recognized as driftwood. Now and then the sloping bank opposite appeared clearly as the smooth surface of the water reflected heat lightning as in a black mirror. The background sounds of the night—the rustling of the reeds, the snoring of the sleeping men, the hum of the mosquitoes, the noise of the current—were from time to time interrupted by a faraway shot, by the splash of a large fish or the crashing of an animal through the thick undergrowth. Once an owl flew along the Terek, and regularly, at every second beat of its flight, one of its wings could be heard brushing against the other. Right over the ambush, it turned toward the forest and flew to a plane tree. It took the owl quite a time to install itself comfortably: the tree kept rustling until it finally settled itself among its branches. Each of these unexpected noises made the wakeful Cossack prick up his ears, narrow his eyes, and unhurriedly reach for his gun.

Most of the night was over. The black cloud had floated westward and had now uncovered from behind its ragged edges a clear, starlit sky, with an upside-down crescent moon shining over the mountains. The coolness grew penetrating. Nazar woke, said something and went back to sleep. . . . Luke, bored, took his knife and started making his twig into a ramrod. All sorts of thoughts passed through his head: he thought of the Chechens living over there, in the mountains, how they came prowling around on this side of the lines without fear of the Cossacks—perhaps even at this very minute they were crossing the river at some other spot. And he stepped out of his hiding place and looked up and down the river, but he saw nothing. After that he only cast occasional glances toward the opposite bank, which was hardly distinguishable from the water under the shy light of the moon. He was no longer thinking of the Chechens. He was simply waiting for the time to wake up the other two and thinking with pleasure of the holiday when he'd go home to his village. Thinking of the Village, he thought of his mistress, Dunia, and the thought was unpleasant. There were unmistakable signs of morning now. A silvery mist appeared over the water. Some young eagles, quite near him, shrieked shrilly and noisily flapped their wings. Finally, the crowing of the first rooster came from a nearby settlement, followed by the protracted crowing of another. Then other roosters joined in.

"Time to give them a shake," Luke said, finishing his ramrod and feeling that his eyelids were growing heavy. He turned toward the others, figuring out which legs belonged to whom. Suddenly it seemed to him that he heard something splash over toward the opposite bank of the Terek. Once more he scrutinized the mountains on the horizon, growing lighter under the upside-down crescent of the moon, the outline of the opposite bank, and the river itself, carrying a piece of driftwood he could now make out clearly. He had the illusion that the Terek and the piece of wood were standing still while he himself was drifting, but this was only for a moment. He started scanning the horizon again. The large floating piece of wood with a single long branch caught his attention. It had a strange way of drifting down the very middle of the stream without rocking or twirling in its course. Then it occurred to him that it wasn't drifting with the current but somewhat across it, toward the shallows. Luke stretched his neck and started watching it intently. The piece of wood reached the shoal, stopped, and moved in a strange way. He thought he saw an arm appear from under the log.

"Looks like I have a chance to kill that Chechen fellow all by myself," he thought. He took his rifle and unhurriedly sighted it on the piece of wood.

"I won't bother to rouse 'em," he decided, but his heart started pounding in his chest so hard that he stopped and listened. Suddenly there was a splash. The log was again afloat. Now toward this bank. "I won't let him through," he muttered. And then, in the light of the crescent moon, he saw the flash of a Tartar head, just in front of the log. He lined up his sight directly on the head. It seemed very close to him, just at the end of his gun barrel. He looked at it once more. "No doubt about it," he decided, pleased. "It's a raider, all right." And he again trained his rifle on the head, muttering, according to Cossack custom acquired in early childhood, "To the Father, to the Son. . . ." And he pressed the trigger.

Lightning engulfed the surrounding reeds and the water for a second. The sharp, abrupt report was carried over the river and somewhere far off turned into a protracted rattle. The log was no longer coming across the current, but drifting downstream, rocking and whirling.

"Stop it!" Ergushev shouted, grabbing his rifle and sitting up.

"Shut up!" Luke hissed through clenched teeth. "It's the raiders!"

"Who were you firing at?" Nazar asked. "Who was it, Luke?"

Luke didn't answer. He reloaded, watching the drifting log. It stopped near a shallow, and a large, staggering shadow appeared from under it.

"What were you firing at? Why don't you tell us?" the Cossacks kept pestering him.

"I told you—raiders——" Luke said.

"Stop telling stories. . . . Did the rifle go off by mistake or what?"

"I tell you I killed one of them. That's what I was firing at," Luke said, his voice breaking and hoarse with excitement. "A man was swimming over there," he said, pointing at the shallow. "I shot him."

"Stop kidding," said Ergushev rubbing his eyes.

"What d'ya mean kidding? Look over there!" Luke seized him by the shoulders and turned him with such strength that Ergushev let out a grunt. Soon, looking in the direction indicated, he made out the body. His tone changed completely.

"You don't say! And I bet there are more of them around. I'm sure," he whispered and started inspecting his rifle. "This one was their scout, and the others are either here or nearby, on this side of the river, mark my words. . . ."

Luke unfastened his belt and took off his shirt.

"What are you up to, you idiot?" Ergushev shouted. "Just show yourself, and that'll be the end of you. And you'll have gained nothing, either, I tell you. If you've killed him, he won't get away. . . . Here, give us a little gunpowder," he said. "Got any? You, Nazar, get to the post and quickly, and keep away from the banks or they'll kill you. I know what I'm talking about——"

"Anything else? If you want to go all by yourself, just go ahead," Nazar answered angrily.

Luke had taken off his shirt and was approaching the bank.

"Don't do it, I tell you," Ergushev said, pouring the gunpowder into his pouch. "You can see he's not moving. In any case, it's almost morning and you can wait till some of our men come over from the guard post. And you, Nazar, go on. Don't be afraid, I tell you."

"Luke, tell us how you killed 'im," Nazar said.

Luke now changed his mind about wading into the river.

"All right, both of you, you go on to the post while I wait here. Tell 'em to send out a patrol. If they're on this side of the river, they'd better be caught."

"I tell you they'll get away," Ergushev said. "They must be caught, that's for sure."

Ergushev and Nazar got up, crossed themselves, and set off toward the post, not along the banks but through the thicket and over the brambles, until they reached the footpath through the wood.

"Look out, Luke. Don't move or they'll cut you down in a moment," Ergushev had said before they left. "And keep your eyes open, I tell you."

And Luke had answered: "Go on, go on, I know. . . ."

And after examining his rifle he sat down on a stump.

Luke remained all alone, sitting and watching the shallows and waiting for the Cossack patrol to come. But the post was quite a distance away and he was impatient. He kept worrying that the raiders following the man he had killed might get away. He kept looking around him, then scrutinizing the opposite bank, expecting to see a man there. He was ready to fire at any minute. The fact that he himself might be killed never occurred to him.

9  IT WAS growing light. The whole of the Chechen's body was now clearly visible. Caught on the shoal, it was gently rising and falling with the water.

Suddenly, quite close to Luke, there was a crackling in the reeds. He heard footsteps and the brushes of the reeds stirred. He muttered softly, "To the Father and to the Son," and cocked his rifle. The footsteps stopped.

"Hey, Cossacks! Don't kill your old uncle," he heard a calm bass and, parting the reeds, Uncle Eroshka came up to him.

"I almost killed you," Luke said.

"What were you after?" the old man asked.

His resounding voice, rolling through the forest and down the river, obliterated in one blast the quiet and the eeriness of the surrounding night. Suddenly everything seemed to grow lighter and more distinct.

"There you are, Uncle—you didn't see a thing and I've shot an animal," Luke said, uncocking the gun and getting to his feet with unnatural calm.

The old man was already looking fixedly at the Chechen's back, now clearly visible amidst the ripples of the river.

"While he was swimming he had that log on his back, hiding . . . but I spotted him and . . . there, see? See his blue pants and that . . . his rifle. . . . Can you see it?"

"Sure I can see!" the old man said angrily, and his face was serious and stern. "You've killed a brave," he said, as if with regret.

"I'm sitting here and I look and guess what I see over there, something black. I made him out way over there; looked like a man to me, as though he'd come up and jumped in. Strange! And the log, a good solid log, comes floating, but instead of floating downstream, it comes crosscurrent. I take a look, and there's a head poking out from under it. A monster! Then I go and stick my head out of the reeds, but I still can't make it out. So I got up and he must've heard me, because then he crawls out on the shallow and takes a look around. 'Oh no,' I says to myself, 'you're not going anywhere!' And he gets out and begins to take a look around. So I got ready my gun, but still I don't budge, I wait 'im out. I stood there and waited and waited and waited. Then he set off again, and when he floated into the moonlight, I could see his back there. So I say 'To the Father, Son, and Holy Ghost,' and fire. And then I see through the smoke that he's floundering around there. Did he really groan, or did it just seem so to me? I can't be sure. 'Well,' I said to myself, 'Praise God, I killed him!' And when he was carried up onto the shoal there, I could see it all. He's trying to get up there, but he can't—no strength left. He was thrashing around and he kept thrashing and then he lay quiet. I see it all clean and clear. Look, he doesn't budge, must've croaked. The others rushed to the post to send the patrol here, so the rest of 'em won't get away!"

"So you got 'im!" the old man said, "and he's far away now, brother." Again he shook his head sadly.

At that moment they heard Cossacks, on foot and horseback, coming along the riverbank. They were talking loudly, dry twigs crackling under their feet.

"You bring the skiff?" Luke called out to them.

"Good boy, Luke! Drag 'im up on the bank!" one of the Cossacks shouted.

Without waiting for the skiff, Luke started to undress, his eyes fixed on his prize.

"Wait! Nazar's bringing the skiff," the Cossack in charge shouted.

"Don't be stupid, Luke. Maybe he's still alive, just shamming. Take along your dagger," another Cossack shouted from a distance.

"Talk away!" Luke shouted, letting down his trousers. He undressed quickly, crossed himself, and leaped with a splash into the river, his white arms thrashing across the current, toward the shoal. From the bank came loud voices.

Three mounted Cossacks went off on patrol. The skiff appeared from around a bend of the river. Luke reached the shallow, stood up, and bent over the body. He poked at it a couple of times.

"He's dead, all right," he shouted sharply to the others.

He had hit the Chechen in the head. The raider wore blue trousers and a Circassian shirt, and he had a dagger and a rifle strapped to his back. And on top of it all was tied the large log which at first had almost fooled Luke.

"That fish was really hooked!" said one of the Cossacks standing in a circle around the body of the Chechen; it had been dragged from the skiff, and lay on the grass.

"Look how yellow he is!" another said.

"Where did our fellows go to look for them? They're probably all still on the other side. This one was a scout— otherwise why'd he have come swimming along like that? No point for a man by himself," a third said.

"Must've been a smart one," got himself caught before all the others. You can see he's a brave all right!" Luke said sarcastically, wringing out his wet clothes on the bank and shivering all the time. "His beard is dyed and trimmed."

"Look at the way he tied his coat in a bag to his back. It made it easier for him to swim," a man said.

The Cossack in charge took hold of the gun and the dagger of the killed Chechen.

"Luke," he said, "you take this dagger and the coat too—and what about three rubles for the gun? What do you say? Look, it's all worn out," he added, blowing down the muzzle. "I want it just as a souvenir, see?"

Luke didn't answer. This begging irritated him, but he knew he couldn't get out of it.

"Ah!" he said, frowning and throwing the Chechen's coat on the ground, "if only the coat'd been good. But this one's nothing but a rag."

"It'd do for collecting firewood," another Cossack said.

"Uncle Mosev, what about me going home?" Luke said, apparently having forgotten his annoyance and wishing to derive some advantage from the present he was forced to make to his chief.

"Sure, go ahead."

Still examining the gun, the chief said to the Cossacks: "Get him out of here, behind the patrol line, boys, and rig up a shelter from the sun over him. Maybe his people'll ransom him!"

"It's not hot yet," someone said.

"What if a jackal gets to him? That won't do, will it?" a Cossack remarked.

"We'll set up a watch. If they come to ransom him, it wouldn't be good if he was all torn up."

"Well, fine, Luke. Go ahead, but you'll have to set up drinks for the lads," the chief said gaily.

"That's right," the Cossacks joined in. "What luck— you haven't seen anything yet, and you kill yourself a brave."

"Buy the dagger and the coat, but give me more money than that. And I'm selling the trousers," Luke said. "I can't get into 'em—he was a skinny devil."

A Cossack bought the coat for a ruble. Another promised two pails of vodka for the dagger.

"Drink, fellows. I'll stand you a pail," Luke said. "I'll bring it from the Village myself."

"And the trousers you can cut up for kerchiefs for the girls," Nazar said. The Cossacks roared with laughter.

"You'll have something to laugh about if you don't watch out," the chief said. "Drag the body away from here. What'd you put the filthy thing here by the hut for?"

"What's the matter with you? Drag him over here, boys!" Luke shouted imperiously to the Cossacks, who reluctantly took hold of the body. They obeyed him as if he'd been their chief and carried the body a few steps, then dropped the legs, which fell with a lifeless jerk. Stepping back, they stood there silently for a while. Nazar went up to the body and straightened the twisted head so that he could see the face of the dead man and the round, bloody wound beneath the temple.

"Whew! What a mark you left! Right in his brains," he muttered. "He won't get lost—his owners'll recognize him."

No one answered, and for some time the Cossacks remained quiet.

In the meantime, the sun had risen and its splintered rays were making the dew-covered leaves and grass sparkle. The Terek burbled in the awakened forest. Greeting the morning, the pheasants called to each other from all around. Silent and motionless, the Cossacks stood around the dead man, looking at him. The brown body, in nothing but its wet blue trousers held by a belt around the sunken stomach, was slender and handsome. The muscular arms lay straight along the sides. The round head, bluish and freshly shaven, with the blood-caked wound on the side of it, was thrown back. The smooth, sunburnt forehead stood out sharply against the shaven skull. The open, glassy eyes, their pupils frozen in a lowered position, gazed, it seemed, past everything. The thin lips, drawn at the corners, stood out under the clipped, dyed mustache and seemed frozen in a faint, condescending smile. The small fists, covered with reddish hairs, were doubled, and the nails were painted red.

Luke still hadn't put his clothes back on. He was wet, and his neck was redder and his eyes shining more brightly than usual. His high-cheekboned face was twitching. From his white, healthy body a hardly perceptible steam rose into the fresh morning air.

"He was a man too!" he muttered, evidently struck by the dead man's appearance.

"Ah, if it'd been him that'd caught you, he'd have given no quarter," one of the Cossacks said sympathetically.

The quiet dissolved. The Cossacks started to move around and to talk. Two of them went off to chop down some bushes to make the shelter. Others went out on patrol. Luke and Nazar hurried off to get ready to go to the Village.

Half an hour later, they were on their way home. They almost ran through the thick forest that separated the Terek from the Village. And all the way they talked without letup.

"Watch you don't tell her now, that I sent you. Just go and have a look around and find out whether her husband's home," Luke said sharply.

"And I'll drop in on Yamka, and perhaps we could all have a good time together?" Nazar suggested.

"And when would we have a good time if not today?" Luke asked.

Arriving at the Village, the two Cossacks had a drink and lay down to sleep until evening.

10 Two days later, two companies of a Caucasian infantry regiment arrived at Novomlinsk. Unhitched transport wagons stood in the square. The cooks had dug a pit and scrounged logs that had been carelessly left in neighboring yards. They had lighted a fire and were already cooking. The sergeant majors were checking their men. Stakes were being driven into the ground to tie up the horses. The quartermasters, like hosts, were scurrying through the streets and alleys, showing the officers

and men their quarters. The picture also included green ammunition crates set up evenly, horses and carts of the service company, and the big cauldrons in which the soldiers' food was cooked. And in the midst of it all stood the captain, the lieutenant, and Sergeant Major Onisim Mikhailovich.

Everything now jammed the Cossack village where it was rumored the companies were to be billeted. In other words, it was to be their new home. Why these soldiers had to be quartered here, among these particular Cossacks, whether the Cossacks liked to have the soldiers among them or not, whether the Cossacks were Old Believers or not—no one cared.

The exhausted, dust-covered soldiers broke ranks, and a noisy, disorderly swarm scattered through the streets and squares. In twos and threes, not even noticing the disgruntled looks of the Cossacks, chatting gaily, their weapons clanking, they enter the houses, hang up their accouterments, unpack their kitbags, and joke with the women. A large group gathers at the soldier's favorite spot, the food cauldron. The soldiers stand there, with their little pipes between their teeth, simply staring at the smoke rising, at first unnoticeably, toward the hot sky, then condensing into a whitish cloud, or at the flames of the fire, trembling in the pure air like molten glass. And they laugh at the Cossack men and women, making fun of them because they don't live the way Russians do. In every yard, the soldiers are seen, and their laughter is heard. And heard too are the hard, piercing shrieks of the Cossack women, protecting their goods and refusing to give the soldiers water or dishes. Little children cling to their mothers and to each other. They follow every movement of these soldiers, men such as they've never seen before, with frightened amazement; they run after them, always keeping a respectful distance. Old Cossacks come out and sit down in front of their houses. In gloomy silence and with expressions of resigned disgust, wondering what will come of it all, they watch the soldiers' comings and goings.

Olenin, who had now been with this Caucasian regiment for three months, was quartered in one of the best houses in the village, that of Ilya Vasilievich, the captain's assistant and schoolmaster—in other words, the house of Grandma Ulitka.

"What on earth will it be like, sir?" Vania, panting, asked Olenin. Olenin wore a Circassian coat and was astride a sturdy Kabarda mount he had bought in Grozny. He was cheerful as he rode into the courtyard despite the five-hour stretch they'd just completed.

"Why, what's the matter, Vania?" he asked, urging his horse forward and looking, amused, at the sweaty, tousle-haired, disgruntled Vania, who had driven the wagon into the yard and was unpacking the things.

Olenin looked a quite different man. On his formerly clean-shaven face a young mustache and beard had sprouted. His complexion was no longer pasty from night life; his cheeks, his forehead, and behind his ears were red with healthy sunburn. Instead of neat, dark suits, he wore a dirty white Circassian coat with wide skirts; and he was armed. Instead of his freshly starched collars, the red collar of a silky shirt was buttoned round his sun-burnt neck. He was dressed like a Circassian—but badly. Anyone would have known him for a Russian and not a Chechen brave. Everything on him was right, but not quite right. Nevertheless, his whole appearance breathed health, happiness, and self-satisfaction.

"You may laugh, sir," Vania said, "but you go and talk to these people yourself. They don't want you around and that's all there's to it. You won't get a word out of 'em." Vania angrily banged an iron bucket down on the door-step. "They're not Russians somehow."

"Well, you should go and ask the Village captain about it."

"How do I find anyone in this place?" Vania asked, offended.

"But who are you so mad at?" Olenin asked, looking around him.

"God knows what kind of people they are! Phoo! The real owner of the house isn't here. They say he's gone fishing somewhere. And the old woman's a real witch, God help us," Vania said, seizing his head in his hands. "How're we to live here? They're worse than Tartars, really, even if they do fancy themselves Christians. A Tartar's bad enough, but he's more polite than this bunch.

'He went fishing!' Why? Where? God knows." Vania turned away.

"What's the matter? Isn't it all like the servants' quarters back home?" Olenin said teasingly. He was still mounted on his horse.

"The horse, please," Vania said. He was puzzled by the new situation but sounded resigned now.

"So a Tartar is more polite, eh, Vania?" Olenin repeated, getting down from the horse and slapping the saddle.

"And you just laugh all the time, sir. You find everything funny!" Vania muttered angrily.

"Oh, don't get angry, Vania," Olenin said, still smiling. "Look, I'll go and see the people of the house, and you'll see, I'll fix things. We'll manage to live nicely here yet, don't you worry."

Vania didn't answer. He squinted his eyes, looked scornfully at his master's back, and shook his head. Vania simply regarded Olenin as his master, just as Olenin regarded Vania as his servant. And they would both have been very much surprised if someone had told them they were friends. And yet they were friends, without knowing it themselves. Vania had been taken into the house when he was a boy of eleven and Olenin was the same age. At one point, when they were fifteen, Olenin had taken charge of Vania's education and had taught him to read French, which made Vania very proud. Even now, in his high-spirited moments, Vania would let out French words, always laughing stupidly when he did so.

Olenin ran up the steps and pushed open the porch door. Marianka, wearing her pink smock—which is all Cossack women usually wear around the house—jumped away from the door, and in fright pressed herself against the wall and covered the lower part of her face with her wide sleeve. Opening the door wider, Olenin saw the tall, well-built girl in the half-light. With the quick, greedy curiosity of a young male, he noted instinctively the firm, female curves outlined under the thin, calico smock and the beautiful, black eyes filled with a childish fear and wild curiosity. "There she is!" Olenin thought. "And there are many more like her to come" flashed through his mind right afterward, as he opened the second door, leading into the house. Old Grandma Ulitka, also wearing just her smock, was sweeping the floor. He could see only her bent back.

"Hello, mother! Here, I've come about lodgings——" he began.

Without straightening up, Ulitka turned her stern but still beautiful face toward him.

"Come for what? To have a good laugh at us? Huh? I'll give you a laugh! A black plague on you!" she shouted, glancing sideways at him from under knitted brows.

Olenin had expected that the gallant Caucasian army, of which he was a member, would be welcomed joyfully everywhere, especially by the Cossacks, their comrades in war. And so he was perplexed by such a reception. However, he was not offended and tried to explain that he intended to pay for the quarters, but the old woman never gave him a chance.

"What'd you come for? Who needs a plague like you? Look at that smooth-shaved snout! You just wait a minute—the master's coming and he'll put you in your place. I don't need your dirty money. You'll smell up the house with your tobacco, and then you'll want to pay it off with money. We know this plague! Go and get yourself shot in the guts," she shouted piercingly, interrupting Olenin.

"I see Vania was right!" Olenin thought. "A Tartar *is* more polite." And, escorted by Grandma Ulitka's invective, he left the house. As he went out, Marianka, still in her pink smock, but with her head wrapped to the very eyes in a white kerchief, unexpectedly darted past him on the porch. Her bare feet tapping rapidly against the steps, she ran down the stairs, stopped, turned back, glanced at him out of her laughing eyes, and disappeared around the corner of the house.

The beautiful girl's firm, youthful stride, the wild look in her shining eyes under the white kerchief, the shapeliness of her strong figure, now struck Olenin more forcibly. "That must be the one," he thought. And thinking even less about the quarters than before, he went up to Vania, all the time looking around for Marianka.

"Whew, what a wild thing!" Vania said. He was still busy with the wagon but he had cheered up a little. "Like a wild mare. *Le femme!*" he added in a loud, solemn voice and burst out laughing.

11 IN the evening the master of the house returned from his fishing and, learning that he would be paid for the quarters, calmed his woman and satisfied Vania's demands.

Everything was arranged: the landlords moved to the winter house and gave Olenin the summer one for three rubles a month. He ate and lay down for a nap. He woke up toward evening, washed, changed, had his dinner and, lighting a cigarette, sat at the window which opened onto the street. The heat was abating. The slanting shadow of the house, with its fretted gable, reached across the dusty street and crept up the lower part of the house opposite. The steep, reed-thatched roof of the other house shone in the rays of the setting sun. The air grew fresher. It was quiet in the village. The soldiers had settled themselves in, and things had calmed down. The village herd had not yet been driven home, nor had the people returned from their work.

Olenin's quarters were almost on the edge of the Village. Occasionally somewhere far away beyond the Terek —in the Chechen or Kumytsk plain—through which Olenin had passed on his way, the dull sound of shots was heard. Olenin felt very comfortable here after three months of camp life. His washed face felt fresh for the first time since his travels; his vigorous body felt clean; each rested limb felt strong and relaxed. And his mind too felt fresh and clear. He thought of the campaign and the danger he had been through. He had faced the dangers well, no worse than the others, and he felt himself to be a full-fledged veteran of Caucasian warfare. His

Moscow memories had almost completely receded, his old life had been erased; a new, a completely new one had begun, and in it he had yet to make a mistake. Here, he was a new man among new people, and he could gain a new, good reputation. He was experiencing for the first time a causeless joy at being alive as he looked out of the window at the boys spinning their tops in the shade of his house; he felt it again looking at his neat new quarters and thinking how pleasantly he would arrange his new life in this Cossack village. Then he looked at the mountains and the sky, and a solemn sense of the greatness of nature pervaded all his memories and dreams. This new life of his had not started the way he had imagined it would when he left Moscow. Actually, it had started unexpectedly well. And in all his thoughts and feelings there was present the sense of the mountains.

"He kissed his dog, he licked the jug clean! Uncle Eroshka kissed his dog!" the children spinning the tops under the window suddenly started shouting, turning toward the side street. "He kissed his dog and sold his dagger for a drink," they cried, crowding together and stepping back.

These shouts were addressed to Uncle Eroshka, who, with his rifle slung on his back and pheasants in his belt, was returning from the hunt.

"I confess it, kids, I confess it!" Eroshka muttered, waving his arms and glancing into the windows of the houses on each side of the street as he passed. "I sold my little bitch for drink, I was wrong and admit it," he repeated, evidently angry but pretending that it was all the same to him.

The boys' behavior toward the old hunter amazed Olenin, and he was still more surprised when he saw the intelligent, expressive face and the powerful build of the man they called Uncle Eroshka.

"Hey, oldtimer! Come over here!" he called to him.

The old man looked over at the window and stopped. "Good evening, dear fellow," he said, raising his cap from his short-cropped head.

"Good evening, friend," Olenin answered, "what's that the boys were shouting at you?"

Uncle Eroshka came up to the window. "Oh, they're

teasing me. Let 'em. I like it. Let 'em have a little fun at their old uncle's expense," he said in the firm, sing-song voice in which venerable people often talk. "You in charge of all these troops by chance?"

"No, I'm just a junior officer," Olenin said. "Where'd you get the pheasants?"

"In the forest. Three hens, I got," the old man said, turning his broad back to the window so that Olenin could see the three pheasants hanging with their heads thrust through his belt. "Seen none around? Take a couple if you like. Here!" And he handed two of the pheasants in through the window. "You a hunter too?"

"Oh yes. On the march I killed four myself."

"Four? That's a lot!" the old man said sarcastically. "And what about drinking? Do you drink *chikhir*?"

"Why not? Sure I drink."

"Ah, you're a good fellow, I can see that! We're going to be buddies," Uncle Eroshka said.

"Come in a while," Olenin said. "We'll have a drink of *chikhir* now."

"Don't mind if I do, but you take the pheasants," the old man said.

The old man's face showed clearly that Olenin was a regular sort, that he'd understood right away that a source of plenty of free drinks had arrived, and that he could well afford to give Olenin the brace of pheasants.

It was only when Uncle Eroshka's figure appeared in the doorway of the hut that Olenin noticed the huge size and the unusual strength of this old man, with his large, silver-white beard and his red-brown, furrowed face. The bulging muscles of his legs, arms and shoulders seemed firm as a young man's. Through his short-cropped hair, deep, ancient scars could be seen on his head. His thick, sinewy neck was a network of folds, like a bull's. His wrinkled hands were bruised and scratched. He stepped lightly into the room, unslung his rifle, and stood it in a corner. He threw a quick glance around, evaluating Olenin's belongings and, turning out his feet in their raw-hide sandals, stepped softly into the center of the room. He brought into the house with him a strong, not un-pleasant mixture of smells—*chikhir,* vodka, gunpowder and dried blood.

Uncle Eroshka bowed toward the icon, smoothed his beard, and, going up to Olenin, held out his thick, dark hand.

"*Koshkildy!*" he said. "In Tartar that means 'Wish you health'—'peace be with you,' in their lingo."

"*Koshkildy!* I know," Olenin said, giving him his hand.

"Oh no you don't—you don't know the proper answer," Uncle Eroshka said, shaking his head. "If they say *koshkildy* to you, then you say, '*Allah rasi bo sun*'—'God save you.' That's the way, my friend, that's what you say and not *koshkildy*. I'll teach you all about it! We had an Ilya Moseich here, one of your Russians, and him and me were real buddies. There was a man! A drunk, a thief, a hunter—what a hunter! And it was I who taught him everything."

"What'll you teach me then?" Olenin asked, growing more and more interested in the old man.

"I'll take you hunting, teach you to catch fish, show you the Chechens, and if you want a girl friend, I'll fix that too. That's the kind of fellow I am . . . I like my fun!" The old man laughed. "Well, I'll sit down now, I'm tired. *Karga?*" he added questioningly.

"What does *karga* mean?" Olenin asked.

"Oh, it means 'all right' in Georgian. But I just said it, like that. It's my byword, my favorite: *karga, karga*. I just say it, just fooling. But look here, tell them to bring the *chikhir*. You got an orderly? You have? Ivan!" the old man shouted. "Well, if a man's a soldier in your army, then he's Ivan. Is yours Ivan?"

"Yes, he's Ivan too. Vania! Please go and get some *chikhir* from the landlord."

"Well, it's the same thing, Vania or Ivan! How come all your soldiers are Ivans? Ivan!" the old man called again, "Ask them for the *chikhir* out of the started barrel. They have the best *chikhir* in the Village. But watch it—don't pay more'n thirty kopeks a pint because that old witch, it'll make her happy. . . . Our people are an unfriendly lot, they're stupid," Uncle Eroshka went on in a confiding tone when Vania had left. "They don't think you're people. You're worse'n a Tartar to 'em. Russian heretics, they call you. But I think even if you're a soldier you're still a human being, and you've got a soul too. That's the way I see it. Ilya Moseich was a soldier, but there was a man! Right, friend? That's why my own people don't like me. But what do I care? I'm happy, I like everyone, I'm Eroshka! That's the way it is, friend!"

And the old man patted Olenin's shoulder affectionately.

**12** IN the meantime Vania, who had finished his settling-in chores and managed to get a shave from the company's barber, was in an excellent mood. He had pulled his pants out of his boots and that made him feel he was at home. He gave Eroshka a close but not too friendly looking-over, as though he was a strange, wild animal, shook his head at the muddy marks Eroshka had left on the clean-swept floor, took a couple of empty bottles from under the bench and went to see the landlords.

"Good evening, friends," he said trying to be very meek, "my master has sent me to buy some *chikhir*. Please pour some for me, won't you?"

The old woman didn't react. The girl, who was tying her kerchief round her head in front of a Turkish mirror, silently turned her head toward Vania.

"I intend to pay for it," he said, jingling the coppers in his pocket. "You be nice to us and we'll be nice to you," he added.

"How much you want?" the old woman asked harshly.

"A pint or so. . . ."

"Go, dear, draw some for them," Ulitka said. "Take it from the already started cask."

The girl took the keys and a jug and went out, followed by Vania.

Olenin caught sight of Marianka as she was passing in front of his window and, pointing to her, asked Eroshka:

"Tell me, who's that woman?"

The old man winked and gave Olenin a shove with his elbow.

"Wait a minute," he said and leaned out of the window. "Hm-hm-hum," he coughed and cleared his throat. "Hey, Marianka, my beauty, hey, my lovely, or don't you love me any more . . . I'm kidding," he added in a whisper, turning toward Olenin.

The girl did not turn her head. She went past, swinging her arms deliberately in the bold gait so characteristic of Cossack girls. For one second only, her dark, burning glance swept over the old man.

"Love me and you'll be happy," Eroshka shouted and, winking, looked questioningly at Olenin. "See how I am? I'm just joking," he said, "but isn't she something?"

"A real beauty," Olenin said. "Call her over here."

"Oh no. That one'll be married off to Luke, a good young Cossack who killed a raider the other day. I'll find you a better one, one all dressed in silk and silver. I'll do what I promised: I'll get you a beauty."

"What are you talking about, old man, it's sinful——"

"Sinful? What's sinful? You think it's sinful to look at a beautiful girl? Is it sinful to love her up a little? Maybe where you come from it's a sin. Uh-uh, brother, it's no sin, it's salvation. God made you and he made the girl, he made everything. So, it's no sin to look at a pretty girl; she's made to be loved and to make us happy. That's the way I figure it, friend."

Having crossed the yard and entered the dark cellar with its barrels, Marianka stopped by one of them, and after mumbling the appropriate prayer plunged a dipper into it. Vania stood by the door smiling as he watched her. He thought it very funny that she should wear just a smock, close-fitted behind and tucked up in front and he found the necklace of silver coins round her neck even funnier. He thought it was very un-Russian and imagined how, back home in the servants' quarters, they would have laughed at her. "This *fille* is *très bien* for a change," he thought. "I'll tell the master, just like that."

"Get out of the light, you fool. Better hand me the jug," the girl suddenly called out to him.

When the jug was filled with the cold red wine, Marianka handed it to Vania.

"Pay Mother," she said, pushing away the hand in which he held out the money.

Vania snorted.

"Why are you dear people so unfriendly?" he said good-humoredly, shuffling his feet while the girl was closing the barrel.

She laughed.

"And what about you, are you people so friendly?"

"Yes, me and my master, we're friendly," he said with conviction, "and wherever we stay, our hosts are always grateful because he's a very nice, generous man."

The girl stood still while she listened to him, then she asked:

"Is he married, your master?"

"No, he's still young and single. In the gentry they never marry very young," he said pedantically.

"Hard to believe! He looks like a fattened-up buffalo, and he's still too young to marry. Is he the big chief here?"

"My master is a second lieutenant, but he's more important than a general because not only our colonel knows him but the Tsar himself. We're no ordinary army trash because our pappy's a senator and has an estate with more than a thousand serfs and sends us a thousand rubles at a time. That's why everybody always likes us. Otherwise, you could meet a captain, but if he hasn't got a penny to his name, what good is he?"

"Move," the girl said, "or I'll lock you in."

Vania took the wine to Olenin and told him, *"la fille très jolee"* and burst into stupid laughter.

13 THE tattoo sounded from the Village square. People were returning from their work. At the Village gate, the herd lowed, raising a gilded cloud of dust. Women and girls rushed busily through streets and yards, driving their

cattle in for the night. The sun disappeared behind the remote, snowy range. A bluish shade spread over the earth and the sky. Imperceptibly, gradually, stars began to light up over the darkened sky, and sounds died out in the Village. The cattle taken care of, the Cossack women gathered at street corners, installed themselves on door-steps, chewing sunflower seeds. Marianka, having finished milking her buffalo cow and the two others, joined one of these groups.

There were several women there, some young girls and an old man.

They were talking about the raider who'd been killed. The man was telling them what had happened; the women were peppering him with questions.

"And will he get a big reward?"

"What do you think?" the man said. "They say he'll get a medal."

"Mosev tried to cheat him and get the gun for himself, but the authorities in Kizlyar heard about it. . . ."

"He never was any good, Mosev."

"I hear Luke has come home," a girl said.

"Him and Nazar are tying one on at Yamka's this very moment. They must've put away at least half a pail by now."

Yamka was a disreputable, unmarried Cossack woman, who sold liquor to men on the side.

"What a stroke of luck for Luke," a woman said, "but I have to hand it to 'im—he's a good lad, smart and straightforward too. Just like his pop, Kiryak, used to be. The whole Village cried when Kiryak got killed. Here they come! And look, that drunkard Ergushev's with 'em!"

Among the three of them, Luke, Nazar and Ergushev had emptied half a pail of vodka, and now they were coming toward the group. Their faces, especially Ergushev's, were red. Ergushev was reeling and kept tittering and nudging Nazar in the ribs.

"What's going on here, girls, why no singing?" he shouted. "I'm asking you to sing for us!"

"Looks as though you've had a few!"

"You seem to be having a good time!"

"Why should we sing?" a woman said, "it's no holiday.

Go ahead and sing yourself! You're the one who's loaded."

Ergushev roared with laughter and nudged Nazar.

"All right, you sing and I will too. I'm good at it, I tell you!"

"What's up, you all asleep or something?" Nazar said. "We've come from patrol to celebrate, to celebrate what Luke did!"

Luke came up to the group, stopped, and slowly raised his sheepskin cap. His high-cheekboned face and his neck were red. He spoke quietly and softly, but in his slow deliberation there was more life and vigor than in Nazar's excited chatter and bustle. Nazar was like a playful colt who suddenly snorts, throws up his tail in a graceful curve, and stops dead as though his hooves had grown roots. Luke was quiet, spoke little, and kept shifting his laughing eyes from the girls to his drunken companions.

When he saw Marianka, he raised his sheepskin cap in a smooth, unhurried movement, stepped aside, and then stood still, looking at her, his feet spread slightly apart, his thumbs stuck in his belt. He was fingering his dagger. Marianka answered his greeting with a nonchalant nod of the head, installed herself on a doorstep, and took out a bag of sunflower seeds. Luke, cracking seeds and spitting out the shells, kept his eyes fastened on her. All the others had fallen silent when Marianka joined the group.

"How long'll you be around?" a woman asked, finally breaking the silence.

"Till morning," Luke said.

"Well, I hope you have a good time," the old Cossack in the group said. "I'm pleased for you, as I was just saying——"

"And I too was saying . . . ," the drunken Ergushev caught him up, giggling. "And look at the guests. . . ." He pointed at a passing soldier. "I love the vodka these soldiers have. Just love it!"

"We've got three of those pigs billeted on us," a girl said. "Grandpa went to complain to the Village authorities, but they say they can't do a thing for him."

"Ha-ha!" Ergushev giggled. "So you got trouble?"

"Bet they've smoked you out with their tobacco," another woman said. "Let 'em smoke outside as much as they like, but I won't let 'em do it in the house. Even if the Village chief orders me to. They'll probably rob you to boot, who knows. And, you'll notice, the Village chief didn't put up any of 'em in his own house, the devil!"

"So you're not happy about it all?" Ergushev said.

"They say that the girls've been told they've got to make the soldiers' beds and give them wine and beer," Nazar said, spreading his feet wider apart and pushing his sheepskin hat back, just like Luke.

Ergushev guffawed and put his arm around the girl closest to him.

"Well, what do you know!" he said.

"Get off, you leech," the girl squealed. "I'll tell your woman!"

"Go ahead, tell her," Ergushev shouted. "And he's telling the truth, Nazar is: they sent a circular around and he can read, you know. . . ."

And he put his arms around the next girl.

"Come on, off with you, you imbecile!" squeaked the rosy, round-faced Ustenka. She warded him off, and snorting with laughter swung at him.

Dodging, Ergushev almost fell over.

"Wow, and they say girls are weak! You almost killed me!"

"What did you have to come back for, you leech?" Ustenka said and turned away, choking with uncontrollable laughter. "So the raider almost got you in your sleep! Wouldn't have been a bad thing if he'd done away with you."

"Then you'd have set up a wail, probably!" Nazar said, laughing.

"Some wailing I'd do for you!"

"Ah, she wouldn't care. You think, really, she'd cry for me?" Ergushev said.

Luke kept looking at Marianka in silence. It obviously embarrassed the girl.

"What's this I hear, Marianka—they billeted their chief on you?" he asked finally, moving closer to her.

As always, Marianka did not answer at once. She slowly raised her eyes and looked up. Luke's eyes were laughing over something that was happening between them, something that had nothing to do with the conversation.

"Yes, it's all right for them—they've got two houses," an old woman butted in, "but another of their chiefs, they billeted him on Fomushkin, and he filled the whole place with his junk, so that the Fomushkin family's got nowhere to put themselves. Whoever heard of such a thing? Herding a whole crowd of them into the Village like that . . . ! They'll spread the plague all over the place!"

"They say they're going to build a bridge over the Terek," one of the girls said.

"And they told me," Nazar said, going up to Ustenka, "that they're going to dig a pit and throw all the girls into it who don't like young fellows." And he made a gesture which made everyone laugh. Ergushev, hugging each girl in turn, skipped Marianka who was next in line, and put his arms round an old woman.

"And why don't you hug Marianka then? It's her turn, isn't it?" Nazar said.

"No, this old one is sweeter," Ergushev shouted, kissing the old woman as she tried to push him away.

"He's strangling me," she cried, laughing.

The regular beat of footsteps at the end of the street interrupted the laughter. Three soldiers in overcoats, their guns on their shoulders, were marching to relieve the guard at the company ammunition depot. The corporal, a decorated veteran, looked angrily at the Cossacks and led his men in a line that meant that Luke and Nazar, who were standing in the middle of the street, would have to move out of the way. Nazar stepped aside, but Luke only screwed up his eyes and pulled his head down between his broad shoulders without budging.

"You can see there are people standing here—go around," he threw out contemptuously at the soldiers, glancing at them from the corner of his eye.

The soldiers passed in silence, stepping out evenly along the dusty street.

First Marianka burst out laughing, then all the other girls after her.

"Eh, they're smart lads," Nazar said. "Just like choirboys in long skirts!" And he marched along the road, imitating them.

Again they all burst out laughing.

Luke slowly walked up to Marianka.

"And where did you put up that chief?" he asked.

Marianka thought awhile.

"We gave him the new house," she said.

"What is he, an old man—or young?" Luke asked, sitting down beside her.

"You think I asked?" she answered. "I went to get him some *chikhir*, and I see he's sitting in the window with Uncle Eroshka—some sort of redhead. They brought a whole oxcart of stuff with 'em."

Marianka lowered her eyes.

"I'm glad I managed to wangle myself some time off!" Luke said, moving closer to the girl and looking her in the eyes all the time.

"How long can you stay?" Marianka asked with a little smile.

"Till morning. Give us some seeds," he said, holding out his hand.

Marianka smiled broadly and opened the neck of her blouse.

"Don't take them all," she said.

"Believe me, I missed you all this time," Luke whispered in a restrained tone, reaching into the bosom of her blouse for the sunflower seeds. He leaned still closer to her and started whispering something, his eyes sparkling.

"I won't come, that's for sure!" Marianka suddenly said aloud, leaning away from him.

"Really . . . I want to tell you something . . . honest," Luke whispered. "Do come, Marianka."

Marianka shook her head but she was smiling.

"Marianka, Marianka! Ma's calling us for supper," Marianka's little brother called as he ran up to the group.

"I'm coming right away," the girl answered. "Go ahead by yourself. I'll be along."

Luke stood up, tipping his sheepskin cap.

"I can see I ought to go home too. It'll be better that way," he said, trying to sound casual but hardly able to hold back a smile. He vanished around the corner of the house.

Night had fallen over the Village. Bright stars were scattered across the dark sky. The streets were dark and empty. Nazar stayed with the group of women, and their laughter continued to ring out. But Luke walked quietly away from them, crouched down like a cat, then broke into a noiseless run, holding his dangling dagger steady. He did not run home but in the direction of the assistant chief's house. He ran through two streets then turned into an alley. Gathering up the skirts of his Circassian coat, he sat down on the ground in the shadow of the fence.

"What a girl!" he thought of Marianka. "She just won't fool around! Well, give me time."

A woman's footsteps approached. He listened, laughing inwardly. With lowered eyes, Marianka was walking straight toward him in a fast, even stride, tapping against the paling of the fence with a switch. Luke got to his feet.

Marianka gave a start and stopped.

"Oof! You scared me. So you didn't go home," she said and broke into a peal of laughter.

Luke put one arm around the girl and took her face in his other hand.

"Oh, what I wanted to tell you. . . ." His voice trembled and broke.

"What kind of talk is this? It's late, Mother's waiting, and it's time for you to go and see your sweetheart."

She freed herself and started to run. At the wattle fence of her own yard she stopped and turned toward Luke, who was running along beside her, still trying to persuade her to stay.

"Well, what'd you want to tell me, night-bird?" And again she started to laugh.

"Don't you laugh at me, Marianka! So I have a girl-friend? So what! Say the word and I'll love you . . . I'll do anything you want. Here"—he jingled the money in his pocket—"let's enjoy ourselves! Others are having fun, but what about me? I don't get any joy out of you, Marianka!"

The girl didn't answer. Standing before him, she rapidly broke the switch into little pieces.

Suddenly Luke clenched both his fists and his teeth. "And why keep waiting all the time. Don't I love you, Marianka? Do what you want with me," he said suddenly, frowning bitterly and seizing both her hands in his.

Marianka's voice and expression remained calm.

"You stop swaggering, Luke, and listen to me," she said, not taking her hands from his but pushing him away from her. "I know I'm just a girl, but you listen to me. I didn't ask for it, but if you love me, here's what I say to you—and you can let go my hands. I'll marry you . . . but don't you expect any sort of nonsense out of me," she said, looking him straight in the face.

"What d'you mean you'll marry me? Marry . . . that's not within our power. You just love me yourself, Marianka," Luke said, abruptly changing his ardently gloomy tone for his former meek, tender, submissive one and looking close into her eyes.

Marianka pressed herself to him and kissed him strongly on the lips.

"Dear!" she whispered impetuously, pressing herself against him. Then she tore herself away, started to run without turning around, and disappeared through the gate of her house.

And although Luke begged her to stay a moment longer and hear what he had to say to her, she did not stop again.

"Go away! They'll see us!" she murmured. "Look over there—the lodger, damn it, is walking around."

"What a girl!" Luke thought. "She'll marry me! Marriage is all well and good, but I want her to love me."

He found Nazar at Yamka's and went off to have a good time with him. Then he went to see Dunia, and although she'd been unfaithful to him, he stayed the night.

**14** OLENIN had been walking in the courtyard as Marianka came through the gate, and he'd heard her say: "The lodger, damn it, is walking around." He'd spent the whole evening with Uncle Eroshka on the porch of his new quarters. He had ordered a table, the samovar, wine, and a lighted candle to be brought out, and, over a glass of tea and a cigar, he had listened to the talk of the old man, who had installed himself on the top step by the porch door. Although the air was still, the candle dripped and the flame wavered, now lighting up a corner of the porch, now the table with its dishes, now the white, short-cropped head of the old man. Moths fluttered about and, scattering dust from their wings, beat against the table and in the glasses, now flying into the flame of the candle, now disappearing into the darkness beyond the circle of light. Between them Olenin and Eroshka drank five bottles of *chikhir*. Again and again, Eroshka filled the glasses, offered one to Olenin, drank to his health and continued to talk untiringly. He told him of the old times, of his father who'd been nicknamed Broad-Shoulders, who could carry a four-hundred pound boar carcass on his back and empty two pails of *chikhir* by himself at one sitting. He told of his own past and of his pal Girchik with whom he'd smuggled felt cloaks from across the Terek during the plague. He told of the hunt when he'd killed two deer in one morning. He told of his sweetheart who would come to him at night when he was away on military duty. And it was all told so eloquently and so graphically that Olenin lost all notion of time.

"So you see, old fellow," Eroshka said, "you didn't know me in my prime. I'd have shown you a thing or two then. Now you see only what's left of Eroshka; but then my name rang throughout the regiment. Who had the fastest horse, the sharpest saber? Who'd get you a drink, who'd give you a good time? Who had to be sent into the mountains to kill Akhmet Khan? Always Eroshka. Who'd the girls love? Again, always Eroshka. Because I was quite a lad: a drunkard, a horse thief, a singer. A jack-of-all-trades, I was. Today you can't find Cossacks like that any more. It's awful to look at them. This high off the ground"—Eroshka indicated three feet—"and he puts on those silly boots and then admires 'em all the time and that's his only pleasure. Or he gets falling-down drunk; he doesn't drink like a man either but I'm damned if I know what he drinks like. And who was I? I was Eroshka the thief. And it wasn't just in the Village that I was known—they knew me in the mountains too. Everyone was a friend of mine—including Tartar princes. For me, a Tartar's a Tartar, an Armenian an Armenian, a soldier a soldier, an officer an officer—it's all the same to me so long as he's a drinker. 'You,' he says, 'should cleanse yourself of worldliness—don't drink with soldiers, don't eat with Tartars.' "

"Who says that?" Olenin asked.

"What d'you mean who? Our preachers. But then, just you listen to a Mullah or a Tartar Cadi who says to you: 'Why do you infidels eat pork?' You see, everyone's got his own laws. But I think it's all the same. God has made everything for man's joy. And there is no sin in anything. Look, for instance, at the wild beast. It lives in the reeds, on the Tartar side and on ours. Wherever it happens to be, there is its home. It eats whatever God sends it. But we're told that as a punishment for our sins we'll be made to lick red-hot pans. Still, I think it's all one big lie," he added after a pause.

"What's a lie?" Olenin asked.

"The stuff they preach. The captain of Chervlena used to be a buddy of mine. Crazy fellow, just like myself. Got killed in Chechenia. Well, he used to say those preachers just invented the whole thing. Once you go, he'd say, grass'll grow on your grave, and that's all there's to it." The old man laughed. "What a man he was!" he said.

"How old are you?" Olenin asked.

"Who knows? Perhaps seventy or so. When you still

had the Tsarina ruling you, I wasn't a kid any longer.
. . . So just figure how many years that makes. I guess seventy at least. . . ."

"I imagine so. And you're still in such good shape."

"Thank God for that—my health is good. Except that a witch has spoiled things——"

"What?"

"Sure, she put a spell——"

"And when you die, grass'll grow over you?" Olenin asked.

Eroshka apparently did not choose to be clearer on this point.

"What did you think?" he shouted, smiling, "come, drink up!"

15 "As I was saying," he went on, "that's the kind of man I am. I'm a hunter and there's no hunter like me in the whole area. I'll find and show you an animal and any bird and what's where. I've dogs and I've two guns and nets and a mare and a hawk—I've got everything, thank God. If you're not just bragging, if you're a real hunter, I'll show you everything. What sort of man am I? Well, if I've found a track, I know the animal: I know where he'll lie, where he'll drink, and where he'll roll on the ground. I rig myself a seat in a tree and sit there throughout the night watching. I'd rather sit there than sit at home. At home I'd only get drunk and then get into trouble and the women'd come and nag my head off and the boys'd shout things at me, enough to drive me out of my mind.

"Oh, it's a different matter to go out at sunset, pick out a good spot, press down the reeds and sit there watching like a self-respecting man ought. And you know everything that's going on in the forest. You can glance at the sky, and there the stars are moving around and telling you how much time has passed. You glance around, and the forest is rustling and any moment there'll be a crackling and a boar will come and wallow in the mud. You hear the young eagles screech and you listen whether it'll be the roosters or the geese that give voice: if it's the geese, that means it's not midnight yet. I know all this. And then, when I hear a far-off gunshot, all sorts of things occur to me: I'll wonder, who fired it—whether it was a Cossack like myself, whether he killed the animal or only wounded him, whether the good beast is now just dragging itself along, smearing the reeds with its blood, all for nothing. Oh, I don't like that, don't like it at all! Why maim an animal? The damned, damned fool! Or perhaps it was a raider killing some stupid Cossack kid. All this whirls around in your head.

"And once I was sitting by the water, and, lo and behold, there was a cradle floating downstream. It was intact—just the edge was broken off. Then all sorts of thoughts began to go through my head. Whose cradle is it? Your miserable soldiers must have come into the village, grabbed the little Chechen, killed it, poor child. One of those bastards just took it by its feet and, crash, just like that, against the wall! You think they don't do it? Ah, people have no hearts! And thoughts came to me that made me sad—they threw the cradle into the water, ran the woman out, burned the house down, and the father took his gun and went killing and looting behind our lines. It all keeps turning around inside your head. . . .

"Then, when you hear a litter of pigs breaking through the thicket, it sets something banging inside you. 'Come on, dearies, come nearer!' you hope, 'don't catch my scent!' And you sit there without stirring and your heart goes boom-boom-boom, hard enough to lift you up in the air. This spring a big litter came so close to me I saw their shadows among the reeds. So I say to myself, 'To the Father and the Son. . . .' And I'm about to pull the trigger when the sow grunts to her piglets, 'Look out children, a man is sitting here,' and off they scatter, crashing through the undergrowth. And she'd been almost close enough for me to bite her!"

"And how did the sow get it across to her piglets that a man was there?" Olenin asked.

"What d'you think? D'you imagine an animal is a fool? No sirree! That animal is smarter than man, even though you call it a pig. It knows everything. Say, for instance, a man crosses your track, he won't even notice it, but if a pig comes across it, it will turn away and run off. What does that mean but that there's intelligence in a pig: it recognized your stench while you yourself don't. And there's this to be said too—you're after a pig to kill it while the pig wishes to go about the forest, to stay alive. You have your laws, and the pig has its own. And although it's a pig, it's just as good as you: it's one of God's creatures just like you are. Ah, dear me, dear me! Man is so stupid—so stupid!"

The old man repeated this several times more, lowered his head, and became lost in thought.

Olenin, deep in thought too, got up, stepped out of the porch and, his hands behind his back, started pacing silently up and down the courtyard.

Opening his eyes, Eroshka raised his head and began to stare fixedly at the moths which were weaving over the fluttering candle flame and falling into it.

"Oh, you foolish thing, where are you off to?" he said. "You silly thing!"

He got up and started to wave the moths away with his thick, awkward fingers.

"Watch out, you'll burn yourself. Fly over here, see, there's lots of room here," he mumbled softly, trying to catch hold of the brittle wings of one of them gently with his thick fingers, and to send it away from the flame.

"You're bringing destruction upon yourself, still I'm sorry for you just the same."

He stayed there a long time, chattering and taking swigs directly out of the bottle while his host kept pacing up and down the yard. Suddenly a whisper beyond the gate attracted Olenin's attention. Instinctively he held his breath and heard a woman's laughter and a man's voice and the sound of a kiss.

Walking as noisily as possible on the grass, Olenin reached the far side of the yard. After a while the wattle fence creaked, and he saw on the other side of it a Cossack in a black Circassian coat and a white sheepskin cap;

at that moment a tall woman in a white kerchief darted past him. Her determined step seemed to say: "You and I have nothing in common!"

He followed her with his eyes until she reached his landlords' house, and he even saw through the window how she removed the kerchief and sat down. And suddenly loneliness, sadness, vague longings and hopes came over him.

The last lights were going out in the houses. The last sounds were dying out in the Village. The fences, the whitish outlines of cattle, the reed roofs, the stately poplars—everything seemed to be engulfed in peaceful, well-earned sleep. Only the ringing voices of the frogs reached the listening ear from their remote, damp places. In the east, the stars were thinning out, fading away in the increasing light. But overhead, they still grew denser and deeper. The old man was dozing with his head in his hand. In the courtyard across the street, a cock crowed. Olenin was still pacing up and down the yard, thinking of something. The sound of a song carried by a few voices reached him. He went up to the fence and listened. It was a gay song sung by young Cossack voices, among which one powerful, young voice stood out.

"Know whose voice it is?" the old man asked, coming out of his doze. "It's Luke, the lad who killed the Chechen raider. That's what he's so pleased about, the fool. Really, what a thing to be pleased about!"

"Have you killed people?" Olenin asked.

The old man suddenly raised himself on his elbows, brought his face close to Olenin's and shouted: "You ask too many questions! Why do you need to ask all those things? It's bad to talk too much! It's not just nothing to destroy a human being, it's not just nothing, oh no! Good night, friend, I've eaten my fill and I'm drunk," he said getting up, "So, shall I pick you up tomorrow when I go hunting?"

"Yes, do come by."

"Don't oversleep then or I'll fine you."

"You'll see, I'll be up before you," Olenin said.

The old man left. The song stopped. Steps and merry talk were still to be heard. After a short while the song was resumed farther off, and among the others, Olenin now recognized Eroshka's loud bass.

"Strange people," Olenin thought.

He sighed and went back into his house alone.

**16** UNCLE EROSHKA had retired from the Armed Cossacks. He was a man on his own. His wife had become converted to the Orthodox Church twenty years before, had deserted him, and married a Russian sergeant major. He had no children. He had not been bragging when he had said that in the old days he had been the finest fellow in the Village. He was still known throughout the regiment for the daring he had shown then. He had brought death to several men, both Chechens and Russians. He would go on forays into the mountains and steal from the Russians; and twice he had served prison terms. He spent most of his life hunting in the forest, where for days he subsisted on a loaf of bread and drank nothing but water. But when he was in the Village, he caroused from morning to night.

Returning home from Olenin's, he slept for a couple of hours, and waking before it was light, lay in his bed thinking about the man he had got to know the evening before. He liked Olenin's "simplicity" very much— by simplicity he meant Olenin's generosity with the wine. And he liked Olenin himself. He wondered how all the Russians managed to be so "simple" and so rich, and why they were all so well-educated and at the same time knew so little. He weighed all these matters in his mind and also pondered what he might wheedle out of Olenin for himself.

Uncle Eroshka's hut was quite large and fairly new, but the absence of a woman was obvious. Unlike most Cossack homes, which were neat and clean, his was very dirty and an incredible mess. All sorts of things had been thrown on the table—a blood-stained coat lay there, and half a rich doughcake next to a plucked, torn crow, food for the hawk. Rawhide sandals, a gun, a dagger, a little bag, wet clothes, and rags were scattered all over the room. In one corner stood a vat of dirty, stinking water in which more rawhide sandals were soaking, and nearby there were a rifle and a hunting screen. There was a net on the floor, along with a few dead pheasants, and near the table the chicken, attached by one leg, was pattering around on the dirty floor. In the unlighted stove stood a crock filled with a milky fluid. And on top of the stove, a screeching falcon tried to tear loose from its string, and a moulting hawk sat quietly on the edge, watching the chicken out of the corner of its eye and from time to time bending its head from right to left. Uncle Eroshka himself, wearing just his shirt, lay on his back on a very short bed which had been squeezed between the wall and the stove. His powerful, muscular legs were raised, and his feet were up on the stove. With his thumb he was picking at the scabs on his hands, which had formed over the scratches made by the hawk he'd trained without using a glove. All over the room, and especially near the old man himself, the air was saturated with that strong, but not unpleasant, mixture of smells which accompanied him wherever he went.

"You in, Uncle?" Eroshka heard a sharp voice outside the window that he at once recognized as that of his neighbor, Luke.

"Yes, yes, I'm home. Come in!" the old man shouted. "Hi, neighbor Luke, have you come just to see your old uncle or are you off to the outpost now?"

The hawk started at its master's shout and flapped its wings, pulling at its cord.

The old man liked Luke—he was the only member of the younger generation to escape Uncle Eroshka's scorn. Besides, Luke and his mother, being his neighbors, often gave the old man wine, clotted cream, and other household products, which Eroshka lacked. The old man, who all his life had given way to his impulses, justified this in a practical way. "Well, what of it?" he would say to himself, "they're well off. I'll give them some fresh meat, or a bird, and they don't forget me either, and maybe they'll bring me a pie, a cake, or something."

"How are you, Luke, I'm glad to see you," the old man shouted cheerfully, jumping up on his bare feet. He took a couple of steps. The floor creaked. He looked down at his turned-out feet and suddenly found them very funny. He laughed, stamped on the floor with his bare heel, stamped again, and did a little dance. "How about that?" he asked, his small eyes shining. Luke smiled faintly. "Well, are you going back to the outpost?" asked the old man.

"I brought you the *chikhir* I promised you at the outpost, Uncle."

"Christ save you," the old man muttered. He picked up his trousers and Circassian coat, which were lying on the floor, put them on, fastened his belt, poured water from the crock onto his hands, wiped them on the old trousers, smoothed his beard with a little bit of comb and stood before Luke.

"I'm ready!" he said.

Luke found a cup, wiped it, poured some wine, and sitting down on a bench, handed it to Eroshka.

"Your health! To the Father and to the Son!" the old man said, solemnly accepting the wine. "May you get what you want, may you be a fine fellow, and earn yourself a medal!"

Luke took a sip of wine, also with a prayer, and put the cup on the table. The old man stood up to get a dried fish, which he placed on the doorstep and pounded with a stick to soften. He grabbed it with his horny hands, placed it on his only plate, a dark-blue one, and put the plate on the table.

"I have everything, even a snack, thank God," he said proudly. "Well, what did Mosev do?" he asked.

Luke, evidently wishing to know the old man's opinion, told him how the Cossack in charge had taken the rifle away from him.

"Don't insist on keeping it, or there'll be no award for you," Eroshka said.

"So what, Uncle? They say that a Cossack with so little service won't get much of a reward anyway, while the rifle's Crimean and may get me up to eighty rubles."

"Eh, let it go anyway. Listen, once I got into trouble

with my commanding officer. 'If you,' he says to me, 'let me have that horse you captured, I'll put you up for promotion.' I refused, and nothing came of the promotion."

"But understand, Uncle, I have to get myself a horse, and they say you can't get one from across the river for less than fifty rubles. My ma hasn't sold our wine yet. . . ."

"Eh, in my time we didn't trouble ourselves with such things. When I was your age, I was already stealing whole herds of horses from the Nogay folk and driving them across the Terek. I've even given away a fine horse for a quart of vodka or a warm cloak."

"Why so cheap?" Luke wanted to know.

"Why? Don't be so stupid. Why do you steal if not so as not to be too stingy. And you youngsters, I bet you've never even seen how people drive off horses. What? Why don't you answer?"

"Well, what do you want me to say, Uncle? I guess we aren't that kind of people," Luke said.

"You're a fool, a real fool, Luke. 'Not that kind of people,' he says," Eroshka mimicked him. "But then, I wasn't the kind of Cossack you are when I was your age, see?"

"How were you different?"

The old man shook his head scornfully.

"Uncle Eroshka was a *simple* man, he never grudged anything. That way, everybody all over the Chechen country was my brother. And if one of my brothers came to see me, I'd make him drunk on vodka, put him up in my house, make him comfortable. And when I myself went over to visit him, I'd take along a present for him, a dagger or something. That's the way people should be and not like they are today: all the youngsters do today to amuse themselves is eat sunflower seeds and spit out the shells," the old man concluded, scornfully mimicking the way the present generation spat out the shells.

"That, I know," Luke said. "You're right about that."

"If you want to be a Cossack brave, be one and don't be a peasant. It's for muzhiks to save up to buy a horse and then hand over all their savings before leading the horse away."

They fell silent for a while.

"And it's so unexciting, Uncle, in the Village and on patrol duty. The fellows are so timid. Take Nazar, for instance. The other day we were in a Tartar village, and there Girey-Khan invited us to join him in a raid for horses in the Nogay steppe. No one else wanted to go, and I couldn't very well go by myself."

"And what about me?" Uncle Eroshka said. "Or do you imagine I'm all dried up by any chance? No sirree, give me a horse, and I'll go to the Nogay steppe this very minute."

"Why waste time on idle talk," Luke said. "You'd better tell me instead how to handle this Girey-Khan. He says all I'll have to do is to bring the horses as far as the river and after that, he says, he can find a place for the whole herd, if need be. But then he's one of them, a shaven-headed Tartar like the rest, and not to be trusted."

"You can trust Girey-Khan, lad. All his kin have been decent people and his father was like a brother to me. Do as I tell you—you know I wouldn't give you bad advice. Make him take an oath just to make sure, and also keep your pistol handy. Especially when it comes to dividing up the horses. Once I almost got killed by a Chechen— I'd asked him for ten rubles a horse. . . . So what I say is: 'trust 'em all right but don't turn up there without your gun.' "

Luke listened attentively to the old man.

"Tell me, Uncle, is it true what they say about you having an explosive grass?" he asked after a pause.

"No, I haven't any explosive grass, but I'll teach you something because you're a good lad . . . and never forget your old uncle. Do you want me to teach you?"

"Sure, Uncle."

"What do you know about the tortoise, lad? You know that the tortoise is a devil, don't you?"

"I know that."

"So then, you must find a tortoise's nest and fence it off so that she can't get back in. Well, she'll turn around for a while and then go off and return with some of that explosive grass and blow up the fence. So you come the next morning, find the place where the fence is broken, and by it there's bound to be some of the grass strewn around. Take it and go wherever you want: there'll be no lock and no door can stop you."

"Have you tried it, Uncle?"

"Well, as for trying, no I haven't, but I've heard it said by reliable people. The only charm I myself ever used was a holy verse when I got on my horse, and so nobody ever killed me."

"What's the verse, Uncle?"

"What, you don't know it? What people! A good thing you asked me. All right, repeat after me then:

> Hail, ye who in Zion are.
> Behold, this is your Tsar.
> Our steeds we mount to ride afar,
> Weeping Sophonius,
> Preaching Zacharias.
> Pilgrim Wanderer
> Loving man forever.

"Forever, forever," the old man repeated. "So you know it now? Repeat it then."

Luke laughed.

"So that's why they never killed you, Uncle! Is that so?"

"You've grown too smart for your own good. But you'd better learn it all by heart and recite it to me. Can't do you any harm in any case. Imagine—you just sing it once and you're all right. . . ." The old man laughed himself. "But you know, Luke, you'd better not go to the Nogay steppe."

"Why?"

"These're not the same times, not the same people. And you're quite a lousy bunch of Cossacks. And then they've sent all these Russians along. It'll land you in jail, I tell you. Better give up the whole idea. But Girchik and I, we used to——"

The old man was about to start telling one of his endless adventures, but Luke looked at the window and said: "It's getting light already, Uncle. Time to be off. Look me up sometime soon."

"God forgive me, I promised to stop by at that army fellow's and take him hunting. He seems quite nice, I think."

**17** FROM Eroshka's, Luke went home. A dewy mist, rising from the ground, enveloped the Village. Everywhere cattle, though still invisible, could be heard stirring. The cocks were crowing louder and more and more often. The air was growing transparent. The villagers were starting to awaken. When he came close to the fence around his house, Luke saw that it was all wet from the mist, as were the porch and the open shed. Through the mist he heard the sound of an ax chopping wood. He entered the house and saw his mother standing in front of the stove, stoking it with pieces of wood. His little sister was still asleep in the bed.

"So you've had your fill of merry-making?" the mother said quietly. "Where've you been?"

"Just in the Village," Luke said reluctantly, taking his rifle out of its holster and proceeding to examine it.

The mother shook her head.

Luke poured some gunpowder into a pan, drew some cartridge cases from a bag, and began filling them carefully. Then he sealed each of them with a ball wrapped in a little piece of cloth. He tested the loaded cartridges with his teeth and put them into a bag.

"Mother," he said, "remember I told you the bags needed mending? Are they ready?"

"Sure, our deaf-and-dumb's been working on them in the evenings. Are you off to the outpost? I haven't seen much of you."

"As soon as I'm ready I must go," Luke said. "And where's the mute? Is she in the house?"

"She must be chopping wood. She missed you. I shan't see him no more, she tried to say. She puts her hand on her eyes, like this, clicks her tongue, and then presses her heart . . . poor thing! Shall I call her? She understood everything—about you killing the raider. . . ."

81

"Do," Luke said. "And then, I had some grease there —could you get it for me, please? I must grease my saber."

The mother left, and a few minutes later Luke's deaf-mute sister came into the room. She was six years older than her brother and would have resembled him very much had it not been for her somewhat obtuse, coarse expression, such as is quite common among deaf mutes. Her feet were bare and muddy, she wore a patched smock, and an old blue kerchief was tied round her head. Her neck, arms, and face were mannish and sinewy —it was obvious that she did a man's work. She brought in an armful of logs, which she threw down by the stove. Then she walked over to her brother with a happy smile that twisted her face, touched his shoulder, and started making rapid signs, using her face and her whole body.

"Good, good, good girl, Stepka," Luke answered, nodding. "She's got everything mended and done. Here, this is for you." Taking two pieces of gingerbread out of his pocket, he handed them to her.

The girl's face turned dark red, and in her joy she let out a sound like a toneless trumpet. She took the gingerbread and gesticulated even more rapidly, pointing in one particular direction and passing her thumb over her eyebrows and her face. Luke understood and nodded with a faint smile. She was telling him to give nice things to eat to the girls, that the girls liked Luke, and that Marianka, who was the best of them all, loved him. She indicated Marianka by pointing rapidly in the direction of her house and at her eyebrows, by smacking her lips and nodding her head. She conveyed "being in love" by pressing a hand against her breast, kissing it, and pretending to be hugging something.

The mother came back, and learning what the deaf mute had been talking about, she smiled and shook her head. The daughter showed her the gingerbread and again let out the joyful trumpeting sound.

"The other day I told Ulitka that I'd soon send a matchmaker to them," the mother said. "She took it well, too."

Luke looked at his mother, then asked:

"And how about selling the wine, Ma? I need a horse, you know."

"I'll cart the wine when I have time, when the barrels are ready," the mother said, obviously resentful of her son's meddling in domestic affairs. "When you go, there's a bag with some things in it by the entrance door. I borrowed it from the neighbors for you to take to the post. Or do you want me to pack it in your big bag?"

"Fine," Luke said. "And if Girey-Khan comes from across the river, ask him to come and see me at my patrol post. I have some business with him."

He started to get ready.

"All right, I'll tell him. But where were you all night? At Yamka's or where? When I got up in the middle of the night to have a look at the cattle, I heard you singing. . . ."

Luke didn't answer. He went out onto the porch, strapped the bags over his shoulders, tucked up the skirts of his coat and took his gun. He stopped for a moment by the gate.

"Good-by, Ma," he said and closed the gate behind him. "Please send me a small barrel with Nazar. I promised it to the boys. He'll come in for it."

"Christ be with you, Luke. God save you! I'll send you some wine from the new barrel."

The old woman walked up to the fence, leaned over it and said, "Listen, one more thing."

Luke halted.

"You've been on a spree. That's fine by me—a young man is entitled to it. Also, God has sent you luck. That's good. But now, mind your step, son, don't get into trouble. Keep on the right side of your superiors—you have to. And I'll sell the wine, save some money, and we'll buy a horse and get the girl for you."

"All right, all right," Luke said, frowning.

The deaf mute let out a noise to attract their attention. She pointed at her head and then at the palm of her hand—which meant a shaven-head, a Chechen. Then, frowning, she pretended to be aiming a gun and trumpeted rapidly, shaking her head. She was trying to tell Luke to kill another Chechen.

Luke understood, smiled, and in a few quick, light

strides disappeared in the dense fog, one hand holding the gun under his leather cloak.

The old woman remained standing by the gate for a few moments, then returned to the house and immediately set to work.

**18** As Luke went off to the outpost, Uncle Eroshka whistled up his dogs and, climbing over the wattle fence, went around to Olenin's quarters by the back way—he didn't like to run into women when he was going hunting. Olenin was asleep and even Vania, although awake, was still trying to decide whether it was time to get up or not. Uncle Eroshka, in full hunting gear, with his gun across his back, opened the door.

"To arms!" he shouted in his thick voice. "Sound the alarm! The Chechens are here! Ivan! Prepare the samovar for your master. Get up, man! Quick!" the old man shouted. "That's the way it's done here, my lad. Look, the girls are up already. Take a peek out the window, take a peek—see, she's going to draw water and you're sleeping still!"

Olenin awoke and jumped up. How fresh and cheerful everything seemed to him at the sight of the old man and at the sound of his voice!

"Hurry, Vania, hurry!" he called out.

"So, that's how you go hunting! People are eating their breakfasts already, and you're asleep. Here, Lam, sit!" he shouted at his dog. "Got your gun ready?" He was shouting as loud as if there'd been a whole crowd of people in the room.

"Well, what can I do? I plead guilty. The powder, Vania! The wads!" Olenin said.

"A fine!" the old man shouted.

*"Du tay voulayvoo?"* Vania said, grinning.

"You're not one of us, damn it, that's not our lingo

you're babbling!" the old man shouted at him, baring his
worn-down teeth.

"I should be forgiven since it's the first time," Olenin
said jokingly, pulling on his boots.

"You're forgiven, for the first time," Eroshka said,
"but the next time you oversleep I'll fine you a pail of
*chikhir*. Once the day gets hot, there'll be no deer
around."

"Well, and even if you find one, he's smarter than we
are," Olenin said, repeating the old man's words of the
evening before. "You can't fool him."

"Go on, laugh! Kill one first, then talk. Well,
hurry up! Hey, looks like your landlord's coming this
way," Eroshka said, looking out of the window. "He's all
dressed up! He's got his new coat on, so's you can see
he's an officer. Ah, what a bunch, what a bunch!"

And, sure enough, Vania came in and said that the
landlord wished to see Olenin.

*"L'argent,"* he remarked significantly to warn his master of the purpose of the assistant chief's visit.

Then the landlord himself entered the room. He wore a
new Circassian coat with an officer's epaulet on the
shoulder and polished boots—a rare sight among the Cossacks. He walked with a roll, smiling. He welcomed
Olenin officially.

The landlord was an educated man who had been to
Russia. He was the schoolteacher and, above all, a
gentleman. He wanted his good breeding to be evident,
but in spite of everything, under this unfortunate veneer
he had imposed on himself—the mannerisms, the show
of self-confidence, the grotesque speech—one felt he was
just another Uncle Eroshka. This came out too in his
sunburnt face, his hands, his reddish nose. Olenin invited him to sit down.

"Hello, Ilya Vasilievich, old fellow!" Eroshka said, getting up and, it seemed to Olenin, making an ironic, ex-
aggeratedly low bow.

"Hi, Uncle! What're you doing here so early?" the
landlord said with a casual nod.

The landlord was about forty, a dry, spare, handsome
man in very good shape for his years, with a graying,

wedge-shaped beard. He was evidently afraid that Olenin
would receive him as if he were just an ordinary Cossack and so tried to make him feel his importance right
away.

"This is our Egyptian Nimrod," he said with a self-
satisfied smile, turning to Olenin and indicating the old
man. "A mighty hunter before the Lord. He's very good
at many things. I see you've met him already."

Uncle Eroshka sat gazing at his feet in their wet rawhide sandals, thoughtfully shaking his head, as if wondering at the composure and learning of the assistant
chief. "Gyptian Nimrod," he repeated. "What'll he think
up next?"

"Yes. As you see, we're off hunting," Olenin said.

"Yes, sir," the assistant chief said, "and I had a little
business to discuss with you."

"What can I do for you?"

"Since you are a gentleman," the landlord began, "and
as I may consider myself one too, since we both have
officer's rank, and since we can always come to an understanding, as among gentlemen. . . ." He stopped and
smiled at Olenin and the old man. "My wife, a simple
woman although of our class, could not quite understand
your words yesterday. But if you wish, you have my consent to your having these quarters. Keep in mind that
they could go to the regimental adjutant, without the
stable, for six rubles. But, being a gentleman, I can always allow free use of the stables. If you wish, both of
us officers, we can come to a private agreement, and I
will fulfill its conditions, even if it's not in strict accordance with our customs, though I myself come from this
region. . . ."

"A fancy talker," murmured the old man.

The landlord continued in this manner for a long time.
Out of it all Olenin finally grasped that the assistant chief
wished to receive six rubles a month in silver for the
quarters. He readily agreed and offered his guest a glass
of tea. The landlord declined.

"According to our silly rites," he said, "we consider
it something of a sin to use a heretic glass. Although
with my education I should . . . but my wife, in her
human frailty. . . ."

"Well, then, perhaps you will have some?"

"If you'll allow me, I'll bring my own glass, my personal one," the landlord replied, and he went out onto the porch. "Bring me my glass!" he shouted.

A few minutes later the door opened, and a youthful, sunburnt hand in a pink sleeve thrust a glass through the door. The landlord went to the door, took the glass, and whispered something to his daughter. Olenin poured tea for the landlord in his personal glass and for Eroshka in a heretic one.

"However, I don't wish to detain you," the landlord said, burning his tongue as he emptied his glass. "I, it so happens, also have a strong liking for fishing and am here only on leave of absence from my duties. I also wish to try my luck and see whether the gifts of the Terek will fall to my lot. I hope that you will come and visit me too, and have a taste of our family's wine, in accordance with our Village's custom," he added.

Thereupon, he begged to take his leave, shook Olenin by the hand, and left. While Olenin was getting ready, he heard the assistant chief giving orders to his household in an authoritative, no-nonsense voice, and a few minutes later Olenin saw him go past his window in an old, torn coat, with his trousers rolled up to his knees and a net across his shoulders.

"What a fraud," Eroshka said, emptying his heretic glass. "But what's this? Surely you're not going to pay him the six rubles? Who's ever heard of such a thing? They rent the best house in the village for two rubles. What a crook! Why, you can have mine for three."

"Oh, I suppose I'll stay here now," Olenin said.

"Six rubles! You can see it's fool's money. Eh-eh!" the old man said. "Ivan! Give us some *chikhir*!"

Olenin and the old man had something to eat and a drink for the road, and before eight, they left the house.

At the gate they came upon a harnessed oxcart. Marianka, her white kerchief down to her eyes and a coat over her smock, wearing boots and carrying a long switch in her hand, was leading the bullocks by a rope tied to their horns.

"Oh my, oh my!" the old man murmured, making as if to grab her.

Marianka waved her switch at him and looked gaily at the two men out of her magnificent eyes.

Olenin grew even more cheerful. "Well, let's go, let's go!" he said, throwing his rifle on his shoulder. He was conscious of the girl's gaze.

"Hup! Hup!" Marianka's voice sounded behind them, and then the wagon started creaking as it moved. They went through the pastures behind the Village, and all the time Eroshka talked. He could not get the landlord out of his mind and kept railing against him.

"Come now, what makes you so angry with him?" Olenin asked.

"He's stingy! I don't like that," the old man said. "He'll knock off and leave it all behind. Who's he piling it up for? He's built himself two houses already. And he got the court to make over his brother's orchard to him. And, you know, when it comes to paper work, he's a real pig too. They come all the way from other villages to have him write their papers for 'em. The way he writes it is exactly the way the business comes out in the end. Exactly. But who's he saving it all for? He's only got the one little boy and the girl—he'll marry her off and then there'll be no one left."

"So then, it must be he's saving for her dowry," Olenin said.

"What dowry! They'll take her all right, she's a beauty. But he's such a devil that he wants to marry her off to some rich fellow. He'd like to land some big fish for her. There's my nephew Luke, a neighbor of mine . . . a fine lad, the one who killed the Chechen. He's been courting her quite a while, but they still won't marry her to him. First it's one thing, then another: the girl's too young, he'll say. But I know what he thinks. He wants 'em to knuckle under to him. It's a damn shame for the girl, the whole thing. But they'll make the match for Luke in the end. He's the best Cossack in the Village, a real Cossack, killed a raider. They'll give him a medal for it."

"But what's this? Yesterday when I was walking in the yard, I saw the landlord's daughter kissing some Cossack or other," Olenin said.

"You're making it up," the old man cried, stopping in his tracks.

"Really!" Olenin said.

"The hellcat!" Eroshka said. Then he added wonderingly, "But who was he?"

"I didn't see who he was."

"Well, what kind of cap did he have? A white one?"

"Yes."

"And a red coat? And how tall, about your height?"

"No, taller."

"That's him!" Eroshka burst out laughing. "That's him, that's my Luke. The very one! Oh, he's a good lad! I was just like him. But it doesn't take much. A girl friend of mine slept with her mother and her sister-in-law, but I got there just the same. She slept in an upstairs room. Her mother was a real witch. Couldn't stand me. I'd come with my friend Girchik. So, under the window, I climbed up on his shoulders, I raise the window, grope around. She slept right there. Once, somehow, she wakes up and yells out. She didn't recognize me. 'Who's that?' And of course I can't speak. Her mother was beginning to stir around. I took my cap and shoved it over her mug, and she knew right away it was me from a patch it had on it. So then she popped right out of there. Those days I wanted for nothing. I used to get clotted cream, grapes—everything," Eroshka added practically. "And she wasn't the only one. That was the life!"

"Well, and what about now?"

"Now? We'll follow the dog who'll tree a pheasant, and then, go ahead and fire away!"

"Would you have gone after Marianka?"

"You just watch the dog now," the old man said, pointing at Lam, his favorite.

They went another hundred paces or so in silence, then the old man stopped again and pointed to a stick that lay across their path.

"And what d'you think that is?" he asked. "You think it's just lying there? No. It's bad the way that stick's placed."

"What's bad about it?"

Eroshka snorted.

"You don't know a thing. You listen to me. When

there's a stick lying like that, don't ever step across it, but either go around it or throw it off the path like this and say a prayer—'To the Father, to the Son, and to the Holy Ghost'—and go your way. That way, nothing will happen to you. That's what the old men taught me in my youth."

"What kind of rubbish is that!" Olenin said. "I'd rather hear about Marianka. So she goes out with Luke, does she?"

"Sh! Be quiet now," the old man cut him short in a whisper. "Just listen. We'll go around, through the forest there."

And stepping silently in his sandals, he preceded Olenin along the narrow path cutting into the wild forest thick with undergrowth. Several times his frowning face turned back toward Olenin who was rustling and thumping along in his heavy boots, his gun getting caught again and again in the overhanging branches.

"Don't make so much of a row. Walk quietly, soldier!" Eroshka kept whispering angrily.

One could feel by the air that the sun was up. The mist was lifting but still brushed the treetops. The trees seemed incredibly tall. With every step forward, the scenery changed. What appeared to be a tree would turn out to be a bush or just a reed.

19 THE mist had lifted somewhat, uncovering wet, thatched roofs, and was also turning to dew, dampening the road and the grass by the fences. All over the Village, smoke poured from the chimneys. People were leaving the Village; some for work, some for the rivers, others for military outposts. Olenin and Eroshka walked along a grass-covered trail. The dogs, wagging their tails, were running along on either side, from time to time looking questioningly at the men. Thousands of gnats

hovered about them, attacking their backs, their hands, and their eyes. It smelled of grass and of woody dampness. Olenin kept glancing back at the oxcart in which Marianka sat, urging on the oxen with her switch.

It was quiet. The sounds of the Village no longer reached them. There was only the crackling of the underbrush as the dogs moved through it and the occasional calls of birds. Olenin knew that the forest was a dangerous place, where Chechen raiders often hid. But he was also aware of the good protection a loaded rifle offered a man on foot. It was not that he was afraid, but he felt that another in his place might have been. He looked around him intently in the damp, misty forest, listened to the rare, faint noises with his hand on his weapon, experiencing a pleasant feeling that was quite new to him. Eroshka was walking in front of him, stopping by every puddle where there were animal tracks and pointing them out to Olenin. He seldom spoke, and when he did, it was in a whisper. The trail they were following had once been made by oxcarts, but it was now completely overgrown with grass. The elms and plane trees to either side were so dense and entangled with creepers that it was impossible to see beyond. Almost every tree was covered from top to bottom with wild vines, and under the trees there were thick patches of brambles. Each clearing was covered with blackberry bushes and gray, feathery reeds. Here and there the tracks of large animals and the little, tunnel-like trails of pheasants ran off from the path into the thicket. Olenin kept marveling at the luxuriant vegetation of this forest still untrampled by cattle. He had never seen anything like it before. The forest, the dangers that lurked in it, the mysterious whispering of the old man, Marianka with her strong, upright body, the mountains—it all seemed like a dream.

"Shsh, a pheasant's settled," the old man whispered, turning back toward Olenin and pulling his cap down over his face. "You cover your mug too." He signaled impatiently to Olenin and moved ahead, crouched almost on all fours. "He doesn't like human mugs," he whispered again.

Olenin was behind him when the old man stopped and started examining the tree. Above, the cock pheasant clucked at the barking dogs, and Olenin saw him. But at that instant a deafening report, almost like a cannon shot, came from Eroshka's huge gun. The bird fluttered up. Some feathers scattered, and it fell to the ground. Running up to the old man, Olenin roused another pheasant. He aimed and fired. The pheasant rose steeply and then came down like a stone, hitting branches on its way.

"Good boy!" Eroshka congratulated him and laughed. He himself was not too good at downing a bird in flight.

They picked up the birds and moved on. Olenin, exhilarated by Eroshka's praise and by the exercise, kept making conversational remarks. The old man paid no attention and then suddenly said, "Wait! This way. I found a deer track here yesterday."

They turned into the thicket, and after some three hundred paces reached a reed-covered, partly flooded glade. Olenin kept falling behind the old hunter, and at one point Eroshka, now about twenty paces ahead of him, stopped and waved to him to come along. When Olenin reached him, the old man pointed out a man's footprint.

"See that?"

"A man's footprint. So?" Olenin said as nonchalantly as he could.

The memory of Fenimore Cooper's *The Pathfinder* flashed in his mind, accompanied by the thought of Chechen raiders. But, as the old man was again creeping ahead stealthily, Olenin did not dare ask, and could not decide for himself, whether such creeping was required by the hunt or by the danger.

"That's my own footprint," Eroshka said, pointing at the grass through which could also be discerned the faint track of an animal.

He set out again, and this time Olenin kept up with him. As they moved down a slope they came to a spreading pear tree. By it, on the black earth, lay the fresh droppings of an animal.

The spot, covered over with wild vines, made Olenin think of a cosy, cool, shady arbor.

"He's been here this morning," the old man said and sighed. "The lair's still damp."

Suddenly, ten yards away, came the sound of a terri-

ble crashing among the trees. They started and seized
their guns. They heard the breaking of branches but still
could see nothing. For a moment they heard the
rhythmical thud of a rapid gallop. Then the sound
changed to a hollow rumble, farther and farther off,
spreading more and more widely through the forest.
Something seemed to have snapped inside Olenin's chest.
He was straining his eyes helplessly, trying to see through
the green screen. Then he looked at the old man. Eroshka
stood motionless, his rifle pressed to his breast, his cap
on the back of his head, his eyes gleaming uncannily, his
mouth frozen half-open showing his worn, yellow teeth.

"A stag," he muttered, throwing down his rifle in disgust. He pulled at his gray beard. "It was just standing
there. We should have come by the path. Goddamn fool,
no-good idiot!" He gave his beard a furious tug. "Imbecile! Pig!" he kept repeating.

And the sound of the fleeing stag came to them through
the mist from farther and farther off.

It was beginning to get dark when Olenin and Eroshka
returned. Olenin felt hungry and invigorated. Dinner was
waiting for them. They ate and drank and Olenin, feeling
warm and fine, went out onto the porch. Again the old
man started on his endless tales about hunting, about
Chechen raiders, about women, about his carefree, reckless life. Again, the beautiful Marianka kept appearing
and disappearing in the yard, her strong body outlined
under her smock.

20 THE next day Olenin went alone to the spot
where he and the old man had startled the stag. Instead
of leaving the Village through the gate, like a native, he
climbed over the thorny hedge, and before he'd even had
time to pull the thorns out of his coat, his dog had
flushed two pheasants. Hardly had he stepped in among

the briers than pheasants began to rise all around him—
the old man hadn't taken him here, reserving it for another time when they'd shoot from behind the screen.
Olenin fired twelve times and brought down five birds.
He worked so hard, clambering after them through the
briers, that he was drenched with sweat. He called his
dog, uncocked his rifle, loaded it with a bullet in addition
to the small shot, and brushing off the mosquitoes with
the wide sleeve of his Circassian shirt, went slowly to the
spot where they'd been the day before. He could not, however, control the dog, who kept coming upon trails on
the very path. So Olenin shot two more pheasants. This
detained him further. It was close to noon when he
began to recognize his surroundings and realized he was
near his destination.

The day was completely clear, quiet and hot. The
morning moisture had dried up even within the forest.
Myriads of mosquitoes literally covered his face, his
back, and his hands. His dog was no longer black but gray
with mosquitoes. Olenin's Circassian shirt was gray with
them too, and they bit through it. Olenin was on the
point of running back to escape them, having come to
the conclusion that this country was uninhabitable in summer. But then he remembered that others managed to
withstand them, and making up his mind to bear the
discomfort, allowed the insects to devour his body. And,
strange as it may seem, by noon the sensation began to
seem almost pleasant. It even seemed to him that the
forest would have lost much of its character and charm
without the mosquito-filled air, without the layer of mosquitoes that, mingled with his sweat, was mashed over
his drenched face, without the tormenting itch that had
spread all over his body. These millions of insects fitted
in so well with the monstrous lavishness of the vegetation, with the multitude of birds and beasts abounding
in the forest, with the dark foliage, with the hot fragrant
air, with the rivulets of rushing water that everywhere
seeped from the Terek, gurgling under the overhanging
branches, that what had at first seemed unbearable now
became pleasant. He circled around the place where they
had found the animal. He saw nothing and decided to
have a rest. The sun now stood directly over the forest

and fell on his back and head whenever he stepped out from under the trees into a clearing or a path. The seven pheasants tied to his belt weighed painfully on his hips. He found the tracks the stag had left the day before, slipped under a bush and into the thicket where the stag had been, and lay down in its lair. He examined the dark foliage around him, the damp place, yesterday's dung, the marks left by the stag's knees, a piece of black earth it had kicked up, and his own footprints left the day before. The place was cool and comfortable, and he thought of nothing and regretted nothing. And suddenly a feeling of causeless happiness and all-encompassing love overwhelmed him so completely that, giving way to a childish impulse, he started crossing himself and thanking somebody.

Then words flashed in his brain, strangely clear:

"Here am I, Dmitri Olenin, a being distinct from other beings, lying all alone, God knows where, in the spot where a handsome old stag used to live. This stag may never have seen a human being, and perhaps no man has ever sat here in thought. Around me are young trees and old, and one of these trees is encircled with wild vines, and pheasants are busying themselves, chasing one another and perhaps scenting their killed brothers."

He reached for his pheasants and looked them over. He wiped the warm blood from his hands onto his shirt.

"Maybe the jackals scent them too, but sense they can't get at them and lope off with dissatisfied expressions. Above me, among those dark leaves that loom up like huge green islands to them, one, two, three hundred thousand, a million mosquitoes are hanging in the air and buzzing, and each of them is buzzing about something, for some reason, and each of them is an individual, a Dmitri Olenin, just as much as I am."

He vividly imagined what the mosquitoes might be buzzing about:

"This way, folks! Here's something edible!"

They buzzed and landed on him. And he felt very strongly that he was not a Russian gentleman, not a member of Moscow society, not the friend or the relative of so-and-so or so-and-so, but simply another pheasant or mosquito or stag like those now around him.

"Like them, like Uncle Eroshka, I'll live awhile and then die, and he's right when he says that grass will grow over me and that's it.

"So what? Let it grow. I still want to live and be happy. I wish for one thing only—happiness. It doesn't make any difference whether I'm simply an animal like the others over whose corpse the grass will grow or whether I'm a frame into which a piece of the one God has been placed—in both cases I must live as best I can. The question is how to live in order to be happy and why haven't I been happy before?"

And he started to think of his former life and began to be disgusted with himself. He saw himself as a terribly self-centered, selfish egotist, although he really needed nothing for himself. He looked around at the sunlight filtering through the foliage, at the declining sun, at the clear sky and felt happy again.

"Why am I happy and what have I lived for until now?" he wondered. "I demanded so much. What didn't I try to think up? And I achieved nothing but disgrace and misery. And now I know that I need nothing to find happiness."

And suddenly he felt as if a mystery had revealed itself to him:

"Happiness consists in living for others. That's obvious. The desire for happiness is innate in every man and is therefore legitimate. When man seeks to satisfy it selfishly by looking for riches, fame, comforts, love—he may find it impossible to attain. Therefore, these particular aspirations are illegitimate—and not the desire for happiness. But what desires can always be satisfied, external circumstances notwithstanding? What are they? Love? Self-sacrifice?"

He was so terribly pleased and excited at having discovered what seemed to him a new truth that he jumped to his feet and began wondering for whom he could sacrifice himself, to whom he could do good, whom he could love?

"Since one can't live for oneself, why not live for others?" he kept thinking.

He took the gun and started out of the thicket. He wanted to get back quickly, to think it all over, and to find an opportunity to do some good. Out in the clearing, he looked around him. The sun could no longer be seen over the treetops. It was growing cooler. His surroundings now seemed unfamiliar to him, quite different from the countryside around the Village. Everything had suddenly changed: the weather and the nature of the forest. The sky was overcast. Wind was rustling the treetops. Olenin stood surrounded by nothing but reeds and battered, maimed trees. He started calling the dog, now out of sight pursuing some animal, and his voice came back to him hollow and empty. It was all quite eerie. He became frightened. He thought of Chechen marauders, of the killings people talked about, and expected a Chechen to appear from behind a bush at any moment and jump at him, so that he would have to fight for his very life, die, or be a coward. This made him think of God and of eternal life, things he hadn't thought about for a long time. And everything around him remained gloomy and bleak.

"And how can it be worth-while living for oneself when we may die at any moment?" he thought. "Die without having done any real good, in a way that no one will ever know the difference?"

He set off in what he assumed to be the direction of the Village. He had forgotten all about hunting. He felt exhausted. He scrutinized each bush, each tree with horror, expecting to find death lurking behind it. He wandered in circles until he stumbled upon a ditch in which flowed cold, sandy water from the Terek. Afraid to lose his way again, he decided to follow it, although he had no idea where it led to.

Suddenly the reeds behind him crackled. He shuddered and gripped his rifle. Then he felt ashamed of himself: his hard-panting dog jumped down into the ditch and began to drink.

He joined it and had a drink too. Then he followed the dog, assuming that it would lead him to the Village. But despite the dog's companionship, his surroundings seemed to grow even more sinister. The forest was getting darker, the wind was increasing, and the noise in the tops of the maimed trees grew and grew. Some large birds circled, screeching above their nests, in neighboring trees. The vegetation was thinning out, there were more and more rustling reeds and bare sandy spots covered with animal tracks. To the howling of the wind was now added another cheerless, monotonous din. He felt depressed. Inspecting the pheasants he had killed, he found that one was missing: only its bloody head and neck was sticking in his belt. He felt more frightened than he had ever felt before in his life. He started praying, horrified at the thought that he might die without having accomplished a single good deed. He wanted so much to live. He longed for self-sacrifice.

**21** SUDDENLY, it seemed as if the sun burst through the clouds inside him. He heard Russian voices, and the fast, rhythmical flow of the Terek. A few steps farther on, the brownish surface of the river ran between its dark-brown sandy banks and shallows. He saw the steppe beyond, the watchtower of the Cossack outpost, a saddled horse picking its way carefully among the brambles, and the mountains. For a moment, the red, setting sun peeked from behind a cloud, and its last rays slipped gaily over the water, the reeds, the watchtower, and a group of Cossacks. Among them, Olenin recognized Luke.

Again Olenin felt supremely happy without knowing why. He had come upon the Nizhneprototsk post on the Terek facing the pacified village across the river. He greeted the Cossacks, but finding no pretext for doing someone a good turn, went into the hut; and there too he found no opportunity. The Cossacks received him coldly. He lighted a cigarette. The Cossacks paid little attention to him, first of all because he was smoking and secondly because they had something else to occupy their attention.

Led by a scout, some hostile Chechens had ridden down from the mountains. They were relatives of the dead raider and had come to ransom the body. They were waiting for Cossack officers to arrive from the Village. The dead man's brother, a tall, well-built man with a clipped, red-dyed beard, had a regal bearing despite his ragged coat and shabby sheepskin cap. He looked very much like the slain raider. He did not vouchsave anyone so much as a look, nor did he glance at the dead man. He squatted on his heels in the shade, smoking a little pipe, spitting from time to time and letting out a few peremptory, guttural sounds to which his companion listened respectfully. Obviously this brave had many times come across Russians under a variety of circumstances, so that nothing about them now surprised him or even interested him. Olenin would have gone closer to the dead man to study him, but the brother looked up at him from under his brows with calm disdain and said something in a sharp, angry tone. The scout hurriedly covered the dead man's face with a coat. Olenin was struck by the brave's stern, majestic expression. He started to speak to him, to ask what village he was from, but the Chechen, hardly glancing at him, spat scornfully and turned away. Olenin was surprised that the hillman wasn't interested in him and decided that his indifference must be due either to lack of intelligence or to a failure to understand Russian. He turned to the scout, acting as interpreter. He was as ragged as the other, but his beard was black instead of red. His teeth were very white and his black eyes gleamed. He was quite nervous, but was perfectly willing to talk to Olenin and asked for a cigarette.

"They five brother," the scout told Olenin in his broken Russian. "Already this third brother Russians kill. Only two left now. He brave, very much brave." He pointed to the Chechen. "When they kill Akhmet-Khan (the dead man's name) he sit on other side in reeds, he sees everything. He see how they put him in skiff and bring him to shore. He sit there till night. He want shoot old man, but others not let him."

Luke came up and sat down beside them. "What Village're you from?" he asked.

"In those mountains there," the scout answered, pointing beyond the Terek to a bluish, misty gorge. "You know Suyuk-su? Be about eight mile beyond."

"Do you know Girey-Khan in Suyuk-su?" Luke asked, evidently proud that he knew him. "He's a friend of mine."

"He my neighbor," the scout answered.

"Really!" Luke seemed very much interested and started talking to the scout in Tartar.

Soon a Cossack captain arrived on horseback with the Village chief and an escort of two Cossacks. The captain, who belonged to the new school of Cossack officers, formally greeted the Cossacks, but got no soldierly response from any of them, only a few even casually acknowledging his greeting. Some, including Luke, got to their feet and stood to attention. The Cossack in charge reported that all was well at the post. Olenin found it all amusing. The Cossacks seemed to him to play at being soldiers. But they soon turned from these formalities to their ordinary ways, and the captain, a Cossack like the rest, began to talk in fluent Tartar to the scout. Some kind of a paper was written out and given to the scout, and the money was taken from him. Then they approached the body.

"Which of you is Luke Gavrilov?" the captain asked.

Luke took off his cap and stepped forward.

"I've written a report about you to the regimental commander. I don't know what'll come of it. I recommended you for a medal. It's too soon to put you in charge of a post. Can you read?"

"No, sir."

"A fine-looking fellow!" the captain said, continuing to play the commander. "Cap on! From which Gavrilov family is he? Broad-Shoulders?"

"His nephew," the Cossack in charge answered.

"I know, I know. Well, let's go! Give them a hand," he said, turning to the other Cossacks.

Luke's face had lighted up with joy and he looked handsomer than ever. He stepped aside, and putting his cap back on, sat down near Olenin again.

When the Chechens had put the body into a skiff, the brother of the slain man approached the riverbank. The Cossacks stepped back to make way for him. He pushed the boat off from the shore with a muscular leg and jumped in. Now, for the first time, Olenin noticed, he threw a quick glance over all the Cossacks and again asked his companion something in an abrupt tone. The man answered something and pointed to Luke. The Chechen looked at Luke and then turned slowly away and gazed at the far bank. There was no hatred in his look, only a cold contempt. He again said something.

"What did he say?" Olenin asked the nervous interpreter.

"Your man kill ours, ours kill yours. It all the same," the scout answered. He bared his white teeth and laughed. Then he jumped into the skiff.

The dead man's brother sat without stirring, gazing fixedly at the other bank. He was so full of hatred and scorn that he was completely uninterested in the Cossacks. The scout, standing in the back of the skiff, steered it skillfully, moving the paddle from one side of the boat to the other, and talking without pause. Beating its way slantwise across the current, the skiff grew smaller and smaller, and their voices soon became inaudible. Finally, the Cossacks saw the hillmen land on the other side of the river, where their horses were waiting. There they lifted the body, and although the horse shied, laid it across the saddle. Then they mounted the other horses and rode at a walk along the road past the Chechen village. A crowd of people came out of their houses to watch them pass.

The Cossacks on their side of the river were very pleased and happy. Laughter and jokes came from every side. The captain and the Village chief went into the hut to refresh themselves. Luke, with a cheerful expression that he tried in vain to make dignified, sat down next to Olenin, and with his elbows on his knees, whittled away at a stick.

"How come you smoke?" he asked, pretending to be curious. "Is it pleasant, or what?"

He must have said it only because he'd noticed that Olenin felt awkward and lonely among the Cossacks.

"A kind of habit," Olenin said. "Why do you ask?"

"Hm! If all of us started smoking there'd be trouble! . . . Those mountains aren't far," Luke said, pointing at the gorge, "yet you'd never reach 'em. How'll you manage to get home by yourself? It's dark. I'll come with you if you get permission."

"A good man!" Olenin thought, looking at the Cossack's cheerful face. He thought of Marianka and of the kiss he had heard outside the gate, and he grew sorry for Luke, sorry for him because he was so uneducated and uncouth.

"What a crazy world," he thought. "Here's a man who's killed another man, and it makes him happy as if he'd accomplished something wonderful. Is it possible he doesn't suspect it's not a cause for happiness, that happiness is not in killing but in self-sacrifice?"

"You'd better not fall into his hands now, brother," a Cossack who'd escorted the skiff said to Luke. "Did you hear how he asked about you?"

Luke raised his head.

"My godson?" he asked, meaning the Chechen he'd killed.

"The godson's quite safe where you've sent him. But the godson's brother. . . ."

"Let him thank God he got away in one piece himself," Luke said, laughing.

"But what are you so pleased about?" Olenin asked of Luke. "If they'd killed your brother, would you be so happy about it?"

Luke looked merrily at Olenin. It was as if he understood just what Olenin wanted to tell him but that he was above such considerations.

"What about it? That happens too! You think they don't kill our brothers?"

22 THE captain and the Village chief rode off. To please Luke and in order not to have to go through the dark forest alone, Olenin asked the Cossack in charge to let Luke go with him, and this was granted. Olenin thought that Luke wanted to see Marianka and, of course, he was glad to have the company of this pleasant, talka-

tive Cossack. Luke and Marianka were linked in his imagination, and he found it pleasant to think about them. "He loves Marianka," Olenin thought, "and I might have loved her too." And as they walked home through the gloomy forest, a strong new feeling of exaltation took possession of him. Luke too was feeling cheerful. And these two very different young men felt something like affection for one another. Every time one caught the other's eye, they felt like laughing.

"Which gate do you use?" Olenin asked.

"The middle one. But I'll come with you as far as the swamp. After that you'll have nothing to fear."

Olenin laughed.

"You think I'm afraid? Thanks, but you go on back. I'll get there alone."

"It's all right. I've nothing special to do. And then, why shouldn't you be afraid? You think we're not?" Luke asked, laughing, to soothe Olenin's wounded pride.

"Come in with me then. We'll have a drink and talk, and in the morning you can go back."

"You think I couldn't find a place to sleep overnight?" Luke asked, laughing. "But I've got to get back right away."

"I heard you yesterday. You were singing a song. And I saw you too. . . ."

"Oh, yesterday. . . ." Luke tossed his head.

"You're going to get married—right?" Olenin asked.

"My ma wants to get me married. And I don't even own a horse."

"You're not in the regular service?"

"How could I be? I just joined. I don't have a horse and can't get one. And that's also why I'm not married."

"How much does a horse cost?"

"They had one for sale the other day, across the river, but they wouldn't take sixty rubles for it even though it was a Nogay horse."

"Will you come and be my orderly? I'll arrange it for you, and I'll give you a horse," Olenin said suddenly. "Really. I have two, and I don't need both."

"What do you mean 'you don't need both'?" Luke asked, laughing. "Why should you give it to me. We'll be rich yet, God willing."

"Is that so! What about it without you being my order-ly then . . . ?" Olenin asked, glad that he had thought of giving the horse to Luke. However, he felt awkward and ashamed somehow. He searched for words but couldn't find anything to say.

It was Luke who broke the silence. "Do you have your own house in Russia, then?" he asked.

Olenin could not refrain from telling him that he had not only one house, but several.

"A good house? Bigger than ours?" Luke asked amiably.

"Much bigger, ten times. It's got three stories," Olenin said.

"And you have horses like ours?"

"I have a hundred head, cost three, four hundred rubles each, but they're not horses like yours. Three hundred in silver! Race horses, you know. . . . But I like the horses here better."

"Well, did you come here of your own free will, or what?" Luke asked, still seeming to be chuckling. "Look, here's where you went wrong," he added, pointing to a trail. "You should've turned right."

"Of my own free will," Olenin answered. "I wanted to see this area and take part in a campaign."

"I'd go on campaign any day," Luke said. "Hey, the jackals are howling," he added, listening.

"But listen, doesn't it scare you to think you've killed a man?" Olenin asked him.

"What's there to be afraid of? And I'd go out on cam-paign anytime!" Luke repeated. "I'd like it, I'd like it very much. . . ."

"Maybe we'll go together. Before the holidays our company's going, and your detachment too."

"And you wanted to come here! You've got a house, you've got horses, you've got serfs. Wow, I'd have gone off and had myself a time, and then some! What's your rank?"

"Probationary second lieutenant, and now I've been put up for confirmation."

"Well, if you're not bragging about the life you've had, I'd never have left for anything if I were in your place.

But I'd never leave home anyway. You like living among us?"

"Yes, very much," Olenin said.

Talking thus, they approached the Village. It was already completely dark. And, as well, they were enveloped in the dark gloom of the forest. High up, the wind moaned in the treetops. The jackals, suddenly seeming to be right beside them, howled, laughed, and wailed. And ahead of them, in the village, they could already hear women's voices and the barking of the dogs. The houses were outlined sharply against the sky. There were lights in the windows. The smell, the special smell, of the smoke of the dung-and-straw fuel floated toward them. And Olenin felt, particularly this evening, that in this Village he'd found his home, his family, his happiness. He felt that never again anywhere would he be as happy as he was here. He liked everyone that evening and Luke especially. Arriving home, Olenin, to Luke's surprise, went to the shed and led out the horse he had bought in Grozny. It was not the one he usually rode. But it wasn't a bad horse, although it was no longer young. He gave it to Luke.

"Why should you give it to me?" Luke asked. "I haven't done anything for you."

"Really, it's nothing to me," Olenin said. "Take it and you'll give me what. . . . There, now we can go on campaign."

Luke was confused. "But what is this? That horse cost a lot," he said, without looking at the horse.

"Take it, take it! If you don't, I'll be offended. Vania, take the gray to his place."

Luke took hold of the horse by the reins. "Well, thank you very much. I never expected, I never thought. . . ."

Olenin was as happy as a twelve-year-old.

"Tie it up here. It's a good horse, I bought it in Grozny. And it gallops well. Vania, bring us some *chikhir*. Let's go inside."

The wine was served. Luke sat down and took his glass.

"God willing, I'll make it up to you," he said, drinking down his wine. "What should I call you?"

"Dmitri."

"Well, Dmitri, God save you. We'll be pals. Now you

come and see us. It's true we're not rich, but friends are always welcome. I'll tell my ma that if you need anything—clotted cream, grapes. . . . And if you come out to the post, I'll be at your service—to go hunting, to go across the river, anywhere you want. Just think, the other day I killed a big boar and divided it up among the Cossacks. If I'd known, I'd have given it to you."

"Well, thank you anyway! But just don't use it as a workhorse, it's never been in harness."

"Use it as a workhorse, indeed! I'll tell you something else," Luke said, lowering his head. "If you like, I have a pal, Girey-Khan—he wants me to lie in ambush with him, on the road where they all come down from the mountains. Let's go together. After all, I won't betray you, you know!"

"Yes, let's go, let's go some time."

Luke seemed to have understood the way Olenin felt about him and was completely calm now. Olenin was surprised by his composure and simplicity and even found it a little unpleasant. They talked for a long while. It was quite late when Luke got up to leave. He wasn't drunk—he never got drunk—but he had had a lot to drink. He shook Olenin by the hand and left.

Olenin watched out of the window to see what Luke would do. Luke walked along quietly with his head lowered. Then, when he had led the horse out of the gate, he abruptly threw up his head, jumped as quick as a cat on to its back, threw the rein over its head, and with a whoop, galloped off down the street. Olenin had assumed that he was going to share his joy with Marianka, and although Luke did not do so, Olenin still felt happier than he'd ever felt before. He was as happy as a child and could not resist telling Vania that he'd given Luke the horse and why he'd given it to him, as well as his whole new theory about happiness. Vania didn't approve of this theory; he declared that *"l'argent il n'y a pas,"* and therefore it was all nonsense.

Luke stopped by at his house, jumped off the horse, and handed it to his mother, telling her to let it graze with the communal herd. He himself was due back at his post that same night. The deaf mute volunteered to take the horse to the herd, and indicated by signs that the next time she met the man who had given it to her brother, she would bow low to him, like that. The mother, on the other hand, simply shook her head on hearing her son's story about the horse. Secretly she was certain that Luke had stolen it, so she told the deaf-mute to take it to the herd before daybreak.

Luke went back to the outpost. On the way he kept wondering what had made Olenin give him the horse. Although he did not think the horse a good one, it was easily worth forty rubles and he was very much pleased with the gift. But since he could not understand why Olenin had made him this gift, he felt not the slightest gratitude. On the contrary, it aroused vague suspicions in him about Olenin's intentions. He couldn't put his finger on any of them, but it seemed to him incredible that an unknown man should, for no reason at all, simply out of the kindness of his heart, give away a horse worth forty rubles. Had Olenin been drunk at the time, it would have made sense. It would have meant he wanted to show off. But this man had been sober, so probably he wanted to buy Luke's assistance in some shady deal.

"But we'll see about that!" Luke thought. "And in the meantime, I have the horse. I'm no fool."

Luke felt he'd better watch his step with Olenin, and so began to develop unfriendly feelings toward him. He never told people how he got the horse. He told some that he'd bought it; with others he was evasive. Soon, however, the truth became known in the Village. Luke's mother, Marianka, her father, and other Cossacks learned about Olenin's unsolicited gift. They were nonplused and ceased to trust him. But although they no longer knew what to expect of him, his gesture aroused great respect for his generosity and wealth.

"You heard about that second lieutenant giving Luke a fifty-ruble horse just like that?" one Cossack would say to another. "That's a rich one for you!"

"I heard," the other would answer pensively. "I suppose Luke did him some favor. He's a lucky one, that Luke!"

"Young army officers are a shifty lot," a third Cossack would say. "Next thing you know, he'll be setting fire to a house or something."

**23** OLENIN's life became monotonous and uneventful. He had little contact with his superiors or his fellow officers. In this respect, it was very convenient to be in the Caucasus as a rich second lieutenant on probation. He was not sent out with working parties, nor was he used as an instructor. After the campaign his commission had been put up for confirmation and until the confirmation came through, he was left very much to himself. His fellow officers considered him an aristocrat and so were rather stiff with him. He, for his part, was not attracted by their life—their card games and their singing and drinking parties—of which he had had a taste when he was with the detachment. So now, in the Village, he tended to avoid them. An officer's life in a Cossack village has long followed a set pattern. Just as, on garrison duty, probationary officers regularly drink port, play cards, and discuss the rewards to be earned on campaign, so, in a village, they regularly drink *chikhir* with their landlords, invite girls in for a little snack, run after Cossack women, fall in love with and sometimes even marry them. Olenin had always gone his own way and had an unconscious aversion for the beaten path. And, here too, he did not fall into the usual rut of an officer's life in the Caucasus.

Quite naturally, he would wake with the first light, drink his tea, admire the mountains, the morning, and Marianka from his doorstep. Then he would put on a torn, old leather coat and soaked rawhide sandals, belt on his dagger, take his rifle and a bag containing food and tobacco, call to his dog, and by six, he would have set out for the forest beyond the Village. Sometime after six in the evening he would return tired and hungry with a half-dozen pheasants in his belt, or with some animal he had killed. The food and the cigarettes in his little

108

bag remained untouched. If his thoughts had been packed in his head like the cigarettes in his bag, it would have been evident that not one of them had stirred in his brain the whole time he'd been out. He returned home feeling spiritually refreshed, strong, and perfectly happy. He could not have said what he'd been thinking about all day. Thoughts, memories and dreams—and sometimes scraps of all three—meandered through his mind. Then he would come out of it, and ask himself what he had been thinking about. And he would find he'd been imagining himself a Cossack working in the orchards with his wife, or a raider up in the hills, or a boar running away from Olenin himself. And all the time he kept eyes and ears open for a pheasant, a boar, or a deer.

In the evening, without fail, Uncle Eroshka would be at his place. Vania would bring a jug of *chikhir,* and they would sit and talk quietly, drink their fill, and finally, both content, would separate to get some sleep. And the next day there would be hunting again, and the same healthy weariness; again the two men would drink their fill and talk, and again they would be happy. Sometimes, on a holiday or a day of rest, he'd spend the whole day at home. Then his main preoccupation was Marianka. Without realizing it himself, he eagerly watched her every movement from his windows or the porch. He looked at Marianka and loved her—or so he thought—as he loved the beauty of the mountains and the sky, and it didn't even occur to him to approach her. It seemed to him that the relations that existed between her and Luke could not possibly exist between her and himself, and still less possible were the sort of relations that exist between a rich officer and a Cossack wench. He thought that if he were to act as his fellow officers did, he would be giving up his utter contentment, his contemplation, for an abyss of suffering, disillusion, and regret. Besides, where she was concerned, he had already performed an act of self-denial which had given him great satisfaction. But the main thing was that for some reason Marianka intimidated him, and he could not bring himself to make a frivolous pass at her.

Once, during the summer, Olenin, instead of going

hunting, stayed home. Quite unexpectedly, a young man he'd met in Moscow came to see him.

"Ah, *mon cher,* how glad I was to learn that you were here!" he began, talking the mixture of Russian and French used in Moscow society. And he continued in the same fashion, scattering French words throughout his conversation. "They told me 'Olenin is here.' What, Olenin? I was so pleased that we'd been brought together again. Well, how are you? What're you doing here?"

And Prince Beletsky told Olenin all about himself: how he had joined the regiment temporarily, how the commander-in-chief had offered him the post of adjutant, and how, after the campaign was over, he would take it, though of course it held no interest for him whatsoever. "If one has to do service here, in this hole, one might as well at least advance one's career . . . a medal . . . rank . . . get transferred to the Guards. It's really quite essential, not for myself of course, but for my family, for my friends. . . . He received me very nicely. A very decent man," Beletsky said, talking without pause. "As for the campaign, I've been recommended for the St. Anne's Cross. And now I'll stay here until the new expedition leaves. It's marvelous here! What women! Well, and how are you doing? Our captain told me—you know Startsev, a kind-hearted, stupid creature—he said you live like a savage, that you never see anyone. I can understand your not wanting to have much to do with the officers here. I'm glad. Now we'll be seeing one another. I'm staying at a Cossack sergeant's. There's a delightful girl there—Ustenka! Believe me, a sheer delight."

And the French and Russian words poured on and on, out of a world that Olenin thought he'd left forever. The general consensus on Beletsky was that he was a kind and amiable young man. And perhaps he really was. But to Olenin, in spite of his pleasant, friendly air, he seemed extremely unprepossessing. He seemed to reek of the vile life Olenin had renounced. And what annoyed him most was that he could not—he clearly did not have the strength to—brush off this representative of that world; it was as if his former life still had some irresistible claim on him. He was irritated with Beletsky and with himself, and yet, against his better judgment, he found himself putting French phrases into his conversation and showing interest in the commander-in-chief and in his Moscow acquaintances. And because they both used this French dialect and referred to their fellow officers and the Cossacks with condescension, he received Beletsky as a friend, promised to go and see him, and asked him to drop in. Moreover, Vania approved of Beletsky, calling him a proper gentleman.

However, Olenin did not go to see him.

Beletsky at once fell into the usual life of a rich officer. In a month, before Olenin's very eyes, he became a veteran of the Village. He got the old men drunk, arranged little parties in the evenings, and went out to such parties at the girls' houses. He bragged of his conquests and even reached a point where the women and girls, for some reason, called him "Grandpa." And the Cossacks, able to clearly assess Beletsky as a man who liked his wine and his women, grew accustomed to him and preferred him to Olenin, who had remained a mystery to them.

**24** It was five in the morning. On the porch Vania was fanning up the flame under the samovar with a kneeboot. Olenin had already ridden off to have a dip in the Terek. He had recently thought up a new pleasure for himself—taking his horse to swim in the river. The landlady was in one of the outbuildings. She had just lighted the stove, and thick, black smoke was rising from the chimney. The girl was in the shed milking the buffalo cow. "She won't stand still, damn her!" her impatient voice could be heard exclaiming, and then the rhythmical sound of milking followed. Out on the street, near the house, the lively sound of hoofbeats was heard, and Olenin, riding bareback on his handsome, dark-gray horse, which was still glossy-wet, rode up to the gate.

Marianka's shapely head bound in a red kerchief popped for a second out of the shed. Olenin was wearing a red shirt and a white Circassian coat, a dagger in his belt, and a tall cap. He sat on the wet back of his well-fed horse with a certain air. Steadying his rifle on his back, he bent down to open the gate. His hair was still wet, his face shone with youth and good health. He thought of himself as handsome, agile, resembling a Chechen brave —but he was wrong. At a glance anyone who knew the Caucasus could have told he was simply an army man. Seeing the girl's head pop out, he bent forward stylishly, threw open the wattle gate, and pulling in the reins and flourishing his whip, rode into the yard. "The tea ready, Vania?" he shouted gaily, not looking at the door of the shed. The horse pranced on the dry clay of the yard. Olenin felt with pleasure how it drew in its flanks, pulling at the reins with every muscle aquiver, ready to take off and leap the fence.

"*C'est prêt,*" Vania said.

It seemed to Olenin that Marianka's pretty face still peeked from the shed, but he didn't look at her. As he jumped from the horse, his rifle got caught against the porch; he made an awkward movement and threw an alarmed glance toward the shed. The regular sound of milking had resumed and no one was to be seen.

He disappeared inside the house and re-emerged onto the porch with a book and his pipe. He sat down with a glass of tea on the part of the porch that was still shaded from the slanting rays of the morning. He wasn't going anywhere before lunch that day and intended to write letters, a thing he had long postponed. But for some reason he was reluctant to leave his place on the porch and go back into a house that suddenly resembled a prison. The landlady had lighted the stove, the daughter had driven out the cattle, and returning, she had started to collect and pile fuel bricks along the fence. Olenin was reading a book but without taking anything in. He kept looking up to watch the young woman coming and going. Whether she flitted into the damp morning shadow of the house or moved into the warm, sunlit center of the yard, where her shapely, bright-clad figure gleamed in the sunshine casting a black shadow—he was equally afraid to miss a single movement. It was a joy for him to see the freedom and grace with which she bent, the way her pink smock, her only clothing, draped itself over her breast and fell along her long, straight legs; how, as she straightened up, her heaving bosom was outlined under the fastened smock; how her slender feet in their worn red slippers rested on the ground without losing any of their shapeliness; how her strong arms, in rolled-up sleeves, the muscles straining, wielded the shovel almost angrily; and how her limpid black eyes from time to time turned toward him. And although her fine brows were knitted, her eyes shone with joy and suggested that she was conscious of her own beauty.

"Hello, Olenin. Been up long?"

Beletsky, in a Caucasian officer's tunic, had come into the courtyard.

"Ah, Beletsky!" Olenin said, holding out his hand to him. "Why are you up so early?"

"Couldn't help it. They kicked me out. I have a party tonight. Hey, Marianka, you coming to Ustenka's?" He turned toward the girl.

Olenin was surprised. How could Beletsky possibly address this woman so easily? But Marianka seemed not to have heard him. She bent her head, and throwing the shovel over her shoulder, walked toward the little hut with her mannish, cheerful stride.

"She's shy," Beletsky said, following her with his eyes. "She's always shy." And smiling gaily he ran up onto the porch.

"What party're you giving? Who kicked you out?"

"At Ustenka's, my landlady's, there's a party. . . . A party, with cake and a gathering of the local girls. . . . You're invited too, you know."

"But we . . . what'll we do there?"

Beletsky smiled slyly, winked, nodded toward the little hut where Marianka was.

Olenin shrugged. "Really, you're an odd fellow," he said, turning red.

"All right! Out with it!"

Olenin frowned.

Beletsky noticed this and smiled insinuatingly. "Come, come, what do you expect me to think?" he asked. "Here you're living in the same house, and she's such a remarkable girl, a real beauty——"

"A striking beauty!" Olenin said. "I've never seen such a woman."

"Well then?" Beletsky asked, completely bewildered now.

"It may be strange," Olenin said, "but why shouldn't I tell you the way it's been? Since I've been here, it's as if women didn't exist for me. And really, it's quite all right. And then, what can there be in common between us and these women? With Uncle Eroshka, it's different. I have something in common with him—our mutual love of hunting."

"What do you mean, nothing in common! And what's there in common between me and Amalia? Exactly the same thing. You may say they're dirty—that's another matter. But *à la guerre, comme à la guerre!*"

"Well, I've never known any Amalias, I've never known how to handle them," Olenin said. "But I have no respect for their kind, whereas I do respect these women."

"All right, go on respecting them. No one's stopping you."

Olenin didn't answer directly. He seemed to be longing to finish what he had started to say—it was so close to his heart.

"I know I'm an exception," he said, obviously embarrassed, "but my life has arranged itself in such way that I see no reason to change the rules. And I couldn't have lived here as happily as I have if I'd followed your way of life. I'm looking for something different in them, and I see in them things that you don't see."

Beletsky raised his eyebrows skeptically.

"Still, do come to my place this evening. Marianka'll be there. I'll introduce you. Please come. If you get bored, you can leave. So, will you come?"

"I would, but to tell the truth, I'm afraid of getting seriously involved."

"Oh, oh, oh!" Beletsky shouted. "Just come, please. I'll keep you out of trouble. Will you come? Promise?"

"I'd come, but really, I can't think what we'll do. How will we act with them?"

"Please, because I ask you, please. Will you come?"

"All right, I'll come. Perhaps."

"I simply don't understand you. They're delightful women, better than anywhere else. So why this monastic life? What's the idea? Why make life difficult and not take advantage of what's at hand? Have you heard your company's going to Vozdvizhenskaya?"

"I doubt it," Olenin said. "I was told that the Eighth Company would be going there."

"I had a letter from the adjutant. He writes that the commander-in-chief himself will take part in the campaign. I'll be glad to see him. I'm beginning to be bored here."

"I've heard there'll be a raid soon."

"I hadn't heard that. What I heard is that Krinovitsin got a St. Anne's Cross for a raid. He hoped to be promoted to lieutenant but . . . ," Beletsky said, laughing.

It was getting dark and Olenin started thinking about the forthcoming party. The invitation tormented him. He wanted to go, but it seemed strange, wild, and somewhat sinister when he thought of what he would be doing there. He knew that there'd be no men there, no old women, no one but themselves and the girls. What would happen? How should he behave? What should he say? What would they talk about? What would be the relations between him and these wild Cossack girls? He remembered Beletsky's stories about their strange, cynical, and, at the same time, rigid relations. . . . It struck him as strange that he'd be in the same room with Marianka and probably have to talk to her. It seemed impossible when he thought of her regal bearing. But Beletsky took it all so much for granted. "Is it possible that even with Marianka, Beletsky will be the same? I wonder," he thought. "No, it would be better not to go. It's disgusting, trite, and above all pointless." But then he was again tormented by the question: "What will it be like?" And he felt tied by the promise he'd made. He went out without having made a final decision, but when he reached Beletsky's house he entered.

Beletsky's house was just like Olenin's. It stood on six-foot stilts and consisted of two rooms. In the first, which Olenin reached by climbing a steep flight of steps, cushions, rugs and blankets were arranged in Cossack style along the wall facing the door. On another wall, brass basins and arms were hanging, and, under a bench, watermelons and pumpkins were stored. In the second room there were a large stove, a table, benches, and some Old Believers' icons. Beletsky slept here on a folding bed, and he also kept his saddle pack and baggage here. His weapons hung on the wall, with a little rug behind them, and on the table were his toilet articles and several pictures. His silk dressing gown was thrown over a bench. Beletsky himself, neat and tidy, lay on his bed in his underwear, reading *The Three Musketeers*.

Beletsky jumped up.

"See how I've installed myself here? Like it? I'm glad you've come. They're already hard at work, you know. Have you any idea what they make their pies of? Pastry filled with pork and grapes. But that's not the main thing. Look at all the fuss there!"

Olenin looked out of a window and saw an extraordinary commotion going on. Girls, carrying all sorts of things, kept running out of the landlord's house and then rushing back again.

"How long will it take?" Beletsky shouted.

"Not long. Sounds like you're hungry, Grandpa." A ringing laugh came from the house.

Ustenka, plump, red-cheeked, pretty, with her sleeves rolled up, rushed into Beletsky's house, carrying the plates.

"Get out of my way, you'll make me break the plates," she squealed at Beletsky. "You could come and help," she said, turning to Olenin and laughing. "And see to it that there are refreshments for the girls."

"Has Marianka arrived?" Beletsky asked.

"Sure, she brought the dough."

"Do you know," Beletsky said, "if one dressed that Ustenka properly, cleaned her up, gave her a little polish, she'd outdo our Moscow beauties. You know Borsheva? She's a Cossack woman and, you know, she married a colonel. *Quelle dignité!* Wonder where it comes from."

"I haven't seen Borsheva, but I think there's nothing finer than their way of dressing."

"My God, I can accommodate myself to any way of

life," Beletsky said, sighing with a smile. "Wait, I must go and see what they're up to."

He put on his dressing gown and ran out of the house.

"And you please see to the refreshments," he said.

Olenin told the orderly to go and buy gingerbread and honey, and as he gave the man the money, he suddenly felt disgusted with himself. He felt as though he were buying someone. And when the orderly asked, "How many mints and how many honey ones?" He answered, "Just as you please."

"Shall I spend it all?" the business-like old soldier asked. "The mint ones are more expensive, sixteen kopeks the——"

"All right. Spend it all, spend it all," Olenin said. He sat down by the window, surprised to find his heart beating strongly, feeling as though he were expecting something important, something evil.

He heard shouts and squeals from the hut where the girls were when Beletsky went in. And a few seconds later, he saw a laughing, shouting Beletsky emerge and run down the steps.

"They kicked me out," he announced.

A few minutes later Ustenka entered and solemnly invited them to come: everything was ready.

When they went over, everything was quite ready, and Ustenka was putting the rugs straight on the walls. On a table covered with a tiny cloth there stood a jug of *chikhir* and some dried fish. The place smelled of pastry and grapes. A half-dozen girls in pretty blouses, without their usual kerchiefs round their heads, were crowding in a corner by the stove, whispering, giggling, and bursting with laughter.

"Please do honor to my saint," Ustenka said, as an invitation to the guests to sit down to the table.

Olenin, surrounded by girls who were all beautiful, looked at Marianka and grew sad because he was meeting her in such vulgar, awkward circumstances. He felt stupid and clumsy and decided to do whatever Beletsky did. Beletsky, somewhat stiffly but with self-assurance and familiarity, approached the table and drank a glass of wine to Ustenka's health, inviting the others to do the same. Ustenka said that the girls didn't drink.

"But I suppose I could do with some honey," a girl's voice said.

They called the orderly who had just returned from the Village store with the honey and other refreshments. The orderly, half-enviously, half-scornfully, looked up from under his brows at his masters "having a good time," dutifully handed over his purchases wrapped in gray paper, and was about to account for the price and the change, but Beletsky chased him away.

They mixed honey into the glasses of *chikhir*. The gingerbread was scattered prodigally everywhere on the table. Beletsky pulled the girls out from their corner, sat them down at the table, and started pressing ginger-bread on them. Olenin noticed Marianka's slender, sun-burnt hand taking two large peppermints and one large gingerbread, then hesitate, unsure of what to do with them. The conversation was awkward and painful despite the easy manner of Ustenka and Beletsky and their at-tempts to get the party going. Olenin felt shy, couldn't think of anything to say, felt that they were curious about him and that perhaps they were sneering at him or that he was infecting the others with his shyness. He was blushing, and it seemed to him that Marianka, especially, felt ill at ease.

"Probably they expect us to give them money," he thought. "How does one do it? How could we give it to them quickly and leave?"

**25** "How do you manage not to know your own lodger?" Beletsky asked Marianka.

"How can I know him? He never comes to see us," Marianka answered, glancing at Olenin.

Olenin was alarmed. He flushed and said, without knowing what he was saying, "It's your mother I'm afraid of. She was so unfriendly the first time I entered your house."

Marianka laughed. "So she scared you off?" She glanced at Olenin and turned away.

It was the first time Olenin had seen her whole face—until then he had only seen her with her kerchief down to her eyes. It was obvious why she was considered the most beautiful girl in the Village. Ustenka was a pretty girl, small, plump, red-cheeked, with merry brown eyes and a constant smile on her very red lips. She was always laughing and chattering. But Marianka wasn't pretty at all—she was beautiful. Her features might have seemed too strong, almost too coarse, had it not been for her tall stature, powerful chest and shoulders, and above all, the severe yet caressing expression in her black, almond-shaped eyes, with their shadowed lids beneath her black brows. And then, her mouth was charming and her smile radiant. She seldom smiled, but when she did it was striking. She gave an impression of strength and health. All the girls were pretty, but they themselves, as well as Beletsky and his orderly who'd come in with the gingerbread, all instinctively looked at Marianka. And when they talked to all the girls, it was she they turned to. She was the proud and cheerful queen of them all.

Beletsky, trying to keep the party going, chattered incessantly, made the girls hand round the *chikhir,* fooled with them, repeatedly made suggestive remarks to Olenin in French about Marianka's beauty, referring to her as *la vôtre,* trying to get Olenin to behave as he did. It was becoming more and more painful to Olenin. He was trying to think up a pretext to clear out and run home when Beletsky announced that Ustenka, whose name day it was, was to offer *chikhir* to the officers with a kiss. She consented on condition that they should put money on her tray as is the custom at weddings.

"What the devil am I doing at this disgusting party?" Olenin muttered to himself and stood up, intending to leave.

"Where're you off to?"

"I must go and get some tobacco," he said, determined to flee, but Beletsky caught him by the arm.

*"J'ai de l'argent,"* he said in French.

"I can't leave now. I must pay up," Olenin thought, and he became terribly embarrassed over his clumsiness. "Why can't I do things the way Beletsky does? I didn't have to come here, but now that I'm here I mustn't spoil it for them. I must drink like a Cossack." And he took a wooden bowl with a capacity of about eight glasses, filled it with wine, and almost emptied it. The girls stared at him in bewilderment, almost fearfully, as he drank. It seemed strange to them and in bad taste. Ustenka offered each a glass and kissed them in turn.

"Here, girls, we'll have a good time from it," she said, jingling the four silver rubles they'd put on her plate.

Olenin no longer felt awkward. He felt like talking.

"Now, you, Marianka, what about you handing the *chikhir* around with kisses," Beletsky said, catching her by the hand.

"I'll give you kisses!" she said, swinging at him jokingly.

"I'd kiss Grandpa even without money," another girl said.

"Clever girl!" Beletsky said and kissed her as she tried to push him off. "Now," he said to Marianka again, "pass it around—give it to your lodger."

He took her by the hand and sat her on the bench next to Olenin. "God! Isn't she beautiful," he said, turning her head to see her profile.

Marianka did not fight him. She smiled proudly and turned her almond eyes toward Olenin.

"What a beauty!" Beletsky repeated.

"I'm a beautiful girl," Marianka's glance seemed to say.

Olenin, without realizing what he was doing, put his arms around Marianka and tried to kiss her. But she suddenly jerked herself loose, jumped up, making Beletsky lose his balance, and took shelter by the stove. This set everyone shouting and laughing. Beletsky whispered something to the girls, and suddenly all of them rushed out into the corridor and locked the door behind them.

"Why," Olenin said, "did you kiss Beletsky and then not want to kiss me?"

"No reason. I just don't want to, that's all," she said, her lower lip and one of her eyebrows quivering. "He's our Grandpa," she added, smiling. She walked over to the door and started banging on it. "What did you lock it for, damn it!"

"Why not? Let them be there and let us be here," Olenin said, approaching her.

She frowned and sternly brushed him away, and again she seemed so majestic and so beautiful to Olenin that he came back to his senses and was filled with shame for himself. He went to the door and started pulling at it.

"Hey, Beletsky, open up! What a stupid joke!"

Marianka laughed again, lightly and cheerfully.

"What, you're afraid of me?"

"You're just as ill-tempered as your mother."

"So you'd better stick to Eroshka. That'll make the girls like you more," she said and smilingly looked him in the eyes. He didn't know what to say.

"And if I came to see you . . . ?" he let fall.

"That would be a different matter," she said, tossing her head.

At that moment, Beletsky pushed the door open, and Marianka started back and bumped against Olenin with her hip.

"All I've been thinking the whole time is just rubbish: love is rubbish, and self-sacrifice is rubbish, and Luke too. There is only happiness and he who is happy is right." This thought flashed through Olenin's head, and with unexpected strength, he took hold of Marianka and kissed her on the temple and on the cheek. She did not become angry but simply burst out laughing and left the room to join the other girls. That was the end of the party. Ustenka's mother came back home from work, rebuked the girls, and sent them home.

26 "If I just," Olenin thought on his way home, "give myself a little rope now, I'll fall desperately in love with this Cossack woman." The thought was in his mind

as he went to sleep, but he felt that it would all blow over and that his usual life would resume again.

But it didn't. His relations with Marianka were no longer the same. The wall that had separated them had broken down. Now Olenin said hello to her every time they met.

When the landlord returned to collect his rent, he had heard about Olenin's wealth and generosity, and he invited him to his house. The old woman received him pleasantly now, and from the time of the party, Olenin often dropped in on his landlords in the evenings and sat there until late at night. Externally, he seemed to be living in the Village, just as before, but within him everything had changed. He spent his days in the forest, and when it began to get dark, by eight or so, he went to see his landlords either by himself or with Eroshka. And they grew so accustomed to him that they felt quite surprised when he didn't turn up. He paid well for his wine and was, in general, a quiet young man. Vania brought him tea, and he sat down with it in the corner by the stove. The old woman went on with her chores without minding him, and over tea or *chikhir* they talked about Village affairs, about the neighbors, asked Olenin about Russia. Sometimes he would take a book and read to them. Marianka crouched like a wild goat in some dark corner with her feet drawn up under her. She took no part in the conversation, but Olenin could see her eyes, her face, could hear her move, hear the cracking of sunflower seeds between her teeth; and he felt that when he spoke, she listened to him with total absorption. Even when he was reading, he felt her presence. Sometimes he felt her eyes were fixed on him and, turning to meet their radiant look, he would fall silent, staring at her. Then she would immediately hide her face, and he, pretending to be deep in conversation with the old woman, would listen to her breathing, to her every movement, and wait for her to look at him again. In the presence of others, she was mostly gay and pleasant to him, but when they were alone she was wild and rude. Sometimes he arrived at his landlord's house before Marianka had returned to the Village. Then he would hear her firm steps, and her blue calico skirt would flash in the doorway. She would enter, see him, and give him a small, gentle, hardly perceptible smile, which both made him happy and frightened him.

He never tried to obtain anything from her, nor did he want anything. Still, with every passing day, her presence became more and more indispensable to him.

Olenin was now so immersed in his life in the Cossack village that his past seemed quite unreal to him while a future not connected with this world was simply inconceivable. He was irritated by the letters he received from friends and relatives because they seemed to consider him a lost man, whereas he believed that it was not he but they, and all those who led a different life from his, who were lost. He was certain that he would never regret having renounced his former existence to settle down in the Village and lead such a solitary, independent life. He enjoyed himself during campaigns or when his company manned advanced positions, but only in the Village, only under the wing of Uncle Eroshka, only in his forest or in his house at the edge of the Village, only thinking of Marianka and Luke, did all the falsity of his former life become fully clear to him, make him angry, seem repulsive and ridiculous beyond words. As the days went by, he felt he was becoming more and more emancipated. The Caucasus differed from what he had imagined. He had found here nothing even remotely resembling his previous ideas about it or the descriptions he had read.

"There are none of those chestnut steeds, abysses, romantic heroes and villains," he thought. "People here live naturally. They die, they're born, they unite and are born again, they fight, they drink, they eat, they enjoy themselves and die again, and they recognize no restrictions except those imposed by nature itself upon the sun, the grass, the beast and the tree. They have no other laws. . . ."

And for this reason, these people, compared to himself, seemed so magnificent, strong and free that, looking at them, he felt sad and ashamed of himself. He seriously considered giving up everything, becoming a Cossack, buying himself a hut and some cattle, marrying a Cossack woman—only not Marianka whom he conceded to Luke

—and living together with Eroshka, hunting and fishing with him and going on raids with the Cossacks.

"Well, why don't I do it? What am I waiting for?" he asked himself. He even baited himself: "Am I too cowardly to go through with something I consider right and proper? Is my longing to become a simple Cossack, to live close to nature, to harm no one, to do good to people—is it more stupid than the dreams I had of becoming a minister of state or a colonel?"

But a voice seemed to tell him to wait, not to make any irrevocable decisions. He was restrained by the vague awareness that he could not live altogether like Luke or Eroshka, that his idea of happiness differed somewhat from theirs—in that happiness lay in self-sacrifice.

He was still very pleased about his gesture toward Luke. And he kept looking for an opportunity to make sacrifices for the sake of others. But he did not find many.

At other times he forgot about this newly discovered prescription for happiness and thought that his life could be identified with Eroshka's. But the feeling never lasted very long. He would return to the idea of deliberate self-sacrifice, and leaning on it, he was able to look serenely down on others and on a happiness he didn't share.

**27** JUST before the grape harvest, Luke rode in to see Olenin. He looked handsomer than ever.

"Well, are you getting married then?" Olenin asked cheerily.

Luke did not answer directly.

"I want you to know I've exchanged your horse over there across the river for another. This is a real horse, a Kabarda. And I know something about horses."

They examined the new horse and put him through his paces in the yard. It was a very fine one, a long, broad gelding with a glossy coat, a thick, silky tail, a soft, fine mane and the crest of a thoroughbred. He was so well-fed that, as Luke put it, "you could go to sleep on his back." His hoofs, eyes, teeth were such as can be found only in thoroughbreds. Olenin admired the horse tremendously; he hadn't come across a more beautiful one since he had been in the Caucasus.

"And you should see him go!" Luke said, patting its neck. "What a pace! And then he's so intelligent, he follows me everywhere."

"How much did you have to pay in addition to the other horse?"

"I didn't count it. I got it from a friend," Luke said, smiling.

"It's really a marvelous horse. How much would you sell him for?" Olenin wanted to know.

"They offered me a hundred and fifty rubles, but you can have it for nothing," Luke said gaily. "Just say the word and you can have it. I'll only take the saddle, and you give me a horse of some sort for my duties."

"No, not on your life!"

"Well then, here's a dagger I've brought for you," Luke said, unfastening his belt. He took off one of the two daggers that hung from it.

"I got it from across the river too."

"Thank you."

"And by the way, Mother has promised to bring you some grapes."

"Why should she? We'll be even anyhow, since I'm not paying you anything for the dagger."

"Of course not, we're friends. It's just like Girey-Khan across the river took me into his house and said: 'Pick whatever you want.' So I took this saber. It's our custom, see."

They went into the house and had a drink.

"Are you going to stay here for a while?" asked Olenin.

"Oh no, I've come to say good-by. I'm being transferred to a Cossack company stationed beyond the Terek. I'm leaving today with my friend Nazar."

"When will the wedding be then?"

"Well, I'll come back soon. We'll get engaged, and then

I'll go back to my company," Luke said reluctantly.

"What do you mean? You won't be seeing your betrothed?"

"So what? What do I have to look at her for? When you're on campaign, ask in our company for Luke. And you know, there're a lot of boars there! I got two of them. I'll take you with me."

"Good-by then and God keep you."

Luke mounted his horse, and without going in to see Marianka, rode in a slow canter down the street, where Nazar was waiting for him.

"What do you think? Shall we drop in there?" Nazar said, blinking and nodding in the direction of Yamka's house.

"All right, you go," Luke said. "Here, take my horse to her place, and if I'm long in coming, give it some hay. I'll reach the company by morning anyway."

"Didn't he give you any other present?"

"Uh-uh! I'm glad I paid him back with the dagger. I think he was on the point of asking for the horse," Luke said, dismounting and handing the reins to Nazar.

He passed under Olenin's windows again, darted into the courtyard, and ran over to the landlord's house. It was already quite dark outside. Marianka was getting ready for bed. She was combing her hair.

"Hey, it's me," Luke whispered.

Marianka's expression, which had been severe and calm, suddenly brightened. She opened the window and leaned out, frightened and happy at the same time.

"What? What do you want?" she said.

"Open!" Luke said. "Let me in for a minute. I've missed you so much. It's awful!"

Through the window he took hold of her head and kissed her.

"Let me in, really!"

"Stop talking nonsense. I've told you I won't let you in. Are you here for long?"

He didn't answer, just went on kissing her, and she didn't ask again.

"I can't even hug you properly through the window," Luke said.

"Marianka, who're you talking to?" They heard the voice of Marianka's mother.

Luke took off his hat, by which she might have recognized him, and crouched down by the window.

"Go away, quickly!" Marianka whispered to him. And then she answered her mother. "It was Luke. He was asking for Father."

"Well, ask him in."

"He's already gone. Said he was in a hurry."

And, indeed, Luke, stooping, passed under the windows in big strides. He was off to Yamka's, and Olenin was the only one to see him go. At Yamka's, Luke drank a couple of glasses of wine with Nazar, and then they rode out of the Village. The night was warm, dark and quiet. They rode in silence, hearing nothing but the hoofbeats of their own horses. Luke started singing a song about the Cossack Mingal, but before he had finished the first verse, he fell silent and said to Nazar:

"Well, she didn't let me in."

"Oh," Nazar said, "I knew she wouldn't. And you know what Yamka told me? Their lodger has started visiting them, and Eroshka brags that he got a gun out of him for Marianka."

"He's lying, the old son-of-a-bitch," Luke said. "She's not that kind. If he doesn't watch out, I'll bruise his ribs for him."

And he started singing his favorite song:

> From out the village of Izmailov, near
> To the garden where a lord abode,
> Out flew a keen-eyed falcon clear,
> And after him the hunter rode.
> He beckoned the keen-eyed falcon down
> To his strong right hand at his side,
> But circling still high o'er the town,
> The keen-eyed falcon replied:
> "In a golden cage you could not keep me,
> Nor on your strong right hand,
> And now I will fly till I reach the sea
> And a swan I'll kill in that land.
> And until my death I meet,
> I'll feed upon the sweet swan meat."

**28** THE betrothal was being celebrated at the landlord's house. Luke came into the Village but didn't drop in on Olenin, and Olenin did not attend the betrothal, although he had been invited by the landlord. He felt more depressed than he had since he'd come to live in the Village. He saw Luke, in his best clothes and accompanied by his mother, enter the landlord's house, and he was tormented by thoughts of why Luke should be so cool toward him. Olenin shut himself in his house and began writing in his diary:

"I have thought over many things and have changed a great deal recently, and I have come back to the simplest of ideas. In order to be happy, we must love and love self-denyingly, and love everyone and everything and spin the web of our love in all directions and catch in it whoever comes our way: Vania, Eroshka, Luke, Marianka."

As Olenin finished his writing, Eroshka came in. He was in great spirits. A few evenings earlier Olenin had been to see him and had found him, with a proud and happy face, in his yard, deftly skinning the carcass of a boar with a small knife. The dogs, including Eroshka's favorite, Lam, lay around wagging their tails slightly as they watched him work. Little boys also watched him from over the fence. They looked at him with respect and didn't tease him as they usually did. The neighboring women, who were not usually too friendly with him, greeted him. One brought him a jug of *chikhir,* another some clotted cream, and a third a little flour. The next morning Eroshka sat in his storeroom, all covered with blood, and dealt out pounds of boar flesh, some for money, some for wine. All over his face was written: "God sent me luck and I killed the beast and now I'm important." Later, of course, he'd spent his whole time drinking and hadn't left the Village for four straight days. And moreover, he'd been drinking at the betrothal.

Now Eroshka arrived from the landlord's house completely drunk, his face red, his beard disheveled, but wearing a new red coat trimmed with gold braid and carrying a balalaika that he had obtained across the river. He had long promised Olenin a treat and now felt he was in the proper spirit. Seeing Olenin writing took him somewhat aback.

"Go on, write on, write on, pal," he whispered. And as if some strange spirit lurked between Olenin and the paper ready to be scared off, he quietly sat down on the floor. Olenin looked at him, ordered some wine, and went on writing. Eroshka found it dull drinking by himself. He wanted to talk to someone.

"I've just come from the betrothal at your landlord's, but they're a bunch of pigs. I don't want to have anything to do with 'em, so I came to see you."

"And where did you get the balalaika from?" Olenin asked, still writing.

"I went across the river and got it," Eroshka said. "I'm good at playing it, you know. I know plenty of Tartar, Cossack, gentlemanly, and soldiers' songs. You just name it."

Olenin glanced at him once more, smiled, let out a little laugh, and went on writing.

His laugh encouraged the old man.

"Come on, brother, stop it," he said suddenly, with determination. "All right, suppose they did offend you? So what do you care? Spit at 'em! What's the good of all the time writing? What's the sense of it?"

And he tried to mimic Olenin by tracing with a thick finger on the floor and twisting his big face into a contemptuous expression.

"What's the good of scrawling down complaints. Better to have a good time, lad."

For in Eroshka anything to do with writing smacked of legal chicanery.

Olenin burst out laughing. So did Eroshka. He jumped up and started to show off his skill on the balalaika, playing and singing Tartar songs.

"Stop writing, old fellow. You'd better listen to me

and I'll sing something for you, or you'll knock off without ever having heard my songs. Come on, let's have ourselves a time."

He started with a song he'd composed himself which had an accompanying jig:

> Ah dee-dee, dee-dee, dee-dim,
> Where on earth did you see him?
> In the market, at the store,
> Selling pins and pins galore.

Then he sang a song which he'd picked up from his friend the sergeant major:

> On Monday I fell deep in love,
> On Tuesday, importuned my fate,
> On Wednesday, went to tell my dove,
> On Thursday, for reply did wait.
> On Friday she sent her reply,
> For me there was in it no hope,
> On Saturday, resolved to die,
> And went and bought myself a rope.
> But O, salvation gay and bright,
> I changed my mind on Sunday night.

Then he sang again:

> Ah dee-dee, dee-dee, dee-dim,
> Where on earth did you see him?

After that, winking, jerking his shoulders and taking little dancing steps, he sang:

> I will kiss you and embrace you
> And red ribbons round you twine.
> Oh, my little Hope I'll call you,
> Now, my little Hope, you're mine.
> So now tell me that you love me
> And our love will be divine.

And he became so excited that he started to skip about wildly, accompanying himself as he danced around the room.

The songs like *Ah dee-dee* and the gentlemanly songs he sang just to please Olenin, but later, after three more glasses of *chikhir*, the old days came back to him and he sang the genuine Cossack and Tartar songs. In the middle of one of his favorites, his voice suddenly began to tremble and he fell silent; only his hand continued to pluck at the balalaika strong.

"Oh, my friend," he said.

Olenin was surprised at the strange sound of the old man's voice. He looked at him and saw tears in his eyes, one of them rolling down his cheek.

"My days are gone. They won't come back," the old man sobbed. Then he suddenly shouted in a deafening voice, without bothering to wipe away the tears: "Come on, drink! Why the hell don't you drink?"

He was especially moved by one Tartar song. It had few words, and its charm lay in the sad refrain: *"Ai! Dai! Dalalai!"*

Eroshka translated the words of the song: "A young boy drove his sheep from the village to the mountains. Russians came, set fire to the village, killed all the men, and drove the women into captivity. The boy came down from the mountains. Nothing remained where once the village had been. No mother, no brothers, no house, nothing but a single tree. He sat under the tree and started to cry. 'I'm alone, just like you, I'm alone.' And he sang: *Ai! Dai! Dalalai!"* And the old man repeated this wailing, heartbreaking refrain several times. As he sang it for the last time, he suddenly grabbed the shotgun from the wall, rushed out into the yard, and fired both barrels, then sang even more mournfully: *"Ai! Dai! Dalalai!"* Then he fell silent.

Olenin followed him out, looking up in silence at the dark, starry sky where the flash from the shots had appeared. In the landlord's house, the lights were on and voices resounded. Out in the yard the girls crowded together by the door of the house and ran back and forth between it and one of the outbuildings. A few men rushed out of the house, and unable to restrain themselves, they echoed the refrain of Eroshka's song, and then they too fired their guns.

"But why aren't you at the betrothal?" asked Olenin.

"The hell with them! The hell with them!" the old man mumbled. He had obviously been offended by something.

"I don't like 'em. What people! Let's go back inside your house. Let 'em stay by themselves, and we'll have a good time on our own."

Olenin went back into the house.

"Tell me, how's Luke? Is he happy? Why didn't he come to see me?"

"Luke? Somebody lied to him. They said I got his girl for you," the old man said. "What do you say? We could get her all right, if we wanted to. Just give me a little more money. I'll arrange it for you. You can trust me."

"No, Uncle, money won't help if she doesn't love me. You'd better forget about it."

"You and me, we're a couple of unloved orphans," Eroshka said and suddenly began weeping again.

While listening to the old man, Olenin had drunk more than usual.

"So, Luke is happy now," he thought. And this made him sad. As to Eroshka, he had drunk so much that now he collapsed on the floor, and Vania had to summon some soldiers to help carry him out. Vania spat, watching them take Eroshka away. He had become so angry at the old man's unseemly behavior that he didn't utter a single word in French.

**29** IT was August. For days the sky had been cloudless. The sun burned down unbearably. Since morning, a hot wind had been blowing. It raised clouds of hot sand from drifts and from the road and scattered it through the trees, the reeds, and the villages. The grass and the leaves of the trees were covered with dust. The roads and the dried-out salt marshes were bare and hard and resounded underfoot. The water of the Terek was very low and was rapidly subsiding further, and the ditches were drying out. The slimy banks of the Village pond, trodden by cattle, were rapidly growing bare, and throughout the day one could hear splashes and squeals of boys and girls bathing there. The sandy reed beds were drying up in the steppe, and during the day the lowing cattle would run back into the cultivated fields. Wild animals had moved into the more remote reeds and into the mountains beyond the Terek. Clouds of mosquitoes and gnats hung over the lowlands and over the Village. The snowy peaks were veiled by a gray mist. The air was close and smoky. It was rumored that Chechen raiders had forded the shallow river and were roving on the near side. Each evening the sun set in a glowing red blaze.

It was the busiest time of the year. Villagers teemed in the melon fields and the vineyards. The vineyards were thickly overgrown and were cool and shady. Heavy black clusters of ripe grapes could be seen through gaps in the broad leaves. Creaking oxcarts, heaped high with grapes, moved along the dusty road between the vineyards and the Village. Clusters of grapes, crushed by the wheels, were scattered in the dust. Boys and girls, in shirts stained with grape juice, with clusters of grapes in their hands and in their mouths, ran after their mothers. Along the road one constantly came across ragged laborers carrying baskets of grapes on strong shoulders. Cossack girls, their kerchiefs tied over their foreheads, drove ox-carts laden high with grapes. Soldiers, meeting these carts on the road, asked for grapes and the girls without stopping their carts would climb up and throw them armfuls. The soldiers would catch them in the skirts of their coats. In some households the pressing of the grapes had already begun, and the air was fragrant with the smell of the crushed skins. Blood-red troughs stood under awnings, and Nogay workers with their trousers rolled up and their calves stained with juice could be seen in the yards. Grunting pigs gorged themselves on the empty skins and rolled in them. The flat roofs of outbuildings were stacked with black and amber clusters of grapes drying in the sun. Crows and magpies crowded around the roofs, picking out the seeds and fluttering from one place to another.

The fruits of the year's labors were reaped gaily, and this year the fruit was unusually abundant and good.

In the shady green orchards, surrounded by the sea of vineyards, one could hear laughter, songs, and gay women's voices and see the flash of the bright-colored dresses of the women.

At noon Marianka was in her orchard. She was taking her family's lunch out of an unharnessed oxcart, drawn up in the shade of a peach tree. Near her, on a spread-out horse blanket, sat her father, who had just returned from the school. He was washing his hands by pouring water on them from a jug. Her little brother, who had run up from the pond, stood wiping his face with his shirt sleeve. He kept looking anxiously at his sister and mother and catching his breath as he waited for his lunch. The mother, her sleeves rolled up over her strong, sun-tanned arms, was laying out grapes, dried fish, and clotted cream on a low, round Tartar table. The father dried his hands, removed his cap, crossed himself, and came to the table. The little boy grabbed the jug and drank greedily. The mother and daughter sat down at the table, crossing their legs under them. It was very hot even in the shade. Over the orchard the air was stale. The strong, warm wind rustling among the branches brought no relief; it only bent the tops of the pear, peach, and mulberry trees of the orchard. The father crossed himself once more, took from behind his back a jug of *chikhir* that had been covered with grape leaves, drank from the opening, and handed it to his wife. He wore just a shirt, open wide and uncovering his hairy, muscular chest. His fine-featured, cunning face was cheerful. There was none of his usual diplomacy in his attitude or in what he said. He was gay and natural.

"Think we'll manage to finish the part behind the shed before evening?" he asked, wiping his wet beard.

"We'll manage," Grandma Ulitka said, "unless the weather stops us. The Demkins, they aren't even halfway through yet. Ustenka's working alone there, and she's killing herself."

"What else can you expect of 'em?" the man said smugly.

"Here, Marianka, have a drink," Ulitka said, handing the jug to the girl. "God willing, we'll have enough to pay for the wedding feast," she added.

"All in good time," said the father, frowning slightly. Marianka lowered her head.

"Why not talk about it?" the mother said. "The business is settled, and it's not so far off."

"Don't get ahead of yourself. In the meantime we have the harvest to get in," the father said.

"By the way, you see Luke's new horse?" Ulitka asked. "The one he traded for the horse Olenin gave him?"

"No, I haven't seen it. But I was talking to the lodger's servant, and he told me he's received another thousand rubles."

"He's a rich one, all right—no doubt about that," the old woman said.

The whole family was cheerful and content.

The work was progressing well. The grape harvest was more abundant and better than they had counted on.

After lunch Marianka threw some grass to the oxen, folded her coat to make a pillow, and lay down on the fragrant, down-trodden grass. Although she wore only a faded blue smock, with a red kerchief round her head, she was still unbearably hot. Her cheeks were afire, she couldn't find a place to put her legs, her eyes were moist with sleepiness and weariness, her lips kept parting, and her chest heaved heavily and deeply.

The busy time had started a couple of weeks before, and the girl had been absorbed continually in the hard work. She would jump up at dawn, wash her face with cold water, and wrapped in her shawl, run barefoot to attend to the cattle. Then she would hurriedly put on her shoes and her coat, and taking some bread along with her, would harness the bullocks and drive away to the vineyards and orchards for the day. There she cut grapes and carried baskets, taking only an hour or so for rest. But in the evening, she returned to the Village gay and apparently untired, leading the oxen by a rope and prodding them with a switch. After putting in the cattle for the night and supplying herself with sunflower seeds, which she carried around in the wide sleeve of her smock, she stood on the street corner cracking them and chatting with the other girls. But as soon as it began to get dark, she returned home, had her supper with her parents and her brother in the dark outbuilding, then went into the house, carefree and healthy, sat by the stove and, half-drowsing, listened to their lodger talk. As soon as he left, she threw herself down on her bed and fell soundly and quietly asleep until morning. And so it went, day after day. She had not seen Luke since the day of their betrothal and was waiting calmly for the wedding day. She had become accustomed to their lodger and enjoyed the intent way he had of looking at her.

**30** THERE was no escaping the heat. Mosquitoes swarmed in the cool shadow of the oxcart. Her little brother, tossing in his sleep, was pushing her. Still, Marianka pulled the kerchief over her face and started to doze off. Suddenly Ustenka, her neighbor, came running up, dived under the cart, and lay down next to her.

"All right, girls, go to sleep," Ustenka said, making herself comfortable under the cart. "No, wait," she said jumping up again. "This won't do!"

She plucked some green branches and stuck them through the wheels on both sides of the cart, then she hung her coat over them.

"You let me in," she shouted to the little boy as she again crept under the cart. "Get out of here, this is no place for a boy—among girls."

When she was under the cart with her friend, Ustenka suddenly put both her arms around her, and holding her close, started kissing her cheeks and neck.

"Oh, my dearie, my dearie," she kept repeating, bursting into shrill, clear laughter.

"Where did you pick that up—from your Grandpa?" Marianka asked, pushing her off. "Come on, stop it!"

And they both laughed so loudly that Marianka's mother shouted to them to be quiet.

"Jealous by any chance?" Ustenka whispered.

"What're you talking about? Go to sleep. Why did you come?"

But Ustenka wouldn't stop. "Guess what I have to tell you?" Ustenka said.

Marianka raised herself on her elbow, arranged her kerchief that had slipped off, and said:

"Well, what is it?"

"It's about your lodger. I know something about him."

"There's nothing to know."

"Oh, you liar!" Ustenka nudged her with her elbow and laughed. "You're keeping it all to yourself. Tell me, does he come and see you?"

"He does—and what of it?" Marianka suddenly blushed.

"Well, I'm straightforward, and I'll tell everybody. Why should I hide it?" Ustenka asked. And her gay, red-cheeked face grew thoughtful. "Who am I hurting? I'm in love, and that's all there is to it."

"Who? Grandpa?"

"Yes, sure."

"It's a sin," Marianka said.

"Oh, dearie, when is one to have a good time if not before one's married? When I marry a Cossack, I'll have children and I'll have to behave. It's like you— when you marry Luke, you can forget about enjoying yourself. There'll be nothing but children and work. . . ."

"So what? Some women enjoy being married. Makes no difference," Marianka said calmly.

"But tell me, what happened with Luke?"

"What happened? He came and asked for my hand. My pa postponed it for a year. And now they've agreed that the wedding will be in the fall."

"And what did he tell you?"

Marianka smiled.

"What could he say? The usual thing. He told me he loved me and kept begging me to go into the orchards with him."

"He seems in a real hurry. But you didn't go, did you? And he's grown so handsome. He's the big hero now, and he's having a good time in the army too, you know. The other day our Kirka came home, and he told us about the horse Luke got himself in exchange for the other. But just the same, I bet he misses you. What else did he say?"

"You want to know everything," Marianka laughed. "Once he rode that horse up to my window at night. He was drunk. He kept asking me—"

"Well, didn't you let him?"

"Let him? I told him once, and that's enough. My word is like a rock," Marianka said seriously.

"He's handsome. If he wanted someone, there's not a girl would refuse him."

"Well, let him go and get 'em," Marianka said proudly.

"But don't you have even a little pity for him?"

"I do. But I won't do such a stupid thing. It wouldn't be right."

Ustenka suddenly dropped her head on her friend's breast, put her arm round her, and shook with smothered laughter.

"You stupid fool," she said, quite out of breath. "You refuse to be happy." And she started tickling Marianka.

"Stop it!" Marianka shouted through her laughter. "You're squashing Lazutka."

"Damn 'em, can't they keep quiet there!" came Grandma Ulitka's sleepy voice.

"So you refuse to be happy," Ustenka said again in a whisper. "You have no idea how lucky you are. They're all in love with you. You, you crusty thing. If I were in your place, believe me, I'd have turned that lodger's head. I was watching him when he came to our party. He was eating you up with his eyes. Even my Grandpa—what didn't I get out of him? And yours is supposed to be one of the richest of the Russians. His orderly was telling us they even have their own serfs."

Marianka rose and smiled dreamily.

"Do you know what he told me once, my lodger?" she asked, biting a blade of grass in half. "He said, 'I'd like to be a Cossack like Luke or like your little brother Lazutka.' Why do you think he said that?"

"Oh, he was just saying the first thing that came into his head. You should hear what mine says. Sometimes he talks as if he wasn't all there."

Marianka put her head down on her folded coat, put

her arm around Ustenka's shoulders, and closed her eyes.

"He wanted to come and work in the vineyard. Father invited him to come along," she said, fell silent, and went to sleep.

**31** THE sun reached them through the pear tree that had been shading the cart. Now its slanting rays had managed to pierce the shield of branches erected by Ustenka and burned the faces of the sleeping girls. Marianka woke up and started arranging her kerchief over her hair. Looking around her, she saw their lodger, his gun thrown over his shoulder, talking to her father. She nudged Ustenka and pointed at him smiling.

"Yesterday I couldn't find a single one," Olenin was saying, looking around anxiously but failing to see Marianka behind her screen of branches.

"But if you go over there, following the circumference . . . over there, in the abandoned orchard known as the Wasteland here, there are always hare to be found," Marianka's father was explaining, in language that had immediately become affected.

"It's not right to go after hares when things are so busy," Marianka's mother said lightly. "You'd better join us and give the girls a hand. Now, girls, come on, time for you to get up!"

Marianka and Ustenka were whispering under the cart, hardly able to stop themselves from bursting into loud laughter.

Ever since it had become known that Olenin had given the fifty-ruble horse to Luke, his landlords had become much more friendly, the father especially. And it seemed as if he welcomed Olenin's friendship with his daughter.

"But I'm not good at working," Olenin said, trying to peer through the green branches screening off the cart, now that he thought he had discerned Marianka's blue smock and red kerchief behind them.

"If you come, I'll give you some peaches," the mother said.

"It's according to the Cossack tradition of hospitality," the father said, feeling he had to redeem his wife's words. "She's silly, not realizing that, back home, you can have not only as many peaches as you want but also pineapple jam and other such things——"

"So there are hares in the abandoned orchard?" Olenin asked. "I suppose I ought to go and have a look."

He threw a quick glance through the green branches, lifted his sheepskin cap, and disappeared among the regular rows of green vines.

When Olenin returned to his landlords, the sun was already hidden behind the hedges of the orchards, and its rays were shimmering through the translucent leaves. The wind was lessening, and a freshness spread over the vineyards. While he was still far off, Olenin recognized, almost by instinct, Marianka's blue smock among the rows of vines. He walked toward her, picking grapes on his way. His excited dog now and again bit at an overhanging cluster, its mouth foam-flecked. Marianka, flushed, her sleeves rolled up, her kerchief fallen below her chin, was quickly cutting the heavy clusters of grapes and throwing them into a basket. Without letting go the vine she was holding, she stopped just long enough to give him a friendly smile, then went on with her work. Olenin came closer, slinging the gun behind his back to free his hands. "And where are the others? My God, you're all alone!" he was on the point of exclaiming, but he simply lifted his cap. He felt awkward alone with her but he forced himself to go over to her, as though he wanted to torment himself.

"That way you might kill some woman with that gun of yours," she said.

"I don't suppose so."

They both remained silent for a while. Then she remarked, "You could just as well give me a hand."

He got out his knife and started cutting the grapes in silence. He reached under the leaves for a heavy, three-pound cluster, so thick with grapes that they pressed against one another. Unable to find a good place to cut it off, he showed it to Marianka.

"Shall I cut it all off? Perhaps some of the grapes are still green?"

"Give it here."

Their hands touched. Olenin took her hand, and she smiled at him.

"So you're about to be married?" he said.

She didn't answer. She turned her head away and looked at him unsmilingly out of the corner of her eye.

"You in love with Luke?"

"What business is that of yours?"

"I'm envious."

"Oh, sure!"

"I'm telling you the truth! You're a beautiful girl."

He suddenly felt terribly ashamed. His words sounded so unbearably trite. He turned red and, at a loss, grabbed her hands.

"Whatever I am, I'm not for you, so stop this fooling," Marianka said. But the way she looked at him made it obvious that she knew perfectly well he wasn't fooling.

"I'm not fooling. . . . If you only knew . . ."

His words sounded even more trite to him. They did not at all express what he felt. Still he went on.

"I don't know what I wouldn't do for you——"

"Stop it, leave me alone, you gluepot!"

But her face, her shining eyes, her swelling bosom, her shapely legs, told him something quite different. He thought that she felt the banality of the things he was saying but that she was above such considerations. He felt that for a long time she had known everything that he wanted, but was unable, to convey to her, but that she wanted to see how he'd put it. And how could she fail to know what he wanted to tell her since she was herself everything he had on his mind? But, he thought, she did not want to understand, she did not want to react.

"Hello!" Ustenka's high-pitched voice came suddenly from behind the vines, followed by her shrill laughter.

"Hey, Dmitri, come over here. I need some help, I'm all alone!"

And her round, innocent face appeared through the leaves.

Olenin said nothing and didn't move.

Marianka went on cutting grapes, but all the time kept throwing glances at her lodger. He started to say something, but stopped, shrugged, shifted his gun to his hand, and walked off hurriedly.

**32** HE stopped twice to listen to the ringing laughter of Marianka and Ustenka. They were shouting something to each other. Olenin spent the rest of the evening hunting in the forest. He killed nothing and returned home as it was getting dark. Crossing the courtyard, he noticed the half-opened door of the landlord's house and saw through it the blue smock. On purpose, he called out to Vania very loudly to let him know that he was back, then he sat down on his porch and waited. The landlords were back from the vineyard. They had been working in the shed. They crossed the yard going to their house, but they didn't invite him in. Twice Marianka went out of the gate, and once, in the twilight, he fancied that she turned to look at him. He followed her every movement intently but did not dare go over to her. When she disappeared inside her house, he left the porch, went out into the yard, and started pacing up and down. But she didn't come out again. Olenin spent the whole night in the yard, listening to every sound that came from the landlords' house. He heard them talking in the evening, eating, preparing their beds and getting into them. He heard Marianka laughing about something. Then everything was quiet. The father and mother were discussing something in a whisper, and somebody was breathing evenly.

He entered his house. Vania was asleep with his clothes on. Olenin envied him. He went out and started pacing

the courtyard again. He was still expecting something.
But no one came out, no one stirred. He could hear
nothing but the even breathing of three people. He could
recognize that of Marianka and kept listening to it and
also to the thumping of his own heart. The Village was
quiet. The late moon rose, and one could see more clearly the snorting cattle, lying down and slowly rising. Olenin
asked himself angrily, "What is it I want after all?" He
was unable to tear himself away from the night and go
inside.

Suddenly he thought he distinctly heard the floor
creak and someone walking inside the landlord's house.
He rushed to the door, but all was silent again except
for the even breathing. And then the buffalo cow would
sigh deeply in the yard, turn over, get up on her front
knees, then on her four feet, swishing her tail; at that
point something would splash against the dry clay, and
the animal would sigh again and lie down in the dim
light of the crescent moon. Olenin kept repeating: "What
should I do? What should I do?" He would make up his
mind to go to bed, but then he would hear sounds and
imagine he saw Marianka stepping out into the moonlit
fog and he would rush to the window hearing her steps.

It was almost daybreak when he went to her window
and pushed at the shutter and then ran over to the door.
This time he really heard Marianka's sigh and the sound
of her footsteps. He took hold of the latch and knocked.
Careful, bare feet were approaching the door. The floor
creaked very slightly. The latch clicked, the door
squeaked, and a whiff of marjoram and pumpkin came
from the room as Marianka's figure appeared in the
doorway. He saw her only for an instant in the moonlight. She slammed the door and he heard her whisper
something and then her light, receding steps. Olenin
rapped lightly on the door, but there was no answer. He
ran over to her window and began to listen.

Suddenly he was startled by the sharp, squeaky voice
of a man:

"Fine how-do-you-do! I saw you! Fine thing!"

A short Cossack in a white sheepskin hat crossed the
courtyard and came up to Olenin.

Olenin recognized Nazar and didn't know what to do or say.

"Fine goings-on! I'll go and report it to the Village council. I'll prove it too! And I'll tell her father. Looks like one fellow isn't enough for her."

"What do you want from me?" Olenin forced out of himself.

"Nothing, but I'll report it to the council."

Nazar was talking very loudly, obviously on purpose. "Aren't you a clever one!" he said.

Olenin was pale and trembling. "Come here, come here. . . ."

He grabbed Nazar by the arm and pulled him toward his house. "You know nothing happened, she didn't let me in and I didn't . . . She's a decent girl. . . ."

"So let 'em find that out."

"Still, take this anyway. . . . Wait."

Nazar quieted down, and Olenin ran into the house and came out with ten rubles.

"Nothing at all took place, but still, I guess I'm to blame. So you'd better take this. Only for God's sake don't let anyone hear about it! Besides nothing happened at all. You know it."

"Good-by and have a good time," Nazar said, laughing, and disappeared.

Nazar had come to the Village on an errand for Luke —to find a place to hide a stolen horse. And on his way home he had heard the goings-on in the yard.

The next day he was back with his company and bragging to a comrade about how neatly he'd earned the ten rubles.

When Olenin saw his landlords the next morning, no one knew anything. He didn't speak to Marianka, and she simply let out a small laugh on seeing him. The following night he again couldn't sleep, again paced up and down the courtyard, again in vain. The next day he spent hunting, and in order to escape from himself, he went over to Beletsky's in the evening. He was afraid of himself and swore silently that he wouldn't go and see his landlords again. The following night he was wakened by the sergeant major. The company was to leave immediately on a raid. Olenin welcomed this and decided never to return to the Village.

The raid lasted four days. The commanding officer summoned Olenin, to whom he was related, and offered him a post at headquarters. Olenin refused. He couldn't live away from the Village. He had to go back. The raid had brought him a service medal that he had once wanted very much. But now it left him quite indifferent. Nor did he care about the confirmation of his commission which had not yet arrived. Accompanied by Vania, he reached the Russian lines without incident a few hours ahead of the rest of the company.

Then Olenin sat all evening on the porch staring at Marianka, and the whole night, without a thought in his head, he aimlessly paced the yard.

**33** THE next day Olenin woke up late. His hosts were already out. He didn't go shooting. He tried to read but kept rushing out, then going back into the house and stretching himself out on his bed. Vania thought he was ill. Late in the afternoon Olenin made an effort, got up, and started to write. He wrote well into the night. He wrote a letter which he didn't send. Anyway, no one could have understood what he was trying to convey. Nor was there any reason why anyone should want to understand except Olenin himself. Here's what he wrote:

"I keep receiving letters of sympathy from Russia. They're afraid over there I might perish, buried in these backwoods. They say that I'll become coarse, lose contact, take to drink, and even marry a Cossack woman. I suppose Ermolov had a point when he said that after ten years of service in the Caucasus anyone would become a drunk or marry a loose woman. Frightening, isn't it? Indeed, just think of it: I may perish that way when my lot might have been the great happiness of marrying the daughter of Count E——, becoming a Court chamberlain, or a local *maréchal de noblesse.*

"Oh, it's hard for me to tell you how silly and pitiable you all seem to me! You haven't the faintest idea about happiness, about life! For that you'd have had to experience life, even once, in all its artless beauty. You should see and understand what I have before me every day: the inaccessible snows of the mountains and a majestic woman of primeval beauty, the same beauty as that of the first woman as she came from the hands of her Creator. Only then, will it become obvious which of us, you or I, is perishing, whose life is real and whose is false. If only you knew how despicable you are in your delusions! When I picture to myself—in place of my house, my forest, and my love—your drawing rooms, your women with their ridiculous hairdos, their unnaturally moving lips, their weak, distorted limbs and their incredible social chit-chat—I feel horrified.

"I can still see those rich, eligible girls with their obtuse faces saying: 'Please go ahead, don't let my riches stop you.' I still remember your shuffling and reshuffling the precedence at table; your shameless matchmaking, your gossip, and your pretenses; your rules of etiquette as to who should be given the hand, who qualifies for a nod, with whom it is fit to converse; and finally the eternal boredom that is in your blood and is transmitted from generation to generation—and all cultivated deliberately, with the conviction that it is indispensable.

"I want you to understand one thing, or at least to take my word for it. All you have to do is to try to understand what is truth and what is beauty. And if you do, everything you say and think, everything you wish for me and for yourself, will all collapse in dust. Happiness is to be with nature, to see it and communicate with it.

"I can hear them saying with sincere pity: 'He may yet, God forbid, marry a common Cossack girl and become altogether *déclassé!* But I have but one aspiration: to be completely lost from your point of view, to marry a common Cossack girl. Only I don't dare to hope for it, because it would be the supreme happiness for which I do not feel I am worthy.

"Three months have passed since I saw Marianka, the Cossack girl, for the first time. Then the concepts and the prejudices of the world to which I belonged were still fresh in me. Then, I could not conceive that I'd fall in love with this woman. I admired her as one admires the mountains and the sky and could not help admiring her because she was beautiful as are they. Then I realized that the contemplation of this beauty had become a necessity in my life, and I began to wonder whether this might not be love. But I didn't find in my feeling for her anything that resembled what I imagined love to be. My feeling for her was not due to restless loneliness; it was not simply the longing to marry; nor was it a Platonic and, even less, a sensual love. All of these I had experienced before. All I needed was to see her, hear her move, and this made me, if not happy, at least tranquil. Then, at a party, I touched her and felt that there was, between this woman and me, an indissoluble link against which I can do nothing. But I still resisted. I tried to persuade myself that it was impossible to love a woman who will never share in the most important interests of my life, that I could not be in love with a woman just for her beauty, be in love with the statue of a woman. But I was already in love with her although I refused to believe it.

"After the party at which I spoke to her for the first time, our relations changed. Before that, she had been an inaccessible and majestic manifestation of nature for me. But now she became a human being. I began to meet her and to talk to her. Sometimes I helped her with her work, sat whole evenings in her father's house. And, throughout these close contacts, she remained just as pure, inaccessible, and majestic. To everything she always answered composedly, proudly, and with a sort of cheerful indifference. At times she was warm and friendly, but mostly she showed indifference—not a scornful indifference but an exasperating and enchanting one. Every day, I affected a smile and addressed her lightly and teasingly while inside me I was feeling the agony of passion. She knew I was acting but still gazed at me simply, unaffectedly, and gaily. I could stand it no longer. I longed to stop pretending to her, to tell her just what I felt and thought. Once I spoke out. I was in the vineyard. I started telling her about my love in words that I am ashamed to think back on. I am ashamed because she was infinitely above my words and above the feeling I was trying to express through them. I fell silent, and from that day on my position has become untenable. I felt that my former, jocular approach had become impossible and also that I was not good enough to have straightforward, simple relations with her. I kept asking myself what I should do. I sometimes imagined her my mistress, sometimes my wife, and then spurned both these thoughts with disgust. It would have been inconceivable to turn her into a loose woman. And perhaps it would have been even worse for her to become 'one-of-the-local-Cossack-girls-who-married-an-officer.' Ah, if only I could become another Luke, a Cossack stealing horses, getting drunk on *chikhir,* bellowing their songs, killing people, climbing drunk through her window at night without caring who I am and what I am—then, it would have been different. Then we would understand each other, then I would be happy. I have tried to adopt their way of life only to become more and more aware of my weakness, my artificiality. I could never forget myself and my complex, unnatural, freakish past. And then my future would loom up even more hopelessly before me.

"And so every day I see before me these remote, snowy mountains and this majestic, happy woman. And I know that, for me, happiness is impossible, that this woman is not for me! The most tormenting and the most delightful part of my situation is that I feel that I understand her while she could never understand me. And she'll never understand me, not because she's beneath me, but, on the contrary, because she does not need to. She's fortunate; she's like nature—even, quiet and independent.

"And I, a weak, distorted creature, I want her to understand me so much!

"I couldn't sleep at night. I spent nights under her windows, without purpose, without realizing what I was doing. On the 18th of this month our company went on a raid. I spent three days out of the Village. I was sad and didn't care what happened. In the army, the singing, the cards, the drinking, the talk about promotions and

awards disgusted me more than ever. Today I came back
and saw her again. I also found my house, Eroshka, the
view of the snowy mountains from my porch, and I was
seized by a violent joy that made me understand everything.

"I love this woman. I love her truly. For the first and
the only time in my life I feel love. I know now what's
happening to me. I'm not afraid to be humiliated, I'm
not ashamed of my love, I'm proud of it. It isn't my fault
that I fell in love. It happened against my will. I tried
to escape in self-sacrifice. I pretended to be happy about
the love between Luke and Marianka. But this only tor-
tured me and exasperated my jealousy. My love is not an
ideal, or what is called a noble feeling. That I've known
before. Nor is it the sort of attachment in which one admires one's own love, feeling that its focus is within
oneself. I've known that too. Least of all is this a longing
for personal gratification. It is completely different.
Maybe in her I love nature herself, everything beautiful
that exists in nature. But I myself have no active will in
this. I am the instrument through which the elements
love her; the whole of nature presses this love into my
soul and orders me: love! I don't love with my intelligence or with my imagination but with my whole being.
Loving her, I feel I am an integral part of God's happy
world. Earlier, I wrote about my new convictions, the
products of my solitary thoughts, but no one can imagine
the labors I had to go through to arrive at them and the
joy I felt when I saw the new path open before me. There
was nothing that was dearer to me than these convictions.

"Well, then came love, and the convictions were swept
away and I do not have them any longer, nor do I have
any regrets at having lost them. It is even difficult for
me to understand how I could consider important such a
lopsided, cold, contrived state of mind. Beauty came and
scattered to the winds all these fruits of my mental labors
and there's no regret in me for them!

"Self-renunciation is nonsense. It's nothing but vanity,
a refuge from the unhappiness that one's earned, nothing
but a way to avoid envying other people's happiness. To
live for others and do good? What for? Why should I,
when in me there's nothing but love for myself and no

desire but to love her, to live with her, to live her life?
Now, it is not for the others, not for Luke that I wish
happiness. I have no affection for them now. Before, I'd
have said to myself that this was wicked. I would have
tormented myself with such questions as these: What
will happen to her? To me? To Luke? Now I don't care.
I'm not independent. There is something leading me. I
suffer, but then, formerly, I was dead. Now I am alive.
And I'm going over now to tell her everything."

**34** OLENIN finished the letter late in the evening and
then walked over to see his landlords. Ulitka sat in a
corner by the stove unwinding silk cocoons. Marianka,
her hair uncovered, sat sewing near a candle. When she
saw Olenin, she jumped up, seized her kerchief, and
moved back toward the stove.

"Why, where're you going, Marianka? Why don't you
stay and sit with us?" Ulitka asked her daughter.

"No, my hair is uncovered," she said and disappeared
behind the stove.

From where Olenin rested he could see only her knee
and her arched foot pointed downward. He ordered
Vania to bring him some tea and offered some to the old
woman. She offered him some clotted cream which Marianka had to fetch. But after she had brought it, she
again went behind the stove. Olenin felt that she was
watching him from there. Ulitka was carried away and
went into an orgy of hospitality. She brought Olenin
grape jam, a piece of grape tart, and some of her best
wine, pressing him to eat and drink with the rough, proud
hospitality of those who lived by physical labor. This old
woman who had at first surprised Olenin by her uncouth-
ness now often touched him by her delicate, simple
solicitude for her daughter.

"No sir! We can't complain, thank God. We have

enough of everything. We've pressed enough *chikhir* and now we can sell about three barrels of wine, and there'll be enough left for us to drink. Don't be in a hurry to leave us for we'll have a good time at the wedding, I can promise you."

"And when is the wedding set for?" Olenin asked. He felt the blood rush suddenly to his head and his heart start beating painfully and irregularly.

Behind the stove something stirred and there came the sound of cracking sunflower seeds.

"Well, I guess it ought to be next week. We're ready. . . ." the old woman said as matter-of-factly and calmly as if Olenin didn't exist. "I've prepared everything for Marianka. She'll have a nice wedding. The only snag is with Luke . . . our Luke has been running rather wild recently. He has been drinking too much for some time, and then he does foolish things. A Cossack came here from his company the other day, and he told us that Luke's been riding into the Nogay steppe. . . ."

"I only hope he doesn't get caught," Olenin said.

"That's what I say. I told him. 'Luke,' I said, 'don't do foolish things. I know you're a young man and all that, but there's a time for everything. All right, let's say you've captured some horses, stolen something, killed a Chechen raider. Good for you! And now the time has come for you to live quietly.' 'Otherwise,' I told him, 'it begins to look bad.'"

"Yes," Olenin said, "I saw him a couple of times with his company, and he was having a wild time. He's sold another horse, have you heard?"

Olenin glanced toward the stove. A pair of shining black eyes were looking at him in stern hostility. He became ashamed of what he'd said.

"What of it? He never harms anyone," Marianka said suddenly. "He pays for his good times with his own money." She jumped down from the stove and left the room, slamming the door.

Olenin followed her with his eyes as she crossed the room, and, after, he kept looking at the door. He was waiting for something and didn't understand a word of what Ulitka was telling him. A few minutes later some guests arrived—Ulitka's brother and Uncle Eroshka. They were followed by Marianka and Ustenka.

"Good evening," Ustenka said to Olenin. "You still on holiday?"

"Yes," Olenin said, feeling somehow ashamed and uneasy.

He wanted to leave but could not bring himself to get up and go. And then he felt he had to say something. Ulitka's old brother helped him by offering him a drink. They drank together, and then Olenin had one with Eroshka, and then another with the brother again. And the more Olenin drank, the more depressed he became, while the old men grew gay and noisy. The two girls climbed onto the stove and looked at the men as they went on drinking. Olenin said nothing and drank more than anyone else. The two others started shouting. Ulitka wouldn't let them have any more wine and in the end threw them out. The girls laughed at Eroshka, and it was well after ten when they all went out onto the porch. The two old men invited themselves to Olenin's for more drinks. Ustenka ran off home, and Olenin handed the two men over to Vania's care. Ulitka went to tidy up the shed. Marianka was alone in the house. Olenin felt fresh and cheerful as though he had just wakened. He was acutely aware of what was happening, and having disposed of the two old men, he went back toward his landlords' house. Marianka was preparing for bed. He came close to her, wanting to tell her something, but his voice snapped. She was sitting on the bed, her feet under her. She moved into a corner and looked at him with wild, frightened eyes. She was afraid of him. Olenin felt it. He felt sorry and ashamed of himself, but at the same time somehow proud and pleased that he could arouse some feeling in her, if only this.

"Marianka, won't you ever take pity on me . . . I can't tell you how much I love you."

She squeezed herself even farther away.

"Listen to him! It's the wine inside you talking. Come on, come off it, that won't get you anywhere."

"But it's not the wine. . . . You mustn't marry Luke. I'll marry you. . . ."

At the same time he thought: "What am I saying?

Will I repeat it tomorrow? Yes, yes, I shall, I shall repeat it now. . . ."

"Will you marry me?" he asked.

She looked at him seriously, and her fear seemed to have gone.

"Marianka, you're driving me crazy. I'm no longer myself. I'll do whatever you tell me. . . ." And mad, tender words formed by themselves.

"Come on, what's this all about?" she interrupted him and suddenly caught his outstretched hand. She did not push it away. Instead she squeezed it firmly with her strong, hard fingers. "You ever heard of gentlemen like yourself marrying simple Cossack girls? Go on now, on your way!"

"But will you? I'd give. . . ."

"Sure, and where would that put Luke?" she asked, laughing.

He snatched away the hand she was holding and put his arm around her young body. But she leaped up like an antelope and rushed out of the house barefoot. Olenin was horrified when he came to his senses. He again seemed inexpressibly vile and base when he compared himself to her. But not for one second did he regret the things he'd told her. He went home, and without even glancing at the two old men drinking there, he lay down and fell asleep. He slept more soundly than he had for a long time.

**35** THE next day was a holiday. At sunset, all the villagers were in the street, their festive dress shining in the setting sun. They had produced more wine than usual and were now through with the hard work. In a month the Cossacks were to start out on campaign, and wedding preparations were going on in many families.

The crowd was thickest in the square in front of the

Village council house and by the two stores, one of which sold cake and pumpkin seeds, the other kerchiefs and cotton prints. On the steps of the council house many old men were sitting and standing. They wore sober gray or black coats unadorned by any trimmings. They conversed quietly in measured tones about this year's harvest, about the young generation, about communal affairs, about old times, and scrutinized the young people with majestic indifference. Passing by them, the women and girls stopped and lowered their eyes. The young Cossacks respectfully slowed down and raised their caps, holding them for a brief moment over their heads. The old men then interrupted their conversation and looked either graciously or severely at those who passed by, slowly taking off and putting on again their sheepskin caps.

The Cossack girls had not yet started their dancing and singing. They were gathered in groups, wearing their bright smocks and white kerchiefs pulled down to their eyes. They squatted on the ground or sat on doorsteps, chatted and giggled, screening their faces from the slanting rays of the sun. Children were playing rounders: a ball would be batted high up into the clear sky and the little boys and girls would rush around the circle, squealing and shouting. Some half-grown girls were already singing and dancing in a circle; their voices were shrill and self-conscious.

The young men who worked as scribes, those who had been exempted from conscription, and those on leave, wearing new red and white, gold-trimmed Circassian shirts, went in twos and threes from one group of girls to another, smiling in their holiday mood, joking and making playful remarks. The Armenian storekeeper, dressed in a Circassian coat of fine blue cloth, stood in front of his store. Through the half-open door were visible piles of bright, folded kerchiefs. The Armenian seemed full of his own importance and waited for customers with the pride of an Oriental merchant. Two red-bearded, barefoot Chechens from across the river had come to see the festivities. They squatted on their heels outside the house of a friend and nonchalantly smoked their pipes, spitting, watching the villagers and exchanging comments in their rapid guttural speech. Occasionally a soldier in his everyday working uniform would pass hurriedly among the multicolored groups scattered across the square. Here and there one could already hear the singing of drunken Cossacks. The houses were locked, and the front steps looked very clean, having been scrubbed the day before. Even the old women were outside. The streets were covered with pumpkin and melon seeds which cracked underfoot. The air was warm and still, the sky deep and clear. The pale white mountain range, which seemed very near, just beyond the roofs, was turning reddish in the sunset glow. Now and then a distant roar of cannon came from beyond the river. But over the Village all sorts of gay, festive sounds floated and mingled.

Olenin had been pacing the yard all morning, waiting to see Marianka. But as soon as she had finished her household chores, she dressed and went to the church service. Then she either stood with her friends in the street, chatting and cracking sunflower seeds, or, in their company, rushed for a few moments into her house. And each time she passed him, she gave Olenin a bright and friendly look. Olenin did not dare address her flippantly nor say what he wanted to her in front of the others. He felt he had to finish what he had started the night before and to get her final answer. He was waiting for another occasion such as he had had then. But it didn't come about, and he felt he couldn't stand the uncertainty any longer. Once as she went out into the street again, he followed her, after hesitating a moment. He passed by the corner where she had installed herself, catching sight of her shiny blue silk smock and hearing the girls laugh as he went by.

Beletsky's house opened onto the square. Passing by it, he heard Beletsky's voice calling him. He went in.

They chatted for a while and sat down by the window. Soon Eroshka, wearing a new coat, joined them and sat down on the floor at their feet.

"There, you see, is the aristocratic group," Beletsky said, smilingly pointing with his cigarette at the corner. "Mine's there, she's wearing red. See her? That's her new blouse.

"Why don't they start their dances?" Beletsky shouted, leaning out of the window.

"Wait till it gets dark and we'll join them, and then we must invite them and organize a party at Ustenka's."

"Yes, I'd like to come," Olenin said determinedly. "Is Marianka coming?"

"She is. Be sure to come!" Beletsky said without any noticeable surprise. "Very beautiful, I must say," he said, indicating the multicolored crowd.

"Very!" Olenin agreed, trying to sound casual. "On holidays I always wonder how people manage suddenly to become so festive and pleased with themselves simply because the date happens to be the fifteenth or something. And one can see it's a holiday by their eyes, their faces, their voices, the way they move, and also by their dress, by the air itself, by the sun. . . . We haven't got anything like it back home."

"Yes," Beletsky said, bored by talk of this kind. "Why aren't you drinking, fellow?" he asked Eroshka.

Eroshka winked at Olenin, pointing at Beletsky. "Your friend is too proud," he said.

Beletsky raised his glass. "Allah be praised," he said and emptied it.

"Good health to you," Eroshka said, smiling, and drank down his glass.

"You were talking about holidays," Eroshka said to Olenin, getting up and looking out the window. "What sort of holiday is this? You should have seen how they enjoyed themselves in the old days! The women came out in gold-trimmed dresses, a double row of gold coins around their necks and gold-cloth diadems on their heads. When one of them walked by, it sounded like this: frr— frrrr-fr. . . . Every woman a princess. A whole herd of 'em would come out and start singing songs and the very air moaned all night. It went on throughout the night. And men would roll barrels into the street, sit around 'em and drink until morning. And then they'd sweep right through the Village, dancing and singing, like lava out of a volcano. And so they'd go from house to house, and sometimes it would go on for three days straight. I can still remember how my pop would come home, all red, his face swollen, hatless, having lost everything, just managing to stagger home and fall asleep. My ma knew what to do: she'd bring him some fresh caviar and some *chikhir* for his hangover and would go into the Village to find his cap. Then he'd sleep for two days. Yes, that's how they were in those days. But just look at 'em today."

"All those girls in their gold-trimmed dresses—did they like to have themselves a good time together?" Beletsky wanted to know.

"Yes, all by themselves. There were times when men came on horse or on foot and tried to break up their dancing. But then the girls grabbed sticks. During carnival week, they'd let a horse have it with those sticks, and many lads too would take a beating. But he'd break through the wall of girls, seize his sweetheart, and carry her off, blows or no blows, and then they'd love each other to their hearts' content. Yes sirree—the girls in those days! They were something, I'll tell you!"

**36** AT that moment two men on horseback emerged from a side street onto the square. They were Luke and Nazar. Luke sat slightly sideways on his well-fed bay Kabarda, which stepped lightly on the hard road, tossing its beautiful head with its fine, glossy mane. His rifle neatly tucked into its holster, his pistol within reach, his cloak rolled behind the saddle—everything indicated Luke hadn't just come from a picnic. The nonchalant way he sat his horse, the careless motion of the hand tapping the horse under its belly with his whip and, above all, his black eyes gleaming under heavy lids as he looked haughtily around—all showed he was quite aware of his young strength and was full of self-confidence. "Ever seen a man?" his eyes seemed to say as he looked around him. The attention of everyone in the square turned to the graceful horse with its silver trappings and to its handsome rider. Nazar, small and thin, was much less dashing. Riding past the old men, Luke slowed down and raised his white, curly sheepskin cap over his cropped, black head.

"You must have driven off quite a few Nogay horses by now," a thin oldster said gloomily.

"And you must have counted them, Grandpa, otherwise why do you ask?" Luke said, turning away.

"Still, I wish you wouldn't drag my lad along with you," the old man said even more gloomily and with a deeper frown.

"The old bastard knows everything," Luke muttered under his breath, and for one second he looked worried. But then he noticed the group of girls standing on the street corner and turned his horse toward them.

"Hi, good evening!" he shouted in his strong, carrying voice, coming to a dead stop in front of them. "You've all turned into real old hags while I've been away!"

"Luke! Hello!" cheerful voices answered him. "Have you brought plenty of cash with you? Buy us some refreshments. How long you home for? It's true—we haven't seen you for a long time."

"Nazar and I, we've come over to make a night of it," Luke said, raising his whip and jokingly urging his horse on the girls.

"Good thing you came. Marianka seems to have forgotten you," Ustenka squealed, nudging Marianka with her elbow and bursting into shrill laughter.

Marianka moved aside from Luke's horse, and throwing her head back, looked at him. Her large, shining eyes were calm.

"Yes, you've not been around for quite some time. Come on, keep your horse off," she said drily and turned away from him.

Luke had been exceptionally gay, boldness and joy painted all over his face. Marianka's coolness seemed to strike him. He knitted his brows.

"Come, put your foot into my stirrup, and I'll take you into the mountains," he shouted to her, making his horse prance among the girls as though to disperse the unpleasant thought that had come to him. He bent toward

Marianka and said: "Come, I'll kiss you . . . oh, I'll kiss you like. . . ."

Their eyes met, and Marianka suddenly turned red.

"The devil with you, you'll crush my feet," she said, and lowering her head, she looked down at her new red slippers with their narrow silver braid and her shapely legs in their tight-fitting blue stockings with clocks.

Luke then spoke to Ustenka while Marianka sat next to a woman holding a baby in her arms. The baby stretched his hand toward Marianka and caught the necklace that hung outside her blue silk blouse. Marianka leaned toward the child, and, in doing so, she gave Luke a quick glance out of the corner of her eye. At that moment he was getting a packet of sweetmeats and sunflower seeds out of his coat pocket.

"Here, I sacrifice it for the good of everybody," he said handing the bag to Ustenka and glancing at Marianka with a smile.

Once again, her face expressed embarrassment. It was as if a fog had gathered in her beautiful eyes. She drew down her kerchief, and bending over the baby's pink face, suddenly began to kiss it ardently. The child, pushing against the girl's chest with its little fists, gurgled, opening its toothless mouth wide.

"Stop smothering my son," the baby's mother said, taking the child away, unbuttoning her blouse and giving it her breast. "You'd better do such things with your boy friend."

"I'll just put my horse away, and then Nazar and I, we'll be back and have a good time till morning," Luke said, whipping his mount and riding away from the girls.

In a narrow street he and Nazar stopped by two houses standing side by side.

"Here we are, don't be long!" Luke shouted to his friend, getting off the horse by the wattle fence and leading it carefully through the gate to his yard. "Hi, Stepka," he said to the deaf-mute who, also in her Sunday best, came out to meet him and to take the horse off his hands. Then he explained to her in sign language that she should give the animal hay without unsaddling it.

The girl made her usual humming noise, smacked her lips as she pointed to the horse. Then she kissed it on the nose. That meant that she thought it was a good horse and that she liked it.

"Hello, Mother, how are you! How come you're still in?" Luke shouted to her, steadying his rifle in place as he bounded up the steps of the porch.

The old woman opened the door.

"Dear me! I never expected you today. Never thought you'd come," she said. "Kirka told us you weren't coming."

"What about getting us a bit of *chikhir*, Ma? Nazar is coming to see me and we could celebrate a bit together here."

"Sure, Luke, I'll get you some. Our girls are off, you see. I believe even the deaf-mute has gone."

She took her keys and hurried to the outbuilding.

Nazar had put his horse away and taken off his rifle, and now he came over next door to Luke's.

**37** "YOUR health!" Luke said, taking a cup filled to the brim with *chikhir* from his mother's hands, raising it carefully to his lips and lowering his head to meet it.

"That's bad business," Nazar said, "Grandpa Burlak talking about the stolen horses. He must know something."

"The old buzzard!" Luke said. "But what difference can it make? The horses are on the other side of the river by now. Where'll they find them?" he added, tossing his head.

"Still, I don't like it."

"There's nothing to it. Here, take some *chikhir* over to him tomorrow, and it'll be all right. Forget it and have a good time. Drink!" Luke shouted the way Eroshka usually did. "We'll go out and see the girls. You go and get some honey for 'em or I'll ask the deaf-mute to. We'll drink until morning."

Nazar smiled.

"How long'll we be here?" he asked.

"Let's have ourselves some fun. Go on and get some vodka. Here's some cash."

Nazar went off to Yamka's.

Uncle Eroshka and Ergushev, circling around like birds of prey and always able to spot wherever any drinking was going on, tumbled into the house one after the other. Both had already put away quite a bit.

"Give us another half pail of wine, Ma," Luke shouted to his mother as the two men greeted him.

"Well, now, tell me all about it. Where, you son-of-a-gun, are you stealing 'em from?" Eroshka shouted. "Good boy, I like you!"

"Sure, you like me," Luke laughed, "That's why you act as a go-between for the officers, taking sweetmeats to the girls. You old. . . ."

"Not true, not true, Luke!" the old man laughed. "You should have heard that stupid ass begging me. 'Go,' he says to me, 'try to arrange it.' He wanted to give me a rifle. The hell with it! I didn't want to do it, for your sake. Now, tell me, where've you been." And the old man spoke in Tartar.

Luke answered him in Tartar too, but Ergushev, who didn't speak it well, would occasionally interject Russian words.

"Yes, you should've seen him drive off those horses! It was something, I want to tell you!" Ergushev would chime in.

"So me and Girey," Luke was saying, "we crossed the river and he keeps bragging that he knows the steppe over there like the back of his hand and that he'll take me right to the spot. But when we set out, the night was foggy and the fellow lost his way, and we kept going in circles. He just couldn't find that Chechen village, and that's all there was to it. We must've gone too much to the right. Then, thank God, we heard dogs howling at last."

"You're a couple of fools!" Eroshka said. "We also got lost in the steppe. Who the hell can find his way out there every time? But then, I'd always ride to the top of a hill and start howling like a wolf. Like this, see?"

Eroshka cupped his hands around his mouth and let out a howl that sounded like a whole pack of wolves stretching out a single note. "And immediately the Village dogs would answer. . . . All right, go on with your story. You found the horses there?"

"Yes, we drove 'em off quickly, although Nazar almost got caught by those Nogay women."

"What do you mean they nearly caught me," Nazar, who had just returned, said in an offended tone.

"When we rode off, Girey lost his way again and almost landed us in the sand dunes. We thought we were heading toward the river, but we had our backs to it all the time——"

"You should've checked by the stars," Eroshka said.

"That's what I say!" Ergushev chimed in.

"Where would you've gotten stars—there were none to be seen. I rode a mare we'd taken and let my horse run free, hoping he'd get us out of the mess. And what do you think? He snorted a couple of times, put his nose to the ground, took off ahead of us and led us directly back home to the Village. And thank God we made it, it was getting light and we had just enough time to hide the horses in the forest. Nogim came and took 'em away."

Ergushev shook his head and said:

"Just as I figured it. Very smart. How much you get for 'em?"

"It's all in here," Luke said, slapping his pocket.

His mother entered the room, and Luke cut short his remarks. Instead he shouted: "Drink!"

"It's like once Girchik and I, we rode out quite late. . . ." Eroshka began.

"I'm not going to be able to hear the end of your story," Luke said. "I'm afraid I have to go."

He emptied his cup, tightened his belt, and left the house.

**38** It was dark when Luke went out into the street. The autumn night was windless and cool. The full golden moon floated out of the black poplars growing on one side of the square. The smoke from the chimneys merged with the mist and spread over the Village. Here and there lights shone from windows. The whole place smelled of smoke, grape pulp and mist. Voices, laughter, and the cracking of sunflower seeds merged, as during the day, but now were more distinct. Clusters of white kerchiefs and sheepskin caps gleamed through the darkness by fences and near houses.

On the square in front of the open door of a lighted store, could be seen the black and white figures of men and women, and one could hear at a distance their loud voices laughing, singing and talking. Girls, hand in hand, danced round and round in a circle, stepping gaily in the dusty square. A thin girl, the plainest of the lot, led off with a song:

> From the dark, dark forest,
> To the gaily flowered lea,
> There came two youthful lads,
> Unmarried and quite free.
> They stopped and argued hotly,
> When from a small bright glen,
> A maiden stepped out lightly,
> And paused between the men.
> "Hear me out, good fellows,
> And I'll pick my husband here,
> I'll marry the fine laddie
> With the shining golden hair.
> He may take me as his wife,
> And he'll be quite proud of me,
> I will fit in with his life,
> And he'll show me off with glee."

The older women stood around listening to the songs. In the darkness, little boys and girls rushed around playing tag. Men were trying to catch the girls each time they passed in their circular dance, and from time to time one of the lads would try to break through the ring and reach the center.

Olenin and Beletsky stood in a dark doorway in Circassian coats and sheepskin caps, but their conversation sounded very different from that of the Cossacks. They were talking quietly and were fully aware of the attention they attracted.

In the round dance, Ustenka and Marianka danced side by side. The plump little Ustenka was in red. Marianka wore her new blouse. Olenin and Beletsky were discussing how best they could snatch the two girls out of the moving ring. Beletsky thought Olenin was just having fun, but Olenin was expecting his fate to be decided. Whatever happened, he felt he had to see Marianka alone that very night and find out what she wanted and whether she would be his wife. Although he felt her answer would be no, he hoped that he'd be able to convey to her the way he felt and that she'd understand him.

"Why didn't you tell me before? I could have arranged it through Ustenka quite easily. You're an odd one!"

"Well, it can't be helped now. One day, I'll explain everything. But now, please, please arrange that she should come to Ustenka's."

"All right, I'm sure it can be arranged without too much trouble. Well, Marianka, so you'll go to a fair stranger and not to Luke?" Beletsky said, addressing Marianka, and then receiving no answer, he began asking Ustenka to invite Marianka to her place. But before he could finish, the thin girl leading the chorus intoned a new song, and the other girls joined in:

> One day, passing by my land,
> A stranger waved at me his hand.
> The second day, imagine that,
> He raised on high his sheepskin hat.
> The third time that he passed my way,
> He stopped to while the time away.

"Three times this house have I passed by,
And still of me you seem so shy.
Come stroll with me, O maiden dear,
And banish every qualm and fear.
Do not mock me, do not scorn me,
When I'm gone, then you will mourn me."
Though I knew what to reply,
I was still so coy and shy,
That I couldn't tell him no,
So I said that I would go.
Then my darling to me said:
"Here's a kerchief for your head,
And for it you will have to pay,
Five kisses on this very day."

Luke and Nazar had managed to break through the circle and were now in the center of the ring of girls. Luke softly joined in the song, and waving his hands in the middle of the circle, repeated from time to time:

"Come on, one of you—over here!"

The girls were trying to push Marianka toward him, but she refused to go. The sound of giggles, slaps, kisses mingled with the singing.

Passing by Olenin, Luke had given him a friendly nod.

"Hello," he had said, "you here too?"

"Yes," Olenin had answered coldly.

Beletsky whispered something into Ustenka's ear. She didn't have time to reply until she completed a full circle.

"All right, we'll be there," she said then.

"Marianka too?"

Olenin leaned toward Marianka and whispered: "You coming? Please come, if only for a minute. I must tell you something."

"I'll come if all the other girls do."

"Will you give me your answer?" he said, leaning toward her again. "You seem so cheerful tonight."

She was already dancing away from him. He followed her.

"Will you tell me?"

"Tell you what?"

"What I asked you the other day. Will you marry me?" Olenin said into her ear.

She seemed to think for a second and then said: "I'll let you know. I'll let you know tonight."

In the darkness her eyes sparkled gaily at him. He kept following her. He enjoyed being close to her, leaning toward her.

But, at one point, Luke, who was singing in the middle of the circle, suddenly caught Marianka's hand and pulled her violently toward him, tearing her out of the circle. He did it without interrupting his singing. Olenin just had time to say: "So don't forget to come to Ustenka's." Then he stepped back to join Beletsky.

The song ended. Luke wiped his lips. So did Marianka. They kissed.

"Not enough! I want five kisses," Luke said.

Chatter, giggles, and horseplay now replaced the rhythmical movements and sounds of the round dance. Luke, who seemed already quite drunk, began to give out candy to the girls.

"Here! There's some for everyone!" he kept saying, clowning. Then he threw a quick, angry look at Olenin and added: "But all of you who go around with soldiers —out of the ring!"

The girls were grabbing pieces of candy and struggling gaily for them among themselves. Beletsky and Olenin moved farther away.

Luke, as though having second thoughts about his lavishness, took off his cap, wiped his brow with a sleeve, and came up to Marianka and Ustenka.

*"Do not mock me, do not scorn me,"* Luke said, addressing Marianka in the words of the song they had just sung. "Tell me, *do you mock me?"* he repeated angrily. *"When I'm gone, then you will mourn me!"* And he hugged both Marianka and Ustenka at the same time.

Ustenka wriggled free, and taking a wide swing, she hit him on the back with such strength that she hurt her hand.

"Will there be another round dance?" Luke asked.

"I don't know about the other girls," Ustenka said, "but I'm going home, and Marianka's coming with me."

Luke kept his arm around Marianka and led her into a dark corner, away from the throng.

"Don't go," Luke said. "Let's have some fun for the last time. Go home and I'll join you there."

"Why should I go home? Holidays are made for having a good time. I'm going to Ustenka's."

"You know I'll marry you whatever."

"All right, all right, we'll see about that when the time comes."

"So you're going?" Luke asked seriously. He held her close and kissed her on the cheek.

"Come on, lay off me, will you!"

Marianka wrenched herself free and walked off.

"There's going to be trouble . . . ," Luke sighed. He shook his head, turned away from her, and shouted to the other girls: "Come on, sing some more!"

But Marianka had heard him and seemed frightened and angered. She stopped and asked him: "What do you mean there'll be trouble?"

"Just that."

"What?"

"Because you go around with your soldier lodger and because you don't love me any more."

"So? I'm free to love or not to love. You're not my father or my mother to tell me what to do. I'll love whomever I wish, understand?"

"All right, I'll remember that," Luke said and walked over to the store. "Hey girls, why aren't you dancing your round? Come, let's have another one. Nazar, go and get us some *chikhir*!"

"Think they're coming?" Olenin asked Beletsky.

"They're coming right now. Let's go. We've got to get ready for the party."

39    IT was late by the time Olenin stepped out of Beletsky's house to see off Marianka and Ustenka. The girls' white kerchiefs gleamed in the dark street. The

golden moon rolled down toward the steppe. A silver
mist hung over the Village. There were no lights to be
seen. Everything was quiet except for the receding steps
of the girls. Olenin's heart beat violently. The damp
night air cooled his burning cheeks. He looked up into
the sky, then turned back and glanced at the house he
had left. Its light went out. He began again to look into
the night at the receding shadows. The white spots of the
kerchiefs dissolved in the mist. He became afraid to
stay there alone. He was so happy! He suddenly started
running after the girls.

"Damn you!" Ustenka said, "someone may see us!"

"I don't care!"

Olenin ran toward Marianka and put his arms round
her. She didn't push him off.

"Haven't you kissed her enough?" Ustenka said. "When
you're married, you can kiss her to your heart's content,
but for the time being you'd better wait."

"Good night, Marianka, tomorrow I'll come and talk to
your father. Say nothing. . . ."

"What did you expect me to tell him?" Marianka said.

The two girls began to run. Olenin stayed behind and
began to think of what had happened. He had spent
the whole evening alone with her, in the corner by the
stove. Ustenka hadn't left the house for a moment and
had been chatting and fooling around with Beletsky and
the other girls. Olenin talked to Marianka in a whisper.

"Will you marry me then?"

"You're trying to trick me. You don't really mean to
marry me."

"But do you love me? Tell me, for God's sake."

"And why shouldn't I love you. You're not squint-
eyed or anything like that," Marianka said, laughing,
and squeezed his hands in her hard strong ones. "Look
at your hands," she said, "they're so white and so soft,
just like clotted cream. . . ."

"I'm not joking, Marianka. Tell me, will you marry
me?"

"Why shouldn't I marry you if my father consents?"

"Remember, I'll go out of my mind if you're laughing
at me. I'll speak to your father and mother tomorrow
and ask for your hand."

Marianka burst out laughing.

"What's happened?"

"Nothing, just it's funny."

"Listen. I promise, I'll buy an orchard, a house and I'll sign on as a Cossack——"

"Mind you don't run after other women. I'll be nasty about it."

Olenin rapturously recalled those words. When he re-lived them, he felt at some moments very hurt, a physi-cal pain; at others, his joy was so violent that it took his breath away. What hurt him was that she had re-mained so calm, talking to him in her usual tone. The new development didn't seem to excite her in the least. It was as though she weren't giving a thought to their future or otherwise didn't believe him. He felt that she loved him only in the present and that he didn't figure in her future. What made him so wildly happy, on the other hand, was that everything she said seemed sincere and that she had consented.

"We shall really understand each other only after she's completely mine," he thought. "For this sort of love, there are no words—it can only be expressed through living, through a whole life. . . . Tomorrow everything will be cleared up. I can't go on like this any longer. To-morrow I'll announce it to her father, to Beletsky, to the whole village. . . ."

After two sleepless nights, Luke had drunk so much that, for the first time in his life, his feet wouldn't carry him. He slept at Yamka's.

**40** THE next morning Olenin woke up early. In the very first moment of waking, he remembered what lay ahead of him and joyfully relived the kisses, the pressure of her firm hands and the remark about the whiteness of his. He jumped up, wanting to go immediately to see her parents and ask for her hand. Although the sun had not yet come up, Olenin noticed there was great agitation in the street; people on foot and on horseback were talking and milling around. His landlords were not up. Five mounted Cossacks rode by arguing quite noisily about something. At their head was Luke on his Kabarda horse. The Cossacks were all talking at the same time, so that it was impossible to make out what they were saying.

"Ride to the upper post . . . ," one said.

"Saddle your horse and catch up," another shouted to someone.

"It's nearer if we go out by the other gate."

"What are you talking about?" Luke said. "We should take the center gate."

"Yes, that's the best way," a Cossack said. He was covered with dust, and his horse was drenched with sweat.

Luke's face was red and swollen from drinking. His sheepskin cap was pushed back. He spoke with authority, as though he were in charge.

"What's happened? Where're you off to?" Olenin said, having difficulty attracting the Cossacks' attention.

"We're off to hunt for raiders. Some were reported hiding in the sand dunes. We've got to go now, but there're not enough of us."

And the Cossacks, calling out to others to join them, rode down the street. It occurred to Olenin that it wouldn't look well if he failed to join them. Besides, he thought, he could manage to get back quickly. He dressed, loaded his gun with bullets, and jumped on his horse, hurriedly saddled by Vania. He managed to catch up with the Cossacks at the village gate. They had dismounted and stood in a circle pouring *chikhir* out of a small barrel into a wooden mug, passing it around and drinking to the success of their sortie. Among them was a smartly dressed young Cossack lieutenant, who happened to be in the village and who had taken charge of the nine Cossacks present. All the others were privates, but though the Cossack lieutenant tried to act like the leader, they listened only to Luke.

And no one paid any attention to Olenin. When they

remounted, Olenin rode over to the lieutenant, a usually affable man; he hardly bothered to answer Olenin's questions and seemed to regard him from the exalted position of his nominal command. It was with the greatest effort that Olenin managed to get from him what was happening.

A patrol sent to find raiders had found some mountaineers in the sand dunes seven miles from the Village. The raiders had taken shelter in a trench. They fired at the scouting party and declared that they wouldn't allow themselves to fall into the Cossacks' hands alive. So the corporal of the patrol remained there with one man and sent the other to the Village to get reinforcements.

The sun was just beginning to rise. The steppe began about three miles outside the Village, after which nothing was to be seen but the bleak, uniform, parched plain, covered with hoofprints of cattle and here and there tufts of sere grass, with short reeds in the flats, occasional, faintly discernible footpaths, and, far off on the horizon, the tents of Nogay nomads. The striking feature of the countryside was the absence of shade. It was forbidding.

The rising and setting sun is always red in the steppe. When the wind blows, it moves whole mountains of sand. When the air is still, as it was that morning, the silence, uninterrupted by a movement or a sound, is quite noticeable. This morning the steppe was quiet and dull, though the sun had now risen. Everything evinced a peculiar desolate softness. No stir in the air, nothing but the hoofbeats and the snorts of the horses and even these sounds came dully and died immediately.

The Cossacks rode mostly in silence. Cossack weapons are always carried in such a way that they will not jingle or rattle. Jingling weapons are considered a disgrace. Several other Cossacks caught up with the detachment, and two or three words were exchanged. Suddenly Luke's horse either stumbled or caught its foot in some grass. It became restive. A bad omen among Cossacks. They turned their heads toward the horse, then turned away again, pretending not to have noticed anything. Luke pulled at the reins, frowned, pressed his lips together, and brandished his whip over his head. The beautiful

Kabarda horse was prancing from one foot to another, not knowing from which to start, as if it wished to fly. But Luke whipped him on his well-fed flanks and then whipped him again and again, and the animal, baring its teeth and spreading out its tail, snorted, reared, and sprang ahead of the rest of the party.

"That's a beauty," the lieutenant remarked.

"A real lion," a Cossack said.

They rode on, now trotting, now at walking pace. They rode silently, and except for the incident with Luke's horse, nothing interrupted their solemn procession.

The only living things they ran across during the seven-mile stretch were a Nogay family moving from one place to another. Their tent was being carried on an ox-cart, and it passed about a mile away from the Cossacks. Then they came across two ragged, high-cheeked Nogay women gathering cattle chips in baskets for fuel. The lieutenant, who did not speak the Nogay dialect well, tried to ask the women something, but they didn't understand him, and obviously frightened, they kept looking at one another.

Luke came up, reined in his horse, and gave them the standard Nogay greeting. This visibly reassured the women, and they began to talk to him freely.

They made some monosyllabic sounds and pointed in the direction the Cossacks were going. Olenin gathered that they were saying that there were many raiders ahead.

Never having taken part in such adventures before, and knowing of them only from Eroshka's words, Olenin had firmly decided not to lag behind in order to see it all. He admired the Cossacks, and he watched everything. But, though he had taken both his rifle and his saber along, he had decided he wouldn't take any part in the action when he'd realized that the Cossacks were trying to ignore him. He decided that his bravery had been sufficiently proved during the campaigns. And then, too, he felt ecstatic that morning.

Suddenly he heard a shot nearby.

The Cossack lieutenant became excited; he started to deploy the Cossacks and to tell them how they should approach the raiders. But the men were clearly not lis-

tening to him. They kept looking at Luke. Luke's face
and figure were solemn. He made a sign to the men and
put his horse to a trot. Soon the others couldn't keep up
with him. But he kept riding ahead, looking in front of
him out of narrowed eyes.

"There's a man on horseback over there," he said,
slowing down his horse and allowing the others to catch
up with him.

Olenin strained his eyes, but he couldn't see a thing.
The Cossacks soon made out two riders and quietly
rode toward them.

"Are those the raiders?" Olenin asked.

The Cossacks didn't deign to answer. Raiders would
have to be crazy to cross over to this side of the river
with their horses.

"That's Rodion, I'll bet—he's signaling to us," Luke
said, pointing at the two riders now clearly visible. "He's
coming this way."

A few minutes later Olenin too recognized the two
horsemen. They were Cossack scouts. And soon Rodion,
the corporal, rode up to Luke.

41 LUKE asked simply: "How far?"

At the same time, about thirty yards away, a sharp,
dry shot resounded. The corporal had a faint smile on
his face.

"That's our friend Gurka shooting at 'em," he said,
nodding in the direction of the gunfire.

A little farther on they saw Gurka sitting behind a
sandy hillock and reloading his rifle. He seemed to be exchanging shots with the raiders simply to pass the time.
The raiders were behind another sand dune. A bullet
came whistling. The Cossack lieutenant was pale and
becoming confused. Luke jumped from his horse, threw
the reins to another Cossack, and walked over to Gurka.

Olenin did the same, and ducking behind the sand dune, followed him. Just as they reached Gurka, two bullets came whistling over their heads. Luke laughingly turned toward Olenin, stooping even lower.

"Better watch out, or you may get killed," he said. "You'd really ought to get out of here. This is no place for you."

But Olenin felt he had to have a look at the raiders.

Then, about two hundred yards away, behind a sand dune, he saw their caps and guns. Suddenly there was a puff of smoke, and another bullet whistled past. The raiders were hiding in a marsh at the foot of the hill. Olenin was struck by their location. It was not so different from the rest of the steppe, but the very fact that the raiders were there made it something special. It seemed to Olenin that it existed especially for the raiders to occupy. Luke returned to his horse. Olenin followed.

"Over there, behind the hill, there's a Nogay cart loaded with hay," Luke said. "We've got to get ahold of it, or some of us'll get killed."

He said this to the Cossack lieutenant, who agreed. The hay cart was brought up, and the Cossacks, sheltered behind it, were pushing it slowly forward. Olenin rode to the top of a hill from which he could see everything. The hay cart was moving. The Cossacks were crowded together behind it. The Chechens—there were nine of them—sat knee to knee without firing. All was quiet. Suddenly from the Chechen side came the sound of a mournful song, something like Eroshka's *"Ai! Dai! Dalalai!"*. The hillmen knew they couldn't escape, and to resist the temptation to flee, they had strapped themselves to one another at the knee, loaded their rifles, and were intoning their death song.

The hay cart drew nearer, and Olenin expected the shooting to break out any moment. But there was nothing to be heard but the Chechens' mournful song. Suddenly it ceased. There was a sharp report. A bullet struck the front of the cart. The Chechens yelled and shouted curses. Shots followed shots, and bullet after bullet smashed into the cart. The Cossacks, no more than five yards away, still held their fire.

Another moment passed. Then the Cossacks, with a

fiendish whoop, emerged from behind the cart on both sides. Luke was in the lead. Olenin heard only a few shots, some shouting, and a moan. He made out what seemed to him to be smoke and blood. He left his horse and frantically rushed toward the Cossacks. Horror veiled his eyes. He couldn't make out what was happening—all he knew was that it was over.

Luke, white as a handkerchief, was holding a Chechen by the arms and shouting: "Don't fire, I want him alive!"

The Chechen was the same red-bearded one who had come to collect the body of his slain brother. Luke was twisting his arms. Suddenly the Chechen wrenched himself free and fired his pistol. Luke fell. Blood appeared on his belly. He leapt to his feet but fell again, swearing in Russian and Tartar. There was more and more blood on him. Some Cossacks ran up to him and began loosening his belt. Nazar was one of them. Before he could do anything, he fumbled for some time trying to sheath his saber. It wouldn't go in. The blade was blood-stained.

The bodies of the red-bearded Chechens with their clipped mustaches lay on the ground, slashed and mauled. Only the one who had shot Luke was still alive, though he too was slashed. He looked like a wounded hawk, bleeding all over—blood gushing from his right eye, his teeth clenched, pale and sinister-looking, and he gazed around him with huge angry eyes as he squatted, dagger in hand, ready to continue fighting. The Cossack lieutenant went toward him, as if to pass by him, then suddenly bent over and shot him in the ear. The Chechen jerked violently and collapsed.

The Cossacks, panting, dragged the bodies to one side and started taking their weapons. Each of the red-bearded Chechens had been a human being, and each had his individual expression. Luke was carried to the cart. He kept swearing in Russian and Tartar. "No! You won't get away. I'll strangle you with my own hands," he shouted, trying to raise himself, but soon he grew limp from loss of blood.

Olenin rode home. In the evening he was told that Luke was dying, but that a Tartar from the other side of the river had undertaken to save him with herbs.

The bodies were carried to the Village council house.

Women and little boys ran up to have a look at them.

Olenin had returned at dusk, and it took him a long time to regain his senses after what he'd seen. Then, later, the images of what had happened overwhelmed him. He looked out the window. Marianka was passing to and fro between the house and the cow shed, attending to her chores. Her mother was in the vineyard, her father with the Village council. Olenin couldn't wait until she'd finished what she was doing. He walked over to her. She was in the house, her back turned to him as he came in. Olenin thought she was embarrassed.

"May I come in, Marianka?" he asked. Suddenly she turned toward him. Scarcely perceptible traces of tears marked her cheeks. Her face was sad and beautiful. She looked at him in silence, majestically. Olenin said: "Marianka, I have come——"

"Leave me alone," she said. Her face remained unchanged, but somehow the tears gushed out of her eyes.

"What's the matter? What's happened?"

"What?" she said in a hard, rough voice. "Cossacks have been killed, that's what's the matter."

"Luke?" Olenin said.

"Go away. What do you want of me?"

"Marianka," Olenin said, coming closer to her.

"Go away, you'll never get anything from me."

"Don't say that, Marianka, please."

"Get out!" She stamped her foot and moved threateningly toward him. There was so much disgust, scorn, and anger in her face that Olenin suddenly realized that he had nothing to expect from her, that his earlier impression of her inaccessibility had been all too true.

He said nothing and ran out of her house.

**42** HE returned home and lay motionless on his bed for two hours. Then he went to his company commander to ask permission to ride over to staff headquarters. Without bidding anyone good-by, he sent Vania to pay his landlord, packed and prepared to leave for the fort where regimental headquarters were set up. Eroshka was the only one to see him off. They had a drink, then another, and then a third. Just as on the night of his departure from Moscow, a three-horse carriage waited at the door. Unlike then, Olenin was no longer absorbed with himself, and, unlike then, he did not repeat over and over to himself that everything he'd been doing was not the "real thing." Now he no longer promised himself a new life. He loved Marianka more than ever and knew that he would never be loved by her.

"Farewell, fellow," Eroshka said. "When you go on an expedition, be smart. Remember me, I'm an old man. When you take part in a raid or something, or find yourself where there's shooting going on, never get in the middle of a group of men, let me tell you. I'm an old wolf and I've had plenty of experience. Because you people, when you get scared, you keep bunching up, as if it were safer when you're clustered together. But that's the worst possible thing. It's at people they're aiming. I've always kept away from crowds. I like to be all by myself. And look at me—I've never been wounded. Believe me, I've seen plenty in my lifetime."

"And what about that bullet that's sitting in your back?" asked Vania, who was fussing around the room.

"That? Just horseplay among Cossacks," Eroshka said.

"What do you mean, Cossacks?" Olenin said.

"Well, it wasn't anything. We were drinking, and there was a Cossack around by the name of Vanka Sitkin. He got drunk, pulled out his pistol, and shot me right there. And I say to him: 'What did you do that for, brother? You've killed me. I won't let you off just like that, you're going to have to stand me a pailful of vodka for that!'"

"Did it hurt?" Olenin asked, listening only vaguely.

"Let me finish. So he paid up. We drank it, and I was still bleeding. I messed up the whole hut with blood. And so old man Burlak says: 'He's finished. Stand us a bottle of wine, or we'll testify against you.' So they brought a bottle, and we drank and drank."

"But did it hurt you?" Olenin asked again.

"What's this hurting business? Stop interrupting me. I don't like being interrupted. Let me tell it my way. So we drank until morning. And I went to sleep drunk on the stove. And when I woke, I couldn't straighten up."

"It must have hurt terribly," Olenin repeated, thinking that now he had finally obtained an answer to his question.

"I never said it hurt. I said I couldn't straighten up, couldn't move—not that it hurt."

"And then it healed?" Olenin asked, unsmilingly, feeling too depressed to smile.

"Sure it healed up. But the bullet's still in there. Here, feel it." Eroshka lifted his shirt, exposing his huge, powerful back where, close to the spine, a bullet could be felt.

"Feel how it rolls around under your finger," Eroshka asked, playing with the bullet as if with a toy. "Here, now it's rolled back, see?"

"Think Luke will live?" Olenin asked.

"God knows. There's no doctor around. They've gone to fetch one."

"Where'd they go? To Grozny?" Olenin asked.

"Oh no. I'd have hanged your Russian doctors long ago if I was Tsar. All they know is how to cut a man up. One of our Cossacks, Balakshov, they cut his leg off, and he's not a man any more. What's he good for now? Proves they're stupid, doesn't it? No, brother, in the mountains over there, there are real doctors. You know, once my pal Girchik was wounded in the chest, up here. Your doctors gave up on him. And then a doc came from the mountains, one Saib, and cured him. They know all about herbs."

"Come on, enough nonsense," Olenin said. "I'll send a doctor from headquarters."

" 'Nonsense, nonsense,' " the old man aped him. "Oh, you're a fool. 'Nonsense, I'll send a doctor from headquarters,' he says. Well, if your doctors were as good as our Cossack ones or the Chechen doctors, we'd go over to your place to get healed. But, as it is, your officers and colonels send for our doctors when they need real help. You're all humbugs, you know."

Olenin didn't bother to argue. He himself knew only

too well that everything was humbug in the world from which he had come and to which he was returning.

"And how is Luke? Have you seen him?" he asked.

"Luke? He just lies there as if dead. Don't take food or drink except vodka. That's the only thing he accepts. But as long as he drinks vodka, he's still with us. It would be a shame if he died. A fine lad, a real brave one, my kind. Once I was dying too, just like him. The old women were already wailing over me. My head was afire. They had already laid me out under the holy icons. So I lay there, and over me a little drum no bigger than this was beating a tattoo. I yelled to 'em to stop but they drummed all the harder." The old man laughed. "Then the women brought a church elder in. They were getting ready to bury me. 'This one has defiled himself with worldly unbelievers,' they said. 'He has gone with women, he has killed people, he has not fasted, and he has played his balalaika. Confess,' they said. So I confessed. 'I've sinned,' I says. And then whatever the priest said, I always answered: 'I've sinned.' He began to question me about the balalaika. 'Where is the filthy thing?' he says. 'Show me and I'll smash it.' 'I haven't got it,' I says to him. But the truth was I'd hidden it in the shed under the fishing net, and I knew they wouldn't find it. And so finally they left me alone. Well, I recovered later and I went on scratching at my balalaika. . . .

"What was I saying?" he asked after a while. "So, you listen to me. Stay away from people when under fire. Otherwise they'll kill you, and that would make me sad. I like you, you're a drunkard. And then, watch out. You Russians, you love to ride up hills and look around. There was one of your fellows stayed here once, and as soon as he saw a hill on the steppe he would ride up it. And once he rode to the top of one, quite pleased with himself, and a Chechen fired at him and killed him. Oh, those Chechens, they shoot straight, you know. Some of them shoot even better than me. I hate it when a guy gets killed so stupidly. Sometimes I used to watch your soldiers, and I used to think to myself: 'There's stupidity for you, if ever there was.' They are driven, the poor fellows, in a clump, and they even sew red on their coats to make themselves better targets! How can they help being hit? And when one of them gets killed, they take him out and squeeze another into his place. What foolishness!" The old man shook his head. "Why not scatter and move one by one? And then, just advance? They won't notice you, and you'll be able to do what you've come for."

"Well, thanks. Good-by, Uncle. Hope we'll meet again one day," Olenin said. He got up and moved toward the door. The old man remained sitting on the floor.

"Is that the way to say good-by? You're a real fool, you are," he said. "Good God, what have people come to nowadays? We've been knocking around together for a whole year and now just good-by and that's it. Don't you understand I like you and I'm sorry to lose you? You're such a sad one and always so alone. You're sort of unloved. When I can't sleep sometimes, I think of you, and I feel so sorry. It's like the song you know:

> It is hard, oh brother dear,
> In an alien land to live.

That's how it is with you."

"Well, good-by," Olenin said again. The old man gave him his hand. Olenin shook it and turned to go.

"No, no," the old man said. "Give me your mug!"

He took Olenin by the head with his big hands, kissed him three times, his wet mustache rubbing against his face, and started to cry: "I like you! Farewell. Good luck to you!"

Olenin got into the carriage.

"You're going to leave just like that? You could give me something to remember you by. What about a rifle? What do you need two for?" the old man said, his voice broken by sobs.

Olenin took out a rifle and handed it to him.

"You give too many things to the old man. He'll never have enough. He's a regular beggar," mumbled Vania. "They're shifty people." Vania wrapped himself in his overcoat and took the seat on the box by the driver.

"Shut up, you stingy pig," the old man shouted, laughing.

Marianka came out of the shed, glanced indifferently

at the carriage, nodded briefly, and went into the house.

*"La fille,"* Vania said, winking and letting out a silly laugh.

"Drive on!" shouted Olenin angrily.

"Good-by, brother, good-by! I won't forget you!" Eroshka shouted.

Olenin looked around. Eroshka and Marianka were talking, apparently about their own affairs. Neither the old man nor the girl turned to look at him.

# THE RAID

1  WAR has always fascinated me. I don't mean the tactical maneuvering of whole armies by famous generals—movements of such magnitude are quite beyond my imagination. I have in mind the real essence of war—the killing. I was less interested in the deployment of the armies at Austerlitz and Borodino than in how a soldier kills and what makes him do it.

The time had long since passed when I used to pace my room alone, waving my arms and fancying myself as the inventor of the best way to slaughter thousands of men in an instant, a feat which would make me a general and earn me eternal glory. Now all that interested me was the state of mind that pushes a man, without apparent advantage to himself, to expose himself to danger and, what is even more puzzling, to kill his fellow man. I always wanted to believe that soldiers kill in anger; since I could not imagine them continually angry, I had to fall back on the instinct of self-preservation and a sense of duty.

I wondered too about courage—that quality respected by men throughout history. Why is courage a good thing? Why is it, unlike other virtues, often met in otherwise quite despicable persons? Could it be that the capacity to face danger calmly is a purely physical one, and that people admire it just as they admire physical size and muscular strength?

Is it courage that makes a horse hurl itself off a cliff because it fears the whip? Is it courage that drives a child expecting punishment to run off into the woods and become lost? Is it an act of courage for a woman, fearing shame, to kill her new-born child and risk facing prosecution? And is it a display of courage when a man, out of sheer vanity, risks his own life in order to kill a fellow creature?

Danger always involves a choice. What then determines this choice—a noble feeling or a base one? And shouldn't it be called either courage or cowardice accordingly?

These were the thoughts and doubts that preoccupied me. I decided to resolve them by taking part in combat as soon as the opportunity arose.

In the summer of 1845 I was at a small fortified post in the Caucasus. On July 12, Captain Khlopov appeared at the low entrance of my hut. He was in dress uniform —epaulets, sword and all. Since my arrival I'd never seen him in that attire. He must have seen my surprise for he explained: "I've come straight from the colonel. Our battalion is to march tomorrow."

"Any idea where?"

"To Fort N—. That's the assembly point."

"And from there, will there be a raid, do you think?"

"Probably."

"Which direction?"

"All I can tell you is that last night a mounted Tartar arrived with orders from the general for the battalion to move out and to take along two days' rations. Why, where, for how long—don't ask me. We've been given our orders and that's it."

"But if they've ordered you to take only two days' rations, that must mean the troops aren't expected to be on the march more than two days—"

"It means nothing."

"What do you mean?" I asked, surprised.

"Just what I say. When we went to Dargi, we took along rations for a week, but we were gone almost a whole month."

"May I come along?"

"Surely, but if you want my advice, don't. Why run the risk?"

"If you don't mind, I'll not take your advice. I've been here a whole month just waiting for an opportunity to see action. And now you want me to miss my chance."

"All right, come along, though I'm sure it'd be better if you waited for us here. You could get in some hunting while we do the job—that'd make the most sense."

He said it so convincingly that at first I was almost persuaded. Nevertheless, I finally decided to go.

"But what's there for you to see?" he asked, still trying to dissuade me. "If you want to know what a battle looks like, read Mikhailovsky's *Scenes of War,* or something. It's a good book and it gives the whole story. It notes the position of every army corps, and you'll get a good idea of how battles are fought."

"Look," I said, "those are just the things that *don't* interest me."

"What are you after, then? Simply to watch how people die? If so, I'll tell you. In 1832 there was another civilian here with us—some kind of Spaniard, I believe. He came with us on two raids, and I even remember that he wore some sort of blue cloak. Well, it's not hard to imagine how it all ended. He got killed. You see, anything may happen."

Although I felt shamed at the way he put it, I didn't try to make excuses.

"Would you say he was a brave man?" I asked.

"God knows, though I must say he always rode out in front, and wherever there was firing, he was sure to be there."

"So he was brave, then?"

"Well, it doesn't necessarily follow that a man's brave just because he pokes his nose into other people's business."

"What would you call being brave?"

"Brave. Brave?" the captain repeated, as though the question had never occurred to him before. "A brave man is a man who does what he has to do," he said after some reflection.

I remembered Plato's definition of bravery as the knowledge of what should and what should not be feared. Now, despite the generality and vagueness of the captain's definition, I felt he wasn't so far from Plato and that, if anything, his definition was more accurate than that of the Greek philosopher. Had he been as articulate as Plato, he might have said that brave is the man who fears not what should not be feared and fears what should.

I wanted to explain this thought to the captain.

"I think," I said, "that a man faced by danger must make a choice—and if his decision is determined by a sense of duty, it is courage, but if it's determined by a base motive, it is cowardice. So a man who risks his life out of vanity, curiosity, or greed is not brave, and, conversely, a man who avoids danger out of an honest feeling of family obligation or even simple conviction is no coward."

As I talked, the captain looked at me with an odd expression.

"That," he said, starting to fill his pipe, "I wouldn't want to have to prove. But we have a young second lieutenant here who likes to philosophize. You should talk to him about it. He even writes poetry, you know."

I had heard of Captain Khlopov back home in Russia, though I'd only met him here in the Caucasus. His mother owned a small piece of land within two miles of my estate. Before leaving for the Caucasus, I went to see her, and the old lady was very happy that I was going to see her Petey (that's the way she referred to the gray-haired Captain Peter Khlopov) and that I, a "living letter," would tell him about her and take him a small package. She fed me some excellent smoked goose and pie, then went to her bedroom and returned with a largish icon in a black bag with a black silk ribbon attached to it.

"This is Our Lady of the Burning Bush," she said. She made the sign of the cross over the icon, kissed it, and handed it to me. "Please give it to him. You see, when he left for the Caucasus, I said a prayer for him and promised that if he stayed alive and safe I would have this icon of the Mother of God made. And the Holy Mother and the Saints have looked after him; he has taken part in every imaginable battle without once being wounded. Michael, who spent some time with him, told me things that made my hair stand on end. You see, I only hear about him second hand—my son never writes me about his campaigns. The dear boy doesn't want to frighten me."

(Later in the Caucasus I learned from others that

Captain Khlopov had been seriously wounded four times. He clearly had never told his mother about his wounds or about his campaigns.)

"So," Mrs. Khlopov went on, "I want him to wear this holy image, which I send him with my blessing. The Mother of God will intercede for him. I want him to wear the icon, especially in battle. You tell him. Just tell him his mother wanted him to."

I promised to carry out her instructions without fail.

"I'm sure you'll like my Petey very much," she went on. "He's such a nice person! You know, a year never goes by without his sending me and my daughter Annie some money. And, mind you, all he has is his army pay! Yes, I thank God with all my heart for having sent me such a son!" she concluded, tears in her eyes.

"Does he write you often?" I asked.

"Seldom, very seldom. Maybe once a year, and usually only to accompany the money. Even then, he doesn't always write. He says that when he doesn't write it means everything's fine, because if something happens, God forbid, they'd let me know soon enough anyhow."

When I gave the captain his mother's present—he had come to my room on this occasion—he asked me for some paper, carefully wrapped up the icon, and put it away. I spoke to him at length about his mother, and during the whole time he remained silent. He went to the far corner of the room and spent what seemed to me an extraordinarily long time filling his pipe.

"She's a nice old thing," he said in a somewhat muffled voice from his retreat. "I wonder if God will ever let me see her again."

There was love and sadness in those simple words.

"Why must you stay out here?" I asked. "Why not ask to be transferred, so you'd be closer to her?"

"I have to serve in the army anyhow, and here I get double pay—quite a difference to a poor man."

The captain lived carefully. He never gambled, seldom went on sprees, and smoked only the cheapest tobacco.

I liked him. He had a simple, quiet Russian face. It was easy and pleasant to look him straight in the eye. And after our conversation I felt great respect for him.

**2** AT four the next morning, the captain came to get me. He wore an old, threadbare tunic without epaulets, wide Caucasian trousers, a sheepskin cap once white but now yellowish and mangy, and a cheap saber. He rode a small, whitish horse, which ambled along in short strides, hanging its head and swishing its thin tail. The captain certainly was not handsome and there was nothing martial about him, but everything in him expressed such calm indifference that somehow he inspired respect.

I didn't keep him waiting. I immediately mounted and we rode together out the fort gate.

The battalion, some six hundred yards ahead of us, looked like a swaying black mass. One could tell only that they were infantry by the bayonets that pointed into the air like needles, by the drums, and by the rhythm of the soldiers' singing that reached us from time to time, led by a magnificent tenor voice from the Sixth Company I'd often admired at the fort. The road led through the middle of a deep, wide ravine, and along a small river now in flood. Flocks of wild doves whirled over it, landing on its rocky banks, taking off, swooping down in circles, vanishing from sight. The sun had not yet come up, although the top of the right slope of the ravine was beginning to brighten. The gray and whitish rocks, the yellow-green moss, the dew-covered bushes of dogberry and dwarf elm stood out very clearly against the transparent-gold background of the morning light. But the opposite side of the ravine, still wrapped in thick mist that floated in smoky, uneven layers, was damp and gloomy and presented a wide range of shades—lilac, black, white, and dark green. Right in front of us, sharp against the dark azure of the horizon, the gleaming white snowy mountains rose with amazing clarity, their shadows uncanny and yet harmonious in every detail. Crickets, grasshoppers, and thousands of other insects woke up in the tall grass and filled the air with their varied and continual noises. It seemed as if thousands of little bells were ringing inside our very ears. The air smelled of water, grass, and fog—the smell of a beautiful summer morning. The captain lit his pipe, and I found the smell of his cheap tobacco mingling with that of the tinder extraordinarily pleasant.

In order to catch up quickly with the infantry, we left the road. The captain appeared absorbed in his thoughts and never once took his short pipe out of his mouth. At every step, he prodded his horse with his heels. Rolling from side to side, it left a hardly perceptible trail in the tall, wet grass. Once, from under its very feet, a pheasant rose letting out a cry and making a noise with its wings that would have set the spine of a hunter tingling; then it began to rise. The captain paid no attention whatsoever.

We had almost caught up with the battalion when we heard behind us a galloping horse, and a young, good-looking officer in a tall, white sheepskin cap overtook us. As he passed, he smiled, made a friendly sign to the captain, and flourished his whip. I only had time to notice his graceful way of sitting his horse and holding the reins, his dark handsome eyes, his fine nose, and thin, youthful black mustache. What I liked especially about him was that he could not resist smiling when he realized that we were admiring him. From his smile alone, one could tell he was still quite young.

"What's he in such a hurry about?" the captain muttered gruffly, without removing his pipe.

"Who is he?"

"Alanin, one of my second lieutenants. He's just a month out of military school."

"I suppose this will be his first time in action?"

"Yes, that's what he's so pleased about," the captain said, slowly shaking his head. "Ah, that's youth for you!"

"How can he help being pleased? I can imagine how interesting it must be for a young officer."

The captain said nothing for a couple of minutes.

"That's just what I meant—youth," he said in a deep

voice. "How else can one be pleased about something one has never experienced? And after you've seen it often, you aren't so happy about it any more. Take today, for instance—about twenty officers will take part in this expedition, and the odds are that at least one of them will be killed or wounded. No doubt about it. Today, it may be my turn, tomorrow his, the next time somebody else's. What's there to be happy about?"

**3** THE bright sun rose above the mountains, lighting up the valley we were following. The wavy clouds of mist scattered and it grew hot. The soldiers, loaded down with equipment and rifles, trudged heavily along the dusty road. From time to time laughter and snatches of Ukrainian reached us. Some oldtimers in white tunics—most of them non-commissioned officers—walked in a group by the roadside. They smoked their pipes and talked quietly. Heavily laden carts, each drawn by three horses, moved laboriously forward, raising a thick cloud of dust that stayed suspended over the road. The officers, on horseback, rode in front. Some of them were putting their horses through their paces: they made them jump, sprint, and come to a dead stop; others were directing the regimental chorus, which, despite the heat and stuffiness, sang one song after another.

A couple of hundred yards ahead of the infantry rode some Tartar horsemen. With them, riding on a large white horse and dressed in Caucasian costume, was a tall, handsome officer. Throughout the regiment he had a reputation for reckless courage and for not hesitating to tell anyone what he thought of him. His soft, black Oriental boots were trimmed with gold braid as was his black tunic under which he wore a yellow silk Circassian shirt. The tall sheepskin hat on his head was pushed back carelessly. A powder flask and a pistol were fastened to silver straps across his chest and back. Another pistol and a silver-mounted dagger hung from his belt next to a saber in a red leather sheath. A rifle in a black holster was slung over his shoulder. From his dress, his style of riding, all his movements, it was obvious that he wanted to look like a Tartar. He was even saying something to the Tartars in a language I couldn't understand. But then, judging by the bewildered, amused looks they exchanged with one another, I guessed they couldn't understand him either.

He was one of those dashing, wild young officers who attempt to model themselves on the heroes of Lermontov and Marlinsky. These officers saw the Caucasus only through such romantic prisms, and in everything they were guided solely by the instincts and tastes of their models.

This lieutenant could surely have enjoyed the company of fashionable women and important men—generals, colonels, aides-de-camp. In fact, I'm certain he was eager to associate with them, being extremely vain. But somehow he felt he had to show such people his rough side, to be rude to them, although quite mildly so. When some lady appeared at the fort, he felt bound to walk under her windows with his pals, wearing a red shirt and slippers and talking and swearing loudly. But this wasn't done so much to offend as to show her by his supreme casualness how easy it would be to fall madly in love with him were he to display the slightest interest.

He also liked to go into the hills at night accompanied by a couple of friendly Tartars, lie in ambush for hostile hillmen, and take pot shots at them. Although in his heart he felt there was nothing particularly heroic about it, he persuaded himself that he had to inflict pain on hostile Tartars, people who had somehow let him down and whom he pretended to loathe and despise.

There were two things that were always with him: a rather large icon around his neck and a dagger fastened to his shirt, which he retained even when sleeping. He had convinced himself that he had enemies, and the idea that he had to avenge himself against someone, wash off some imaginary insult with blood, was very pleasant to him. He was sure that hatred, revenge, and scorn for men in general were refined, romantic feelings.

However, his Circassian mistress, whom I got to know later, told me that he was really a very kind and gentle man and that every evening, after he'd written saturnine thoughts in his diary, he would carefully draw up his accounts on ruled paper, and then get down on his knees and pray to God. And yet this man went to so much trouble to appear as one of his heroes, if only to himself. As to his brother officers and the soldiers, they never saw him in such a light anyway.

Once, on one of his nighttime sorties, he shot a hostile Tartar in the leg and brought him back a prisoner. He kept the Tartar in his house for seven weeks, nursing him and looking after him as though he were his dearest friend. Then, when the prisoner recovered, he gave him all sorts of presents and set him free. Later, during a raid, he was fighting a rearguard action, firing back at attacking Tartars, when he heard his name called from the enemy ranks and saw his former prisoner ride forward, signaling to him to do the same. The lieutenant complied and they shook hands. The mountaineers remained at a distance and did not fire. But as soon as the lieutenant turned his back, several shots were fired from their side, and a bullet grazed the lower part of his back.

On another occasion when I was present myself, a fire broke out in the fort. Two companies of soldiers were detailed to put it out. Suddenly, lit by the red glow of the flames, there appeared among the crowd a tall man on a black horse. Pushing people out of his way, the rider rode right up to the flames, jumped off his horse, and entered the burning house. Five minutes later the lieutenant reappeared. His hair had been singed and his forearm was badly burnt when he emerged carrying two pigeons clutched to his breast.

His name was Rosenkranz. He often spoke of his ancestry, which he traced back to the Varangians—the Scandinavian princes who were invited to rule over the Slavs in the earliest era of Russian history. He wanted it clearly understood that he and his ancestors were pure Russians.

**4** THE sun was midway across the sky. Its hot rays, piercing the incandescent air, beat down upon the dry earth. Overhead, the dark blue sky was completely clear, although the base of the snowy mountains was already draped in white and lilac clouds. The air was motionless and seemed to be impregnated with a sort of transparent dust. The heat was becoming unbearable.

When we were about halfway to our destination, we halted by a stream. The soldiers stacked their rifles and rushed toward the gurgling water. The battalion commander picked a shady spot where he sat himself on a drum. His whole bearing showed that he was constantly aware of his rank and importance, as he waited to have something to eat with a number of the officers. Captain Khlopov lay on the grass under his company's cart. Lieutenant Rosenkranz and a few other young officers arranged themselves on their outspread cloaks. To judge from the bottles and flasks placed among them, they intended to have a good time. The regimental singers formed a semicircle around them and sang a song of the Caucasus army.

> Recently Shamil decided
> That against us he could rise
> But, of course, he was misguided
> And quite soon we'll make him wise. . . .

Also among these officers was Second Lieutenant Alanin, the youngster who'd overtaken us during the morning. He was very amusing; his eyes sparkled, his words became garbled. He wanted to hug everyone and say how much he liked them. Unfortunately, far from making others like him, his naive warmth provoked nothing but sarcasm. Nor did he realize how touching he looked when at last, hot and exhausted, he threw himself down

193

on his cloak, pushed his thick, black hair out of his eyes, and rested his head on his bent arm.

Two officers sat in the shade of a wagon playing cards.

I listened with interest to the conversations among the men and among the officers; I kept observing their expressions. In none could I discover the slightest trace of the anxiety that I myself felt; their jokes, their laughter, the stories they told, all expressed a complete lack of concern for imminent danger. It never seemed to occur to any one of them that he might no longer be around when we passed this very spot on our return.

**5** IT was past six in the evening when, tired and covered with dust, we gained the entrance to Fort N—. The declining sun cast its slanting reddish rays on the picturesque little cannon, on the poplar groves around the fort, on the yellow fields, and on the white clouds which, huddled together near the snowy mountains, formed another range just as snowy, fantastic, and beautiful. The new moon hung above the horizon like a small transparent cloud. In the Tartar village, the faithful were being summoned to prayer from the rooftop of a hut. Our singing soldiers, filled with renewed enthusiasm and energy, were giving their all.

After a brief rest, I cleaned up and went over to see an aide I knew. I wanted him to obtain the general's consent for my plans. Walking to the fort from the outlying village where I had my quarters, I had time to notice around Fort N— things I never expected to find there. I was passed by a pretty two-seater carriage, within which flashed a fashionable lady's hat, while my ear caught snatches of French. Then, going by under the windows of the commandant's house, I heard the measures of a polka played on a piano that needed tuning.

After, in a café, I saw some clerks sitting before glasses of wine and I heard one of them say:

"No, my dear chap, speaking of politics, I must insist that Maria Gregorievna is the first among our ladies. . . ."

Further on, a stooped, threadbare, sickly looking Jew dragged along a screeching, broken-down barrel organ, and the whole street resounded with the finale of *Lucia*. Two ladies in rustling dresses, silk kerchiefs on their heads and bright umbrellas in their hands, floated gracefully past me on the planked sidewalk, while two bareheaded women, one in blue, the other in pink, stood by the porch of a small house giggling loudly, obviously to attract the attention of the officers swaggering up and down the street in new tunics with flashing epaulets and white gloves.

I found my friend the aide on the lower floor of the house occupied by the general. I had just time to tell him what I wanted and to hear that he was sure it could be arranged when the pretty carriage I'd noticed earlier rattled past the window and stopped. A tall, straight-backed infantry major got out and entered the house.

"Excuse me," the aide said, "I must go and report to the general—"

"Who is it?" I asked.

"The countess," he said, buttoning his tunic and hurrying upstairs.

A few moments later, a short, very handsome man in a tunic without epaulets but with a white cross in his buttonhole appeared on the porch. He was followed by a major, the aide, and two other officers. From the way the general moved and from his voice, one could tell he did not value lightly his exalted position.

*"Bon soir, madame la comtesse,"* he said, thrusting his hand through the carriage window.

A small hand in a kid glove pressed his, and a pretty, smiling face appeared under a yellow hat.

Of their entire conversation, I only heard the smiling general say as I passed:

"You know, Countess, that I have sworn to fight infidels. Do please be careful—I want no infidelity in you. . . ."

Laughter came from the carriage.

"*Adieu donc, cher général.*"

"*Non, au revoir,*" the general said, walking up the steps, "and please don't forget that I've invited myself to your teaparty tomorrow."

The carriage rattled away.

"There's a man," I thought on my way home, "who has everything anyone could want—rank, wealth, and fame. And now, on the eve of a battle in which no one knows how many lives may be lost, this man is off flirting and promising to take tea tomorrow."

I thought then of the remark I'd heard a Tartar make: only a poor man can be brave. "When you become rich," he said, "You become a coward." But then, the general had much more to lose than most people, and, even among the Tartars, I'd never seen such elegant indifference in the face of possible doom. This thoroughly confused my theories about courage.

Later, in the house of the same aide, I met a young man who surprised me even more. He was a young lieutenant from another regiment, a man of almost feminine docility and shyness. He had approached the aide to complain indignantly against some people who, he said, had conspired to leave him behind during the coming operation. He said it was disgusting to act that way, that it was poor camaraderie, that he'd always remember it, etc. I watched his face carefully and listened to his voice, and I was fully convinced that he was not putting on an act—he was honestly indignant and depressed because they wouldn't let him fire at Tartars and be exposed in turn to their fire. He felt like a child unjustly spanked. To me, none of it made any sense.

**6** THE troops were to move out at ten P.M. At eight-thirty, I mounted and rode over to see the general. But then I decided that both the general and the aide must be busy, so I tied my horse to a fence and sat down on the doorstep where I would catch the general as he was leaving.

The cool of evening replaced the heat. The glaring sun had gone, and in its place the crescent moon formed a pale silvery semicircle in the dark starry sky. It was beginning to set. Lights appeared in the houses and earthen huts and shone through the cracks in the shutters. Beyond the moonlit, whitewashed huts, the tall, slender poplars looked even taller and darker.

The long shadows of the houses, trees, and fences lay in beautiful patterns on the white, dusty road. From the river came the strangely reverberating croaking of the frogs. In the streets, one heard hurried steps, voices, and hoofbeats. From the outlying village came the sounds of the barrel organ playing some aria from an opera and then a waltz.

I won't go into my thoughts, mostly because I'm ashamed of the gloom that pervaded me amid the joyful excitement of the others and also because they have nothing to do with this story. Still, I was so deeply immersed that I never noticed the town clock strike eleven and the general and his retinue pass by.

I hastily jumped on my horse and hurried to catch up with the detachment.

The rearguard was still inside the fort, and I had difficulty making my way across the bridge which was cluttered with gun carriages, ammunition wagons, the supply carts of various companies, and, in the midst of it all, officers shouting orders.

Finally, I managed to get past the gates. I had to ride

197

in the darkness past the detachment, which stretched
over almost a mile, before I caught up with the general.

As I was passing by the guns drawn out in single
file with officers riding between, I was shocked at the
discord wrought in the quiet harmony of the night by a
harsh voice shouting with a German accent:

"Hey, you—give us a light!"

This was followed by the eager voice of a soldier:
"Shevchenko, the lieutenant wishes a light."

The sky gradually became overcast with long, gray
clouds which left but a few scattered gaps for the stars.
The moon had disappeared behind the black mountains
on the nearby horizon to our right; but the peaks were
bathed in its pale, quivering light while the foothills
were plunged in deep black shadows. The air was
warm and so strangely still that not the smallest cloud,
no blade of grass stirred. It was so dark that one could
not recognize objects even close at hand. On the sides
of the road, I kept seeing crags, animals, strange people,
and I realized they were bushes only by their faint rustle
and the freshness rising from the dew with which they
were sprinkled. In front of me I saw an uninterrupted
wall sinking and rising, followed by a few moving shapes
—the mounted vanguard and the general with his retinue.
Behind me another dark but shorter mass was swaying—the infantry.

The troops were so silent that one could hear clearly
all the mysterious sounds of the night: the sad wail of a
faraway jackal, now desperate sobs, now mad guffaws;
the ringing, monotonous sounds of crickets, frogs, and
quail; a curious approaching rumbling for which I could
not account; and all the nocturnal, hardly audible sounds
of nature which can be neither understood nor explained.
All blended into that harmony one refers to as the
stillness of night. The dull thudding of hoofs and the
rustling of the tall grass given forth by the slowly moving
force dissipated into this harmony.

Only now and then could the rumbling of a heavy
gun carriage, the clang of bayonets, a few brief words,
the snorting of a horse be distinguished.

Nature breathed out peace and strength.

Was it possible that there was no place for men in this

beautiful world under this immense starry sky—that hatred, vengeance, and the passion for destruction could lurk in the hearts of men amid such natural beauty? Surely all these evil instincts should vanish in contact with nature—the most direct expression of beauty and goodness.

**7** WE had been riding for more than two hours. I was drowsy and shivering. In the darkness I kept seeing the same vague objects: a way off a black wall and moving shapes; near me the crupper of a white horse, its swishing tail and widespread hind legs, and a back in a white Circassian coat, crossed by the black line of a swaying rifle and the white handle of a pistol in an embroidered holster. The glow of a cigarette threw light on a blond mustache, a beaver collar, and a hand in a kid glove. I'd let my head droop toward the horse's neck, close my eyes, and forget myself for a few moments. Then, I'd be jolted awake by the familiar tramping and rustling; I'd look around and feel that I was standing still while the black wall was moving toward me or that the wall remained fixed and I was about to smash into it. On one of these occasions I was struck by the increase in the rumbling which I'd been unable to account for. And now it dawned on me that it was the sound of water. We were entering a deep gorge and approaching a mountain stream in flood. The rumbling became louder, the damp grass grew thicker, there were more and more bushes, and the horizon narrowed. Now and then bright lights flared up at various points, then vanished immediately.

"Do you know what those lights are?" I whispered to one of our Tartars who was riding next to me.

"You really don't know?"

"I do not."

"The enemy. They tie straw to poles, fire them, and wave them about," he said.

"Why do they do that?"

"To tell everyone Russians are coming. There's a little running around going on in that village over there," the Tartar said and laughed. "Everybody's grabbing his belongings and going down into the ravine. . . ."

"How do they know, off in the mountains, when a detachment's on the way?"

"How can they not know? They always know. That's the kind of people we Tartars are."

"Then their leader Shamil must be getting ready to fight?" I asked.

"No," he said, shaking his head. "Shamil won't take part in the fighting himself. He'll send his aides to lead the fight while he watches the battle through a spyglass."

"Where's his home, do you know? Far away?"

"No, not far. About eight miles over there to the left."

"How do you know? Have you ever been there?"

"I've been there. All of us have been in the mountains."

"Have you ever seen Shamil?"

"No, one doesn't see Shamil that easily! There are a hundred, three hundred, maybe a thousand guards circling around him and he's always in the center," the Tartar said with obvious admiration.

Above, the sky, now clear, was growing lighter in the east. The Pleiades were sinking below the horizon. But the ravine through which we moved remained damp and dark.

Suddenly, a little way ahead of us, there were several flashes, and a moment later bullets whistled past. The silence was pierced by shots fired close by and shrill cries. The advance patrol of enemy Tartars whooped, fired at random, and scattered.

All became quiet again. The general summoned his interpreter. The white-clad Tartar rode up to him and for a long time whispered and gesticulated. Then the general issued an order.

"Colonel Khasanov, have the men deployed in open order," he said in a quiet but clear drawl.

The detachment reached the river. By daybreak the black mountains and the gorges had been left behind. The sky, strewn with pale stars, looked higher. The east was a glowing red; a cool, penetrating breeze came from the west; and a white mist floated like smoke above the river.

8  A NATIVE guide led us to a ford. The cavalry vanguard started across. The general and his retinue followed. The horses were up to their chests in water, which gushed violently between protruding, whitish rocks, foaming and rushing around the animals' legs. The horses, bewildered by the noise of the water, kept lifting their heads and pricking up their ears, but they made their way smoothly and carefully over the uneven riverbed. The riders pulled up their feet and their weapons. The foot soldiers stripped down to their shirts and tied their clothes in bundles to the end of their rifles. Then, carrying their rifles above their heads, each holding onto the man in front, they entered the river in groups of twenty. The physical effort required to withstand the current could be seen on their faces. The artillerymen, shouting loudly, drove their horses into the river at a trot. Water splashed over the guns and the green ammunition cases. Wheels rang against the stony bottom. The heavy horses pulled determinedly, and, with water foaming around their wet tails and manes, finally clambered up onto the opposite bank.

The crossing completed, the general's expression became thoughtful and serious. He turned his horse, and followed by the cavalry, he rode off at a trot through a glade that opened out before us. Cossack patrols were dispatched around the outskirts of the forest.

Suddenly, among the trees, we saw a man on foot wearing a Circassian shirt and a tall sheepskin cap. Another followed, then another. . . . I heard one of the officers say:

"Tartars. . . ."

A puff of smoke appeared from behind a tree. . . . Then the sound of a shot, followed by another. The noise of our fire drowned out that of the enemy. But now and then, a bullet would zoom by like a bee, as if to prove that we were not doing all the shooting. The infantry raced to take their positions. The gun carriages moved at a trot to their chosen emplacements. Then came the booming report of the guns, followed by the metallic sound of flying grapeshot, the hissing of rockets, and the crackle of rifle fire. Cavalry, infantry, and artillery scattered all over the vast clearing. The puffs of smoke from the cannon, rifles, and rockets fused with the dewy greenness and the mist. Colonel Khasanov arrived at full gallop and stopped his horse abruptly in front of the general. He saluted and said:

"Shall I order the cavalry charge, sir? They're carrying their banners. . . ." He pointed with his riding whip at a mounted detachment of enemy Tartars led by two men on white horses. The men had long poles in their hands, with bits of red and blue material tied to them; these the hillmen use as banners, though any chieftain can make himself such an emblem and carry it around.

"All right," the general answered. "Good luck."

The colonel whirled his horse about, drew his saber, and shouted: "Hurrah!"

"Hurrah! Hurrah! Hurrah!" came from the ranks as the cavalry followed.

Everyone watched tensely. There was one banner, then another, another, and yet another. . . .

Without waiting for the attack, the enemy fled, disappearing into the forests and then opening fire. Bullets continued to whistle through the air.

"A beautiful sight," the general remarked, bouncing gracefully up and down in the saddle, on his thin-legged black horse.

Striking his horse, a major rode up to the general and said with an affected lisp: "It is indeed beautiful, sir. War in such beautiful surroundings is a delight."

*"Et surtout en bonne compagnie,"* the general said with an amiable smile.

The major bowed.

At that moment, the sharp, unpleasant hissing of an enemy cannon ball sounded above our heads. It hit somewhere behind us, and there was a cry. A soldier had been wounded.

This cry affected me in a strange way. The battle scene immediately lost what beauty it may have had for me. But no one else seemed particularly concerned: the major, whose conversation was punctuated with laughter, seemed to laugh even louder; another officer in the middle of explaining something repeated the last few words, fearing his audience might have missed them. The general didn't even glance in the direction from which the cry had come; looking elsewhere, he said something in French.

The officer in charge of the artillery rode up, saluted, and asked: "Shall we give 'em a taste of their own medicine, sir?"

"All right, give 'em a scare," the general said nonchalantly, lighting a cigar.

The battery took up its position and the barrage began. The earth groaned, there were constant flashes of light, and the smoke, which almost completely hid the gun crews, stung our eyes.

The village was being bombarded. Then Colonel Khasanov reported to the general again and was ordered to lead the cavalry to the village. With warlike hurrahs, the cavalry disappeared in its own cloud of dust.

The show may have been really impressive to an initiate. But to me, an outsider, the whole thing was spoiled by the fact that all this commotion, enthusiasm, and shouting seemed rather pointless. It made me think of a man violently swinging an ax and hitting nothing but air.

**9**  WHEN the general and his retinue, to which I had attached myself, reached the village, it had already been occupied by our troops, and all its inhabitants had disappeared.

The neat, oblong huts, with their flat, earthen roofs and picturesque chimneys, were scattered over irregular rocky ground. Between hills flowed a small river. On one side of the village were green orchards of large pear and plum trees while, on the other, strange shadows thrown by the perpendicular gravestones of a cemetery and the long poles surmounted by multicolored balls and pennants marked the graves of warriors.

The troops were assembled by the village gate.

"Well," the general said, "what do you say, Colonel, shall we let them do a bit of looting? These fellows here look as though they wouldn't mind at all," he added with a smile, pointing at the Cossacks.

I was struck by the contrast between the flippant tone of the general's words and their grim implication.

A minute later, a stream of Cossacks, dragoons, and foot soldiers was pouring with obvious delight along the winding lanes of the empty village, bringing it to life. Then, a roof collapsed somewhere; an ax resounded against a heavy wooden door; a stack of hay, a fence, a whole hut—went up in flames; a Cossack came running, dragging a bag of flour and a carpet; a soldier, beaming with pleasure, emerged from a hut with a tin basin and some bright piece of material; another, with outstretched arms, tried to corner a couple of chickens which, cackling madly, rushed up and down along a fence in a panic; another soldier found an enormous jug of milk, drank some of it, and, laughing loudly, threw it on the ground.

The battalion with which I had come from Fort N— had also entered the Tartar village. Captain Khlopov had installed himself comfortably on top of a flat roof and was puffing thin whiffs of cheap tobacco smoke from his short pipe with such detached equanimity that the very sight of him made me forget that I was in a conquered village and made me feel completely at home.

"Ah, there you are," he said, seeing me.

Rosenkranz' tall figure kept appearing and disappearing in various parts of the village. He kept issuing orders and looked very busy and preoccupied. At one point I noticed his triumphant air as he emerged from a hut followed by two soldiers leading a tied-up Tartar. The Tartar was very old and wore only a tattered shirt and a pair of patched, threadbare trousers. He was so frail that his arms, tightly bound behind his hunched, bony back, seemed barely attached to his shoulders. He could hardly lift his deformed, bare feet. His face and even a part of his shaven head were covered with deep furrows and his twisted, toothless mouth, set between a cropped mustache and beard, kept opening and closing as though he were trying to chew something. But in his red, lashless eyes, there was a stubborn spark indicating an old man's indifference to life.

Through the interpreter, Rosenkranz inquired why he hadn't left with the rest.

"Where could I go?" the old man asked, calmly looking away.

"Where the others have gone."

"The warriors went to fight the Russians, and I'm an old man."

"Aren't you afraid of the Russians?"

"What can they do to me? I'm an old man," he said tonelessly, looking at the circle of men that had formed around him.

Later, I saw this same old man jolting along tied behind a Cossack's saddle. And he continued to look around with the same detached expression. They needed him to exchange for Russian prisoners.

I climbed onto the roof of the hut where the captain was and sat down next to him.

"There don't seem to be many of the enemy around," I said, in the hope of finding out what he thought about the battle that had taken place.

"Enemy? There aren't any," he said, surprised at my question. "You haven't seen the enemy yet. Wait until evening; there'll be plenty of 'em to see us off over there." He pointed with his pipe toward the woods we had crossed in the morning.

"What's going on?" I interrupted the captain, pointing to a group of Don Cossacks clustered together.

From the center of the group I heard something that sounded like the cry of a child and the words: "Stop it, don't flash your saber that way, they may see you over there. . . . Hey, Evstigneich—got a knife?"

"They're up to something, the bastards," the captain said calmly.

At that moment, young Second Lieutenant Alanin, his face flushed and horrified, rushed toward the Cossacks from around a corner.

"Leave him alone! Don't hurt him!" he shouted in a boyish voice.

Seeing the officer, the Cossacks stepped aside, and one of them let loose a little white goat. The second lieutenant stepped in front of the men overcome with embarrassment. Then, seeing the captain and me on the roof, he turned even redder and ran toward us.

"I thought they were killing a child," he said with an awkward smile.

10  THE general and the cavalry left the village first. Our battalion formed the rearguard. Khlopov's and Rosenkranz' companies were to move out together.

Captain Khlopov's prediction proved correct. No sooner had we reached the narrow woods than enemy Tartars, both on horseback and on foot, started popping up all around us, so close that at times I could clearly see some of them darting from one tree to another, their backs bent very low, their rifles clutched in both hands.

The captain removed his cap and crossed himself. Some old soldiers did the same. From among the trees came the high-pitched shouts of the enemy baiting our men. There was a succession of dry, crackling rifle shots; bullets whizzed by from both directions. Our men fired back in silence, except for a few muttered remarks that the enemy had it easy among the trees and what the devil was the artillery waiting for.

And soon the artillery did join in. The cannon spat grapeshot into the forest. This seemed to weaken the enemy. But no sooner had our troops gone a few more yards than the enemy fire again increased, along with the war cries and the baiting.

Before we were even half a mile from the village, enemy cannon balls started screaming over our heads. I saw one of them kill a soldier. . . . But why dwell on that horrible scene which I myself would give anything to forget?

Lieutenant Rosenkranz, firing his own rifle, kept galloping from one end of the line to the other, shouting instructions to his men in a hoarse voice. He was somewhat pale, and this pallor seeemed to suit his well-formed, manly face.

Second Lieutenant Alanin was in ecstasy: his handsome dark eyes shone with daring, his mouth was slightly twisted into a smile. Several times he rode up to the captain to ask permission to charge.

"We'll stop 'em," he pleaded. "I'm sure, sir, we'll throw 'em back."

"No need for it," the captain answered tersely. "All we're to do is cover our withdrawal."

Khlopov's company was holding a sector at the edge of the forest. The men were lying on the ground, firing at the enemy. The captain, in his threadbare tunic and shabby sheepskin cap, sat on his dirty-white horse, the reins loose in his hands, his knees sharply bent in the short stirrups. He sat there immobile, saying nothing; his soldiers knew their business and there was no need to order them around. Only now and then did he shout sharp reminders to some to keep their heads low.

There was nothing very martial about Captain Khlopov's appearance, but its directness and simplicity struck me. "Here's one who's really brave," I felt instinctively.

*He was the same as ever;* the same quiet movements, the same even voice, the same lack of affectation on his plain, straightforward face. Possibly, though, his eyes were somewhat more intent as a result of his total concentration; he looked like a man quietly and efficiently going about his business.

Yes, he was just as he always was—whereas in the others I could detect at least some difference from their everyday behavior: some wanted to appear calmer, others more determined, still others more cheerful than they'd have been under ordinary circumstances. But from the captain's face it was obvious that it had never even occurred to him that he might need to disguise his feelings.

The Frenchman during the battle of Waterloo who said, *"La garde meurt mais ne se rend pas,"* and other heroes, often French, who coined such historic phrases were really brave and may have actually made their memorable statements. The main difference, however, between their courage and the captain's is that even if resounding words stirred inside his heart, he'd never have uttered them, because for him they'd have spoiled a great deed. And the captain must have felt that when a man senses within himself the strength to perform a great deed, words become superfluous. This, I believe, is a peculiarity of Russian bravery. And how can a Russian not be offended when he hears Russian officers spouting French clichés in imitation of obsolete concepts of French chivalry?

Suddenly from the platoon under Second Lieutenant Alanin there came a rather uncoordinated and subdued "hurrah." I looked that way and saw a score or so of soldiers, their rifles in their hands and their equipment on their backs, running with difficulty across the plowed field. They stumbled again and again but kept going, shouting as they ran. The young second lieutenant rode at their head, holding his unsheathed saber high in the air.

Then they all vanished into the forest. . . .

After a few minutes of whooping and crackling, a frightened horse emerged from the trees. Then I saw some soldiers carrying the dead and wounded. Among

the latter was their young officer, Second Lieutenant
Alanin. Two soldiers held him under the arms. His pretty-
boy face was ashen, and bore only a faint trace of the
enthusiasm that had animated it a minute earlier. His
head was unnaturally pulled in between his shoulders
and hung down on his chest. Under his unbuttoned
tunic, a small bloody stain showed on his white shirt.

"Ah! What a shame!" I said, involuntarily turning
away from the sight.

"Sure, it's a pity," an old soldier next to me, leaning
on his rifle, said gloomily. "That kid wasn't afraid of
anything. And it doesn't make sense, does it?" He looked
intently at the wounded youngster. "Still, he was stupid,
and now he's paid for it."

"And what about you, are you afraid?" I asked him.

"What do you think?" he asked.

11 Four soldiers were carrying the second lieutenant on a stretcher. Behind them, a medical orderly led a
thin, old horse loaded with two green cases containing
medical supplies. They waited for the doctor. Officers
kept riding up to the stretcher, trying to comfort the
wounded youngster.

"Well, Alanin, old man, it'll be a while now before
you can dance again," Rosenkranz said to him with a
smile.

He must have assumed that these words would cheer
up Alanin. But Alanin's cold, sad look showed that they'd
not produced the desired effect.

Captain Khlopov rode up. He looked closely at the
wounded man, and his usually cold, indifferent face expressed honest sorrow.

"Well, dear boy," he said, with a warmth I hadn't expected of him, "looks like it was God's will that it should
happen this way."

The wounded man turned toward him. A sad smile brought his pale features to life.

"Yes. I disobeyed you, sir."

"You'd better say it was God's will," the captain said again.

The doctor arrived. He took bandages, a probe, and some other instrument from the medical orderly, rolled up his sleeves, and, smiling cheerfully, approached the wounded man.

"Looks like they drilled a neat little hole in you," he said in a light, casual tone. "Let me have a look at it."

The young man complied. He looked at the doctor with a reproachful surprise that passed unnoticed. The doctor started to examine the wound, pressing so hard all around it that the young man, at the limit of his endurance, pushed his hand away with a moan:

"Leave me alone," he said in a hardly audible voice. "I'll die anyway."

Then he fell back. Five minutes later, when I passed by him again, I asked a soldier:

"How's the second lieutenant?"

"He's dying," the man said.

**12** IT was late when the detachment approached the fort in a wide column. The soldiers were singing.

The general rode in front and, to judge by his satisfied expression, the raid must have been a success. And indeed it had been; for the first time the Russians had succeeded in setting foot in the village of Mukay—and had achieved this at the cost of very few lives.

Rosenkranz silently thought back over the day's action. Captain Khlopov, deep in thought, walked with his company, leading his little whitish horse by its bridle.

The sun sank behind the snowy chain of mountains, casting its last reddish beams on a long thin cloud that hung motionless in the clear, translucent air above the horizon. The snowy mountains began to vanish in the violet mist, and only their upper reaches stood out with uncanny clarity in the crimson glow. The moon had already risen and was beginning to whiten and detach itself from the darkening azure of the sky. The green of the leaves and grass turned slowly to black and became wet with dew. The dark masses of moving soldiers produced rhythmical waves among the rich green meadows. Drums, tambourines and songs resounded over everything. The chorus leader of the Sixth Company sounded forth in full voice, and the notes of his pure, vibrating tenor, filled with feeling and power, floated through the clear evening air.

# AFTERWORD

"Nice fellow, Olenin," one of the two staying behind said. "But why did he decide to go to the Caucasus, and with the army? I wouldn't do it for anything. By the way, you dining at the club tomorrow?"

"I am."

And each went his way. (P. 13)

Against a background of sophisticated indifference and social irresponsibility, young Olenin sets out for the Caucasus to overcome an unhappy love affair, to escape the fruitlessness of society life, and, perhaps, by a life of boldness and daring in a "real" world, to find himself. The world he leaves behind is no more concerned with him or his quest than the real Moscow world was one night in May 1851 when Leo and Nikolai Tolstoy, after a night spent "parmi les plebs, dans les tentes bohémiennes," set out for Kazan, Saratov, a trip down the Volga to Astrakhan, and finally the Cossack village of Starogladkovskaia, where Nikolai's army detachment was stationed.

Leo Tolstoy's life so far had not been what he wanted. He had left Kazan University and gone to Yasnaya Polyana to prepare for the final examinations and to institute certain reforms among the peasants. But all this added up to zero, Tolstoy thought, for, as he wrote to his Aunt from Tiflis in 1852, he felt pursued by a demon of failure:

I have only to recall the disappointments experienced

212

in the managing of the estate, the studies that I would
begin and be unable to finish, the constant bad luck I
have had when I gambled, and a host of other schemes
that were never realized.—I confess that in most of
these reverses of which I complain I can accuse myself as much as Fortune, but it is not less true that
there exists a small demon who is always busy making
me fail in all my projects.

As his diary indicates, he was continually listing new
precepts and injunctions for himself to live by, but they
had amounted to nothing. Two entries he put down on
his diary, three years apart (June 17, 1850 and June 16,
1847), summarize the contradictions he experienced in
himself with regard to his social life:

> I spent the winter before last in M[oscow], lived a
> very irregular life, without a job in the service,
> without anything to do, without a goal; and I lived like
> that not because, as many say and write, everybody in
> Moscow lives like that, but simply because I liked that
> sort of life. —Partly, the position of a young man in
> Moscow society disposes him to laziness. . . .

In the earlier entry, he had jotted down a feeling which
well illustrates the "other" side of his moral character:

> Will I ever get to the point of being independent of
> any outside circumstances? In my opinion, this is a
> great accomplishment, for in the man who is inde-
> pendent of any outside influence, the spirit necessarily
> by its own requirements overcomes matter, and the
> man will then achieve what he is cut out for.

Twenty-three years old, dissatisfied with what he had
—and had not—done, filled with affection for his brother
and a sense of adventure, and obsessed with discovering
himself—as he said his Aunt Tatiana asserted, "je suis
un homme à épreuve"—he headed for the Caucasus.

His arrival in the North Caucasus is handsomely described in *The Cossacks*. The little village in which his
brother was stationed was on the shore of the Terek
River, which ran between the territories of the Greben
Cossacks on the left bank and of the Tartar mountaineers

on the right, on the edge of the Kumytsk Plain, about eighty miles from where the Terek empties into the Caspian Sea. As described in Chapter 4, the Cossacks were descendants of a group of Old Believers—those who had split from the Orthodox Church in the seventeenth century—and still proudly maintained the old traditions: the women worked and ruled the family; the men drank, fought, hunted, chased women, and scorned Russian peasants and Russian soldiers. The paragon of the Cossack for Tolstoy was Epishka [Epifan] Sekhin, the Eroshka of *The Cossacks*. Once a horse thief and fighter against both the Chechentsy and the Russians, he now hunted, drank, and told countless stories about his life and his people. Many of his "real-life" stories are picked up or are referred to in the novel, such as the story about his "pal" Girchik, referred to in Chapter 14. The descriptions of Eroshka—particularly in Chapter 14—are almost literally those of Epishka. One old Caucasian "hand" certified that

> in the village of Starogladkovskaia, I found a contemporary of "uncle" Epishka and, reading *The Cossacks* to him, tried to hear from him anything that would round out the image of Epishka—"Eroshka." Everything that Lev Nikolaevich said about him is portrayed with photographic accuracy.

Tolstoy's brother Nikolai, in his *Hunting in the Caucasus,* published in *The Contemporary* in 1857, characterized Epishka as

> extraordinarily interesting, most likely already the last of the old Greben Cossacks. Epishka, according to what he himself said, was a bold young fellow, a thief, a swindler, rustled horses, sold people off, lassoed Chechentsy; now he's a lonely old man, nearly ninety. What that man didn't see in his life! . . . His whole life is a series of the strangest adventures. . . . Hunting and carousing—these are our old man's two passions: they were and still are his only occupation; all his other adventures are merely episodes.

Tolstoy's life up to his arrival in the Caucasus had vacillated between good intentions and straight self-indulgence. His splurges with women and cards had always caused him pangs of conscience, but, like Olenin, having left Moscow, he had left his Moscow memories behind—almost. Naturally, aspects of the "old" life returned. Tolstoy notes in his diary on July 3, 1851:

> I went to Chervlionnaia, got drunk there, slept with a woman; all this is very bad and torments me deeply. So far I haven't once spent more than two months well—in such a way that I was satisfied with myself.

The good intentions—to study philosophy and literature, to help the peasants, to stop being dissolute—all amounted, as he put it, to "nothing done." But Epishka Sekhin cast everything in a new light, for he believed, as Tolstoy describes him in this novel, that "God made everything for man to enjoy," that "there's no such thing as sin," that "everyone's got his own laws." There was life to be lived, the old man asserted, horses to be stolen, wars to be fought, and girls to be loved. As Eroshka tells Olenin:

> "I'll find you a better one, one all dressed in silk and silver. I'll do what I promised: I'll get you a beauty."
> "What are you talking about, old man, it's sinful——"
> "Sinful? What's sinful? You think it's sinful to look at a beautiful girl? Is it sinful to love her up a little? Maybe where you come from it's a sin. Uh-uh, brother, it's no sin, it's salvation. God made you and he made the girl, he made everything. So, it's no sin to look at a pretty girl: she's made to be loved and to make us happy. That's the way I figure it, friend." (P. 60.)

Eroshka seemed a wholly natural man, the sort Tolstoy wanted to emulate. He wanted to get free of the modes of high society, the pretentiousness of its men and girls (in his diary for June 16, 1847 he noted that women "in this immoral, vicious age are worse than us [men]"), and to become immersed in the untrammeled, strong, and beautiful life of these men of nature.

He meant it when he said (in his diary, July 4, 1850) that

> consciousness is the greatest moral evil, which only man can comprehend. It's painful, very painful, to know ahead of time that an hour from now, I'll still be the same person, the same images will still be in my memory, but my outlook will have changed independently of myself, and consciously at that.

He wanted to become as pure, brave, and noble as he imagined the Cossacks to be, but he could not drop the furniture of culture, could not help but write, and could not escape the constant gnawings of remorse for what he always felt, after the fact, was his weak and morally reprehensible profligacy.

Indeed, Tolstoy's entire life is characterized by a haunting dilemma: a conflict between standards of hedonism and puritanism which made any situation he was in finally unbearable—or, at least, unsatisfactory—and which was resolved, in the sense of comprehended, only in his creative writing. You might say that the double standard by which he judged his own life and the lives of those he met were subsumed in the standards of his art, that the moral fervor and inappropriate indignation which he applied, for example, to Shakespeare, was frustrated, even relieved, by the excellence of his own literary skill.

All his life Tolstoy felt that he did not "fit," that he was "outside" society in a way he could neither avoid nor overcome. As he noted in his diary on March 29, 1852,

> There's something in me that forces me to believe I wasn't born to be the same as all the rest.

But what the source of this feeling was he did not know. He wrote willingly, he said, but, once he had written something, he loathed it, loathed himself, and even the public who would read it. He wrote, he asserted once, to avoid boredom, to acquire the habit of work, and to please his Aunt Tatiana.

Of course, everyone carries in himself a sense of his

own individuality; the difference is that Tolstoy was pursued by it and, having talent, was compelled to translate his experience into literature. In this sense, Tolstoy is one of the most autobiographical writers. Time and again the central character, episode, feeling, or attitude in one of his stories, or whole parts of his novels, essays, and plays, are a faithful, imaginative, evangelical, astonishing transformation of what was going on inside him. In this sense, we may say that Olenin in *The Cossacks* is Tolstoy, who went to the Caucasus to find life, found it, and found that he finally did not fit in.

I suppose the easiest way to separate the fiction from the autobiography is to remember that Tolstoy understood and dramatized his position through Olenin; but that where Olenin was, so to speak, free to leave, Tolstoy had still to live on. What Tolstoy says about Olenin, as Olenin quits the forward company after the last and sudden fight and Lukashka's wounding, directly reports what he had discovered for himself:

> Just as on the night of his departure from Moscow, a three-horse carriage waited at the door. Unlike then, Olenin was no longer absorbed with himself, and, unlike then, he did not repeat over and over to himself that everything he'd been doing was not the "real thing." Now he no longer promised himself a new life. He loved Marianka more than ever and knew that he would never be loved by her. (P. 177.)

Eroshka says good-by to him, criticizes him, indeed, for the cold and indifferent manner with which he, Olenin, takes his self-confident farewell. The old man declares openly:

> "Don't you understand I like you and I'm sorry to lose you? You're such a sad one and always so alone. You're sort of unloved. When I can't sleep sometimes, I think of you, and I feel so sorry. It's like the song you know:
> > 'It is hard, oh brother dear,
> > In an alien land to live.'
> That's how it is with you." (P. 180.)

Olenin simply says good-by, the old man kisses him three

times, Olenin gets in the cart, the old man asks for something to remember him by, Olenin gives him his rifle, Marianka bows to him, Olenin drives off and looks back:

> Eroshka and Marianka were talking, apparently about their own affairs. Neither the old man nor the girl turned to look at him. (P. 181.)

The story that began with Olenin's entry into the fabled Cossack world, such as that described in the earlier and popular romantic work of Pushkin, Bestuzhev-Marlinsky, and Lermontov, ends with his exit; but in the meantime the hero's point of view has somewhat shifted, just as had Tolstoy's.

In 1852 (see his diary for October 19 and 21), Tolstoy had thought of writing a historico-descriptive "Caucasian Sketches," the fourth part of which was to be based on "the amazing stories" told by Epishka. Other writing, his life with the army, his transfer to the Danubian army and the siege of Sevastopol interrupted. He returned to it sporadically in 1856, 1857, 1858, in Hyères in 1860 after his brother Nikolai's death, and then finally in 1862. For a while, after his return from the Caucasus, Tolstoy had turned to moralistic writings and had lost much ground with the public. "Thank God," he had written to Botkin, "I didn't listen to Turgenev, who was trying to prove to me that a writer must be a writer." Turgenev's reply summed up the situation:

> . . . I can't imagine what you are if not a writer: an officer? a landowner? a philosopher? the founder of a new religious doctrine? an official? a business man? . . . I'm joking—but indeed I very much would like to see you going along, at last, under full sail.

Tolstoy was both disliked by the radical critics and out of favor with the government; his ideas on education had not only antagonized it but even led (on the basis of a spurious report) to a police search of Yasnaya Polyana. The trilogy on his childhood and the Sevastopol stories, all behind him, seemed to have been forgotten.

Then, in Moscow in January 1862, he lost a thousand

rubles gambling and, pressed by the debt, secured an advance from the publisher Katkov for *The Cossacks*. As he wrote to Botkin on February 7:

> ... I got 1000 rubles from Katkov and I promised him my novel this year—the Caucasian thing—which, having thought about it seriously, I'm very glad of, for otherwise this novel, of which way over half is written, would have lain around forever and been used for pasting up windows. ...

On December 19, Tolstoy noted: "I've finished the first part of *The Cossacks*." The next January he recorded having made final revisions and added: "It's terribly weak. No doubt the public will therefore be pleased." The first part appeared in the first volume of Katkov's *The Russian Herald* in 1863. The story that had started out as one man's quest for life ended up as an aspect of the author's search for himself.

Tolstoy's involvement in his work at Yasnaya Polyana had taken him somewhat out of the literary spotlight. In May 1861, there had occurred his famous quarrel with Turgenev—a quarrel which had burst out violently with (according to Tolstoy's wife and one of Tolstoy's letters) Turgenev's threat to "punch Tolstoy in the mug" for Tolstoy's criticism of the way Turgenev was bringing up his daughter. Tolstoy's hot temper provoked him to challenge Turgenev to a duel (Tolstoy affirmed this in a letter to Fet and in a subsequent letter to Turgenev, in which he renounced the challenge), but the whole episode finally quieted down, and the two writers broke off relations for seventeen years. What lay behind the argument was Tolstoy's scorn of Turgenev's lack of intimacy with Russia and Turgenev's sense of Tolstoy's having quit the profession of literature for that of animal husbandry. Tolstoy, indeed, was looking for something—for truth, for God, for happiness—but he had no conviction that he would find it. His diary entry for August 24, 1862 runs, in part:

> ... Afterwards I was as sad as I haven't been in a long time. I have no friends, none! I'm alone. I had friends

when I served Mammon, and none, now I'm serving truth.

The entry for August 28 begins: "I'm 34. I got up with the habitual feeling of sadness. . . ." On September 23, however, he married Sophie Behrs in the Court Church of the Kremlin, and a new period in his life began—that period of "family happiness" of which he had long dreamed, a period, also, of much and great writing.

When he had first arrived in the Caucasus in the early summer of 1851, Tolstoy had been enchanted by the beauty of the landscape and tempted by the habits of the officers. Despite all his resolutions to lead a clean and wholesome life, he spent many nights with Cossack women and gambled away a good deal of money. (His diary entry for March 20, 1852 is a catalogue of some of his activities and a reproach of himself for his "sensuality" and "vanity," which "had spoiled the best years of my life.") He soon went with his brother from Starogladkovskaia to the outpost Staryi Iurt, about 60 miles upstream and away from the river. In June, General Bariantinskii led a detachment on a raid against the Chechentsy and allowed Tolstoy to go along as a volunteer. The objective was a Chechen hill village. The action is literally described in *The Raid*: an incursion by Russian infantry, artillery, and cavalry, sacking of the abandoned town, and the return of the Russians under sniper fire. First conceived in April 1852 and originally entitled "A Letter from the Caucasus," the story was written between May and July, dropped, and finished in December.

Of his own part in the foray, Tolstoy commented in his diary (July 3, 1852): "I was on a raid. —Also, I acted badly: unconsciously was even afraid of Bariantinskii." Bariantinskii, however, subsequently commended him for bravery and recommended he petition to enter the army.

In July 1852, Tolstoy sent his story *Childhood* to Nekrasov, the editor of *The Contemporary*. Toward the end of the summer, he received Nekrasov's reply:

I read your story. It is of such interest that I am

going to print it. Without knowing the continuation, I cannot say absolutely, but it seems to me that the author has talent.

The autobiographical story came out in October, was widely read and highly praised. A second letter from Nekrasov, dated September 5, 1852, included the statement that he had read the proofs of *Childhood* and "found this story much better than it seemed to me at first." Tolstoy wryly commented in his diary (September 30): "Got a letter from Nekrasov—praise, but no money."

Encouraged by the praise, Tolstoy sent Nekrasov the story *The Raid* in December, and it appeared in *The Contemporary* in March 1853. The episode around which the anecdote is built was actual and personal; the substance of the story, however, goes beyond mere naturalistic description. The romantic military life in the Caucasus is not portrayed romantically. The "romantic hero" is played down; the realistic virtues of prudence and patience, played up. The soldier's rôle is summed up by Khlopov's sitting bravely, expertly, wisely on his horse while the young Alanin plunges daringly and foolishly into the forest to return wounded and die. The young officer admits he disobeyed Khlopov, but Khlopov, in his remove, understands more than mere obedience, duty, and adventure, and says simply that it was God's will. Even in such an early story, Tolstoy deeply questioned conventional standards of bravery—witness the opening discussion of bravery between Khlopov and the narrator —and the usual glorification of war and of heroism. The vanity of the young would-be hero—of Alanin, or better, of the *poseur* Rosenkranz—is exposed by contrast to the reliable and steadfast honesty of Khlopov, who is in the army because he must be in service, who is in the Caucasus because of double pay, and whose only concern is to do his job well. How can there be glamor about it, he tells the narrator, when you know that on every raid one or more of your comrades will be killed. This same understanding runs through all of Tolstoy's works involving war and led finally to his condemnation of all violence.

*The Cossacks* and *The Raid,* these two pieces of early Tolstoy prose, will present by their themes, their characters, and their author's explicit point of view what young Tolstoy thought and felt, what he saw and experienced, and, above all, how well he could write. For all the diary jottings and moral tergiversations, for all the outbursts of temper and outspoken pacifism, what remains about Tolstoy is this striking fact: he was a great novelist because he *wrote* so well.

F. D. Reeve
University of Illinois

# SELECTED BIBLIOGRAPHY

## Other Works by Leo Tolstoy

*Childhood*, 1852 Novel
*Boyhood*, 1854 Novel
*Sevastopol*, 1855 Stories
*Two Hussars*, 1856 Novel
*Youth*, 1857 Novel
*Family Happiness*, 1859 Story (Signet CD13)
*War and Peace*, 1869 Novel
*Anna Karenina*, 1877 Novel (Signet CT34)
*The Memoirs of a Madman*, 1884 Story
*A Confession*, 1884 Essay
*The Death of Ivan Ilych*, 1886 Story (Signet CD13)
*The Power of Darkness*, 1889 Play
*The Kreutzer Sonata*, 1889 Story (Signet CD13)
*Master and Man*, 1895 Story (Signet CD13)
*What Is Art?* 1896 Essay
*Father Sergius*, 1896 Story
*Resurrection*, 1900 Novel (Signet CD63)
*The Devil*, 1911 Story

## Selected Criticism and Biography

Berlin, Isaiah. *The Hedgehog and the Fox: An Essay on Tolstoy's View of History*. London: George Weidenfeld & Nicholson; New York: Simon and Schuster, 1953; The New American Library (Mentor Books), 1957.
Gorky, Maxim. *Reminiscences of Tolstoy, Chekhov, and An-*

*dreyev*. New York: The Viking Press, Inc. (Compass Books), 1959.

Hoffman, Modest and André Pierre. *By Deeds of Truth: The Life of Leo Tolstoy*. New York: Orion Press, Inc., 1958.

Mann, Thomas. *Three Essays*. New York: Alfred A. Knopf, Inc., 1929; London: Martin Secker Ltd., 1932.

Maude, Aylmer. *The Life of Tolstoy*. New York and London: Oxford University Press, 1932.

Simmons, Ernest J. *Leo Tolstoy*. Boston: Little, Brown and Company, 1945; New York: Alfred A. Knopf, Inc. (Vintage Books), 1960.

Steiner, George. *Tolstoy or Dostoevsky: An Essay in the Old Criticism*. New York: Alfred A. Knopf, Inc., 1959.

Zweig, Stefan. *Adepts in Self-Portraiture: Casanova, Stendhal, Tolstoy*. New York: Viking Press, Inc., 1928.